Readers love *Whiskers of a Chance* by TEMPESTE O'RILEY

"*Whiskers of a Chance* was a cute story that incorporated a few different tropes that I enjoy, melded together seamlessly."

—Joyfully Jay

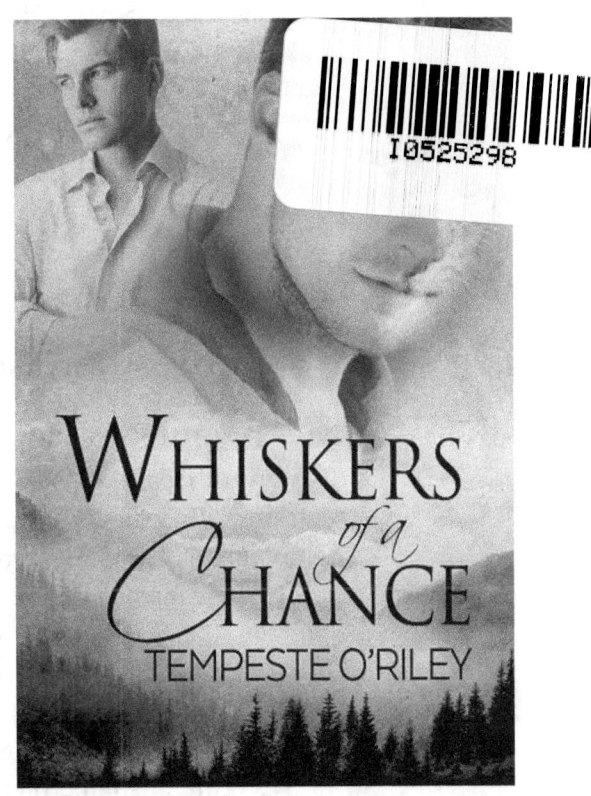

"Okay, let me just say that Tempeste O'Riley has done it yet again. I really enjoyed this book."

—Love Bytes

"The characters were complex, enjoyable and relatable—the sex was hot—the attraction and tension between Keith and Jason was palpable—and overall it was a lot of fun."

—MM Good Book Reviews

"A thoroughly entertaining love story—*Whiskers of a Chance* gives Keith and Jason the chance of a lifetime. An excellent adventure."

—Joyfully Reviewed

By TEMPESTE O'RILEY

Caged Sanctuary
Dreamers' Destiny
Grand Adventures (Dreamspinner Anthology)

CHAIN OF FATE
Whiskers of a Chance
Fangs with a Heart

DESIRES ENTWINED
Designs of Desire • Bound by Desire
Desires' Guardian • Desires' Pride
Temptations of Desire • Truth in Lace
Signs of Desire

Published by DREAMSPINNER PRESS
www.dreamspinnerpress.com

FANGS *with a* HEART

TEMPESTE O'RILEY

REAMSPINNER
PRESS

Published by
DREAMSPINNER PRESS

5032 Capital Circle SW, Suite 2, PMB# 279, Tallahassee, FL 32305-7886 USA
www.dreamspinnerpress.com

Fangs with a Heart
© 2017 Tempeste O'Riley.

Cover Art
© 2017 Catt Ford.
Cover content is for illustrative purposes only and any person depicted on the cover is a model.

ISBN: 978-1-63533-500-2
Digital ISBN: 978-1-63533-501-9
Library of Congress Control Number: 2016920832
Published May 2017
v. 1.0

Printed in the United States of America
∞
This paper meets the requirements of
ANSI/NISO Z39.48-1992 (Permanence of Paper).

ACKNOWLEDGMENTS

I WOULD like to thank all my wonderful readers for their love and desire for my lynx boys. When I wrote *Whiskers of a Chance*, I had no idea it would touch so many (or that I would get so many demands for Trace and Sasha's story beginning on release day for *Whiskers*, lol). Thank you for making my dive into shifters so fun and rewarding.

I would also like to thank Grace R. Duncan and Nikki Prince, without whom I would never have written any kitties. And of course Ginnifer, Elizabeth, Lynn, and the entire DSP staff.

AUTHOR'S NOTE

THE TOPIC of domestic abuse is dealt with within these pages. How much of Trace's past to show and how to let you see his ongoing issues due to the "long-ago" domestic abuse wasn't an easy decision. While I never nearly died, I was abused, so this was very personal for me in places. Sadly, abusers come from all races, genders, religions, walks of life, etc. There is a misconception that women are the ones abused. While women often are, they are by no means the only ones. Unfortunately, there is a stigma if a man seeks out help, admitting to being the abused. Trace may be a figment of my imagination, but he is by no means alone as a victim of domestic abuse. There is also a belief by some that women won't abuse other women. The sad truth is that all genders can and do abuse and all genders can be and are abused. No one is "safe" or "bad" simply due to gender.

If you are hurting—mentally, physically—from mental, emotional, sexual, and/or physical abuse, don't listen to the perpetrator. There are people willing to help. There are programs that can help you get away and back on your feet. Check with your local LGBT center, on the Internet, your church/temple/circle, your family, etc.

Don't try to go it alone. Don't stay, believing you have nowhere to go. No one has the right to hurt you. Ever.

To find help, here are a few links. These are by no means the only ones, but these are a few of the ones I know:

DomesticShelters.org (https://www.domesticshelters.org/)

National Domestic Violence Hotline: 1-800-799-7233

Gay Men's Domestic Violence Project (http://gmdvp.org/gmdvp/): 1-800-832-1901

CHAPTER ONE

"SIR, ARE you sure there's nothing any of us can do to lighten your mood?" Jalin asked as Sasha stared out the window next to his chair. The view outside wasn't any better or worse than from his suite of rooms, but seeing the worried look on his most trusted assistant's face hadn't gotten any easier in the last few years. Not that an answer on how to solve the issues facing him would appear no matter where he looked. He knew because early on, he'd tried.

The view outside his window was magnificent, even if it was lost on him. The grounds at his covenstead were always perfectly maintained— his people would do no less for their prince, of course. This year the gardens were filled with roses in a vast array of colors and types, as well as climbing vines and other flowering plants complementing the benches and statuary, depending on which area you viewed. The mountains in the distance were glorious, no matter how many decades or centuries one looked upon them. But with no one to share them with....

Jalin sighed, something that not that long ago would have annoyed Sasha. Until recently, Jalin would never have done such within Sasha's hearing, believing it was beyond inappropriate to show such attitude and emotion to his liege. But Sasha understood, even if he didn't seem to be able to care. He was worrying them, those closest to him. Probably some of the others in his coven as well, which wasn't the best thing to do. If any of his enemies found out about his distraction or morose attitude of late, he would be putting his friends, family, and more in danger. Even that truth failed to stir much within him, though.

"My lord—"

"Your worry is duly noted, Jalin. But I can't fix things how you want me to." Sasha took a deep breath and pasted on a smile. "Now, do you have today's agenda for me?"

"Yes, sir. Also Jason called and would like, and I quote, 'my best friend to get off his little fanged ass and call me.'"

He couldn't help it. Even with how he felt, Sasha still found himself chuckling. "That was a pretty good impression of Jason, actually. Keith would love to see you do that."

The gulp he got for a reply only made him laugh harder. "See, you wanted me lighter, and you found a way. By the way, why did Jason call you instead of me?" Even in the years since Jason had learned of who and what Sasha truly was and had met Jalin (Sasha's valet and assistant) and Summer and Dimka (his personal guard, though they had spent a few years guarding Jason until he had met and been claimed by his lynx shifter mate, Keith Skyler), Jason still always sought Sasha first, no matter what.

"I believe he did call you, but you didn't answer. You've been doing that a lot as of late, sir. It's, well… we're worried. Dimka said your… distraction, along with some of your other more—" He paused, head cocked to the side as he seemed to think for a moment. "—worrisome behaviors started about the same time you ran into that cat, um, Trace— the council representative—not that long ago. You've always seemed to get along well enough with him, even if you two do appear a little cool toward one another. But since that night, you seem…."

Jalin continued talking, but Sasha couldn't make himself pay attention. Sasha knew the night Jalin referenced, and yes, that was part of the problem. He'd been out, Dimka and Summer his loyal shadows as usual, when he'd run into Keith Skyler's council representative cat, Trace. The lynx had been dressed to kill. His pale blond hair had been artfully arranged in spikes so he resembled some fanciful manga character, only more lovely. Trace had worn skintight black jeans, a slim-fitting pale green turtleneck sweater that made his jade eyes nearly glow, and a pair of low-cut black boots with silver buckles. Unfortunately the other accessory he had was a cute human, probably in his early thirties, hanging all over him.

Sasha and Trace weren't a couple. They never had been, never would be, and yet Sasha still felt the sting of betrayal. Again. And it was stupid to be upset a damn cat wanted to hang out with a human instead of him when they'd mutually rejected the idea of bonding with the other. Sadly that didn't help him feel any better.

Instead of dwelling on what would never be, Sasha pulled his cell out of his pocket and tapped the screen, then frowned when it didn't light up. He tried clicking the side button but again, nothing happened.

"Dammit. I think I let it die. That might explain why he couldn't get me. I suppose I should be glad he didn't show up worried." Or angry.

Jalin held out his hand. When Sasha handed his phone over, he checked Jalin's face, but it gave nothing away. Of course, that was one of the reasons Sasha's father had chosen Jalin to be Sasha's assistant and, well, valet, basically, when he was a younger prince. Jalin disappeared for a moment, then returned and handed Sasha the cell back, except it lit up this time.

"Um...."

"I have a couple of replacement batteries for all your devices, just in case. The battery that was in there is on the charger now and will be ready soon. As for the rest of your day, you need to call Jason, as I said. You have a formal meeting with Alpha Keith this afternoon at his home on the tribe lands. Your coven members would like to see you out and about, especially if your old, playful, princely self could make an appearance." Jalin sounded so hopeful, and for that alone, Sasha resolved to do better at hiding his pain.

At least it wasn't like human royalty. He didn't have a king or queen to cater to. As the ruling prince, he was the ruler of all vampires in the area, just as Keith was the ruler of all the lynx in his tribal area. Actually in Keith's case, because he was a Chosen of Baast, other alphas were starting to swear loyalty to him, something Sasha knew he needed to keep an eye on if he could just manage to keep his attention on anything other than his issues, thanks to Trace.

"And I sent Summer to investigate a couple of possibly rogue vampires new to the area."

Rogue? Sasha pinned Jalin with a glare, not amused to only just now be learning of this. He never allowed any vampires who might jeopardize his coven, his allies in his territory, or Jason. "Why wasn't I informed of their presence immediately?"

"I only learned of them just before coming in to speak with you, my lord—sir." Jalin would learn, dammit. Sasha worked in the human world and couldn't have his personal assistant using nobility terms around the humans. Hospital CEOs, while pompous at times, simply didn't have their workers use *my lord* or *liege* in the normal course of their day. It would cause undue curiosity and concern—things he and his allies did not need. "They haven't done anything, that we know of, to warrant anything but Summer checking on them. They haven't even been in the city long enough to have broken protocol. They are still within time constraints about entrance versus presentation, sir. I merely wished to gather the information you would need and to alert you to their presence."

"I want to know the moment Summer reports back."

"Yes, sir. Also your mother's uncle sent word again that he wishes an audience with you about your rejection of the proposed betrothal between yourself and Princess Tatiana."

Sasha spun back to face Jalin as he clenched his fists so tight he felt flesh give to nails. "If I ever bond, it will be for love and love only. He will not force my hand in this!"

"Y-yes, my lord," Jalin squeaked. "I-I-I—"

"Mother would never have allowed him to try this, and I will not be browbeaten or guilted into bonding to some girl for his gain."

Jalin trembled where he stood as he continued to stare at Sasha. Sasha knew he needed to control his temper better, but bonding was a sore point, and not just because of Trace. He'd always hated the idea of forced marriage—and this wasn't his uncle's first attempt.

Sasha knew how much even his friends feared his temper when he unleashed it, not that he had ever harmed any of those closest to him, be they friend or servant. Only Jason, of all his friends alive, had never seen the true power held within him, and he'd once watched as Sasha held a feline twice his size off the ground as he strangled him unconscious. Sasha found out later the lynx shifter in question had since lost the ability to make a sound in either his human or his cat skins. The point was, Jalin didn't deserve Sasha's anger or pain, as none of this was Jalin's fault.

"Dammit, Jalin," he said, pitching his voice as soft and calm as he could manage. "I'm not upset with you and should not have taken it out on you like that."

"It's all right, my—"

"No, it's not, and being your prince makes what I just said and did even less forgivable."

"But understandable considering what he's trying to do to you."

There was that. Sasha had never approved of forced, arranged marriages, even when they were commonplace. He knew his father, the previous prince, had felt the same, and his parents had been a true bond pair, or what vampires called fated hearts. Sasha had always held out a tiny little hope he would find his own fated partner—even if such destined bondings were so rare that many didn't believe them to be more than children's stories, like the fairy tales told to human children about fairy godmothers and princesses. However, since both his parents and his sister had found their fated heart, the child within him had hoped. Unfortunately, like them, that hope was now gone.

"Maybe if you took a consort? Even if only in name, maybe your uncle would give up and find something useful to do instead of frustrate you with women you have no interest in?" Jalin then flushed a light pink. Vampires never colored much, but it was still both fetching and amusing. "I didn't mean to speak out of turn about your uncle. Forgive me, please."

Sasha waved away Jalin's worries and instead addressed the true issue. "I can't do that to someone—make them believe they have my affections but then withhold the same."

"Surely there's someone—"

"No, and there won't be." Not as long as Trace lived—and lynx were a rather long-lived race. Not that Sasha thought Trace was all that old for a man, much less for a shifter, nor could he tolerate the thought of anything happening to the infuriating cat.

Unlike Trace, the thought of touching anyone else made Sasha physically ill. He'd tried a couple of times over the last few years to ignore what should have been between them. They had never done anything more than shake hands once, so he had hoped he could have a normal life still. Unfortunately he'd had to face the truth: not only did Trace not want to bond with Sasha, but Trace was out trolling bars for companionship. He still couldn't figure out how Trace could do that when Sasha could barely manage to touch his own coven members in a platonic sense since meeting the damnable feline—not without the horrible sense he was somehow filthy down to his core after, and that was from nonsexual touching. Sex wasn't possible. Not since the day he'd met Trace.

"Not even for—"

"Jalin, don't."

"But—"

"For the love of all that's holy, please don't continue that sentence." *Please*. Sasha wasn't even safe from Trace in his dreams or imaginings now, so no, he doubted he could take Jalin's hopes right then. "Now go be positive somewhere else so I can call Jason."

"As you wish."

Sasha waited for the door to close before he grumbled, "And you are *so* not Westley."

He pinched the bridge of his nose. *Wouldn't even get the* Princess Bride *reference, would you*? He knew Jason would have laughed. The thought almost made him smile. He pulled his cell back out and pressed speed dial two—Jason on his contacts list. It only took a moment for the call to connect, and then his best friend's voice came through the line. "Sasha! Where were you?"

"Sorry, hon, just a stupid battery snafu." He did his best to maintain his upbeat, playful tone like he always had. One day maybe it would even feel natural again. "What's up?"

"Not much. I know you're coming out to talk to Keith, but I'd hoped you'd have some time to spend with Sean and me too."

Sasha couldn't help it. He snorted into the phone. "Like I've ever not had time for you and, since the little tyke came along, for him too. He's my favorite nephew, after all."

"He's your only nephew, Sasha," Jason deadpanned.

"He'd still be my favorite even if you had others." Besides, Sasha figured he'd need a pick-me-up by the time he finished dealing with Keith. Or more precisely, finished with who else he would likely have to deal with. "And I don't discriminate. I claim little Zeke too." Zeke was Keith's sister's son, making him Jason's nephew, but as far as Sasha was concerned, both boys were his nephews.

"I know you d-do, but you've been quiet lately, and I'm w-worried."

Oh no, no no no no no. "Hon, relax. I'm all right, so you can calm yourself down right now."

"I'm not upset," Jason groused, then huffed. "Stupid stutter giving me away."

"It does, but I've not heard you do that with me in years and years, so what gives? Do I need to come over early?" Was something wrong with Jason or Sean?

"No. We're fine. It's you I'm worried about. You're brooding, not that I know why. And quiet. And… I don't know, being all not-Sasha. You know, not being you."

Sasha counted to ten in his head before letting out a slow breath. "Jason, hon, I don't know what's gotten into that head of yours, but I can't be anyone but Sasha, as that's who I am. Now how about I come out a little early and we chat before I deal with whatever it is your lovely hubby wants a formal meeting between the vamps and the kitties over, huh? You'll feel better, and Summer and Dimka can have a chance to say hi before they have to check out security. They'll enjoy getting to talk with Keith's guards, Chance and Kelley, and do the whole protection detail thing they all do. Everyone's happy that way."

Almost everyone. Since it would be a formal meeting, Trace would most likely be there. That meant Sasha would have to see him, smell him, hear him... all around deal with being in the presence of the male he couldn't have but wanted on a level that made him ache in ways he had never thought he could that fateful day five years ago.

"Well, can't say that I've ever turned down time with you, so of course you and your group can come out early."

"Sweet. Then once Summer is back and I've had time to catch up on a few things to do with the hospital, I'll head out to your tribe lands."

"Cool. See ya in a bit, then. Hugs."

Once the cell phone was quiet again, the room seemed more oppressive than before, something Sasha hadn't thought possible. He pocketed his phone as he stood. He needed to finish dressing for the day and then head over to the hospital before driving out to the lynx shifter tribe lands where his best friend, human or vampire, lived. He knew he could delegate all his administrative duties, but he liked to be a part of the human world and the fact that what he did helped heal humans, even if he wasn't a healer himself. Most of his kind thought little of humans—some covens even cultivated humans as humans did cattle—but his parents had raised him better than that. They were people, just like vampires or shifters, and while some saw him and his coven as a little odd, they couldn't exactly say much to criticize one of the most powerful in the Americas in strength, abilities, and money.

Sasha still remembered asking his mother once when he was young why they didn't hunt the shifters like other covens did. Her answer whispered through his thoughts on a regular basis. *All creatures belong to the world, and while we need to live and feed, so do they. Shifters do nothing inherently that denies us the right to live, therefore we do not have the right to deny them their right to live.* It was similar to why his father insisted humans shouldn't be killed or treated as cattle. Vampires could make feeding pleasurable for a human and did not need to kill in order to satiate themselves, and as such it was both gluttonous and murderous to deny humans the right to live. The harming of humans and shifters had been outlawed in that area for so long all vampires knew it, and even rogues knew not to challenge a Tolstoi rule unless they wished death.

Sadly the human propensity for cruelty and corruption led to Seattle still having a high crime and death rate....

Sasha shook off thoughts of his parents and death and focused on the day ahead.

As he gathered his wallet and keys, his gaze fell on the stupid silver Baast-inspired bangle bracelet he'd bought a couple of nights before. In fact, it matched some of the ones he had on, except for the tiny paw prints at the hinge locks. Each of Sasha's was the more traditional type, as they fit over his hand without the need of a clasp. This one would pop open if pushed from inside, such as if a shifter forgot to take it off before shifting. Sasha had had it made for Trace in a fit of idiocy. It wasn't as though a lynx's paw was larger than a human's, but with rings and such they risked losing a finger or toe if they forgot to take it off. He knew the cat liked bangles, bracelets, rings, and the like, but, being a shifter, he didn't wear such things unless he knew for sure he wouldn't be shifting—such as the first time he had met Jason. Too much risk, he'd been told. Of course Sasha had never met a shifter who wore anything like that either, though most shifters didn't talk much with vampires. He had heard of a wolf shifter that had a missing ring finger due to wearing a wedding ring for his human wife and forgetting once, so he made sure all of the pretties he had made for Trace were safe.

This wasn't even the first one of these Sasha'd had made for Trace. All with either the singular pressure hinges or with magnetic clasps, depending on the exact item. He'd even had some of them delivered to Trace, anonymously of course. Not even Jason or Jalin knew about Sasha's unfortunate insanity where the cat was concerned. Well, Jalin knew some, but not the full extent, thankfully.

He couldn't even explain why he had them made or sent. He didn't want Trace. Trace didn't want him. They were never going to be a couple. So why send him tokens...? Yeah, even in his own head, it sounded insane. With a resigned sigh, Sasha shoved the bangle into one of his desk drawers before he turned and left his suite, resolving, again, not to let Trace get to him and to live his life as he always had. Now if he could only convince his heart to listen.

CHAPTER TWO

TRACE PROWLED from treetop to treetop, unable to settle either his nerves or his body. His alpha, Keith Skyler, had ordered him to shift and go relax before their meeting with Aleksandr "Sasha" Tolstoi, Prince of the Konstantin Coven. Ha! Right, like he could do any such thing knowing he would have to spend the next few hours, most likely, with Prince Sasha. The infuriating vampire got under his fur even when he wasn't around.

He brushed against the trunk of another tree, loving the feel against his fur, the tug and scritch of the bark of the huge old trees in the forest around Seattle, Washington. Trace had been to older forests, to ones technically nicer, better, et cetera, in Canada—where he was from—but in the years since he'd moved to Seattle, he'd found a love for the forest, the shifters, and the other beings here he'd never expected. Unfortunately he'd also found his mate. An utterly unwanted and unacceptable mate. Trace had no place in his life for such things, no place in his heart now, and fated or not, there was no way any vampire, even if he was sex on two legs, would change his mind. Ever.

If they'd met when Trace was younger... but wishes weren't fishes, and he didn't even want a long-term partner, much less a vampire mate!

"Trace?" Jason's voice rang up through the trees.

Huh? Wonder what the human could want with me? Trace bounded down from branch to branch, curiosity cooling his ire at them for sending him outside as if he were a naughty kitten. He stopped, balancing on a branch just above Jason, and batted at Jason's hair, careful to keep his claws away from Jason's skin—Alpha Keith was not the forgiving sort when it came to his mate.

Jason's chuckle was warm and sweet. "You're all so playful when in your fur." He smiled up at Trace, and the open and honest appreciation there made Trace relax a little more. How he wished he could have found a mate when he was younger, like how Keith had Jason. Not that he wanted Jason, he never had, but once upon a time, he wished for someone to share his life with. Someone who would dote on him the way Jason did Keith, who would look at him how they did each other.

Shaking off that horrible train wreck of a thought, he mewled at Jason, curious why he was out looking for Trace instead of inside his home with his mate and kit.

"You know I can't understand you when you're a lynx, Trace, so don't ask me what I want via mewing."

And yet that's exactly what I asked.... Trace cocked his head and twitched one tufted ear at Jason and waited.

"Oh, fine. Like I don't know what you want to know. Anywhozit, Sasha and his people will be here soon, and I thought you might wish to meet the fanged and fabulous with pants on instead of fur, though lovely fur it is. If not, you're free to stay out until the meeting."

They're coming early? Dammit! Trace thumped down onto the ground beside Jason, landing on his feet, but still not as cleanly and daintily as he would have liked. *So much for relaxing.* He head-butted Jason's leg before rubbing against him a few times, trying to get the man moving.

Trace didn't appreciate the laughter, but he held his head high as he stalked back to his little house so he could shift and re-dress before having to deal with the damn vampires.

"Sorry, Trace, but this is my home, ya know. You don't have to herd me back with you like I'm one of the children."

No, but you're more vulnerable than a shifter, and something might be around that could hurt you. Trace had smelled and felt the presence of something unknown to him out in the forest a few days prior. It hadn't been on the part that was tribe land, but it still unnerved him. He'd told Keith, but no one else had, as of yet, found the scent he'd noticed.

It didn't take long before Jason and Trace were back at Jason's home. Once he was certain Jason was inside, Trace darted back to his own home, which was thankfully close by. He slipped into the kitchen via the cat door—something most all the homes on the tribe land had—then stood still as the shift washed over him. His fur receded as his body broke apart and reformed. Thankfully Baast, in Her infinite wisdom, had made the process painless. It was more a tickle and rush of sensation than anything, at least for him. He'd heard it was different for others, but he'd keep how it felt, thanks.

Naked and crouched, he twitched and stretched, reorienting himself to his human body and limbs before standing. He hated going too fast and falling—which he'd done more than once when younger. The pops felt good, though, as did his human muscles flexing. "Clothing, then back to Keith's and to dealing with the vampires." He could do this. He was certain if he just chanted it enough in his head, it would stick, and eventually it would all be okay again.

It didn't take long to get dressed, as he'd laid out his clothing earlier in the day, knowing about the meeting and that Sasha would be there. The fact they would not mate didn't stop him from making sure he looked damn fine in his slate-gray suit pants with a starched white shirt and the jade-green tie and accents. Shoes on and assorted extras gathered, his gaze fell on the strange gathering of jewelry sitting on top of his tall dresser. That he had an admirer was obvious, but he'd never found out who it was—not really. He suspected Sasha at times, but why would a prince send him anonymous gifts? No, that made no sense, so he always ended up back at square one when trying to figure out who would send the presents. Bangles, bracelets, necklaces, and even a torc had arrived sporadically over the time since he moved to Seattle. He didn't often wear any of the items, as most shifters didn't wear jewelry of any kind, though all the pieces were made specifically with a shifter's needs in mind. Still....

Without allowing himself to consider why, Trace gathered up a set of bangles and quickly slipped them onto his right wrist, making sure they settled over his sleeve properly before he slipped outside. He took a deep breath, taking in the clean air and fresh scent of the various pines, oaks, and other trees in the area, then sauntered over to Keith and Jason's.

No one lived too close to their alpha and alpha's mate, though Taylor, Keith's sister, was the next closest. Then there were the homes of Keith's closest friends; Vance, his second; Chance and Kelley, his enforcers/guards; and Trace, his adviser and council representative. After that the tribe chose their own layout of homes, with tribe council and members intermixed as they saw fit, though Keith and Jason did insist on proper roadway plans and such. Trace had enjoyed watching as Chance and the wolf shifter Caleb had worked together to map out the lynx tribe "town" of sorts. This was the only tribe he knew of who worked so closely with wolf shifters or with vampires.

And thinking of vampires, Trace caught sight of the prince's sleek metallic off-black Charger Hellcat, followed by a black SUV coming down the road as he reached the front porch of Keith and Jason's home. He bit back a sigh and turned away to knock on the door, refusing to acknowledge he'd seen the vampires coming. The polite thing to do would have been to wait, he knew, but he didn't think his nerves could manage it. He needed the other lynx around him if he had any hope of surviving the meeting. They and the topic should serve to distract his need and his unease at being near Sasha.

"You can come in," Keith's voice boomed from the other side of the door. "No need to knock, Trace. I can both hear and scent you out there."

Trace turned the knob and pushed the door open, then stepped inside. "It's your home, Alpha. It's only polite."

"I sent for you."

"And I am here as requested, sir."

Keith shook his head but smiled. "Did your outing do you any good at all?"

With a shrug, Trace replied, "No good was needed. I'm all right. The vampire coven representatives are arriving now. Are we ready?"

Jason came out of the side hall that led to the bedrooms. "Yeah. Sean is down for his nap and the oak door is closed, so he shouldn't hear anything."

"You don't really think there will be any yelling, do you?" Keith asked, a sudden frown marring his handsome face. "He's your best friend and our ally, but I won't have him scaring Sean."

"You know I can hear you," Sasha said as he sauntered into the large, open-space-layout living room they were all standing in. "Pardon my intrusion, as I know this is official, not a personal visit, but I was the topic of discussion and the door was open."

Dayum! Trace fought not to shiver as he took in all five feet six inches of Sasha Tolstoi, vampire prince and walking wet dream. His clothes had to have been made for him, how they hugged his body and accentuated every curve and plane. It took a moment for Trace to fight down his lynx, who didn't like that Trace refused to go get their mate and claim him. His lynx didn't understand how unsuitable Sasha was or why it wasn't possible for Trace to take a mate. No one knew why, and no one ever would! Not if he could help it.

"Sasha!" Jason squealed and threw himself at his much shorter friend, quickly wrapping him in a tight hug. "You know you're always welcome here."

"He is," Keith said, but his voice was hard, not the soft or indulgent tone it usually was with his mate. "However, Prince Tolstoi is also correct in that he should have waited to enter. He's here officially, so he should have been announced, not have just come on in like he usually does, Jason. You know that."

Jason released Sasha—which did *not* make Trace's lynx happy! Honest!—and pouted. "But—"

"No, hon, he's right. I should have waited, but the thought that I would do anything to hurt or scare Sean made me reckless." Sasha looked from Jason to Keith. "Forgive my rudeness, but why would you think I would hurt my nephew? I would rather give up my fangs than hurt him or Jason. I thought you knew that."

Keith shook his head and looked around at his gathered members, then at Trace, and motioned to him. "Trace, please."

Trace nodded. "If everyone would please take their places. Prince Tolstoi? Would you and your entourage please join us? We have much to discuss, and our alpha would like to do so before his son wakes and wants to come out and visit his favorite uncle."

Sasha gave a small smile but nodded. Jalin moved to stand beside where Sasha sat. Dimka and Summer stood behind Sasha, his ever-present and usually silent guards. Keith and Jason sat on a loveseat. Vance, as Keith's second, sat in a plush chair to Keith's right. Taylor, Levi, Gloria, Darla, and Neil—all part of the tribe council—sat in chairs around them. Chance and Kelley stood to the sides of Keith and Jason as their guard.

"In the normal course of events," Keith began, looking from Sasha to his council and back, "I would not alert the vampire coven to what was going on, much less invite you to a discussion about the situation, but you are both our allies and involved in a way, so it would be both impossible to hide and ill-advised to try."

Trace listened to Keith but watched Sasha intently, for once not because of his *not a crush*. The confident, near-haughty look slowly slid off his face, replaced by one of worry. Sasha leaned forward, his hands clutched to the armrests. "What's wrong?" He quickly shifted his gaze to Jason. "Hon? He mentioned Sean before. What's wrong with my nephew? I'll call my doctor right now. Jalin?"

Huh. That wasn't the reaction Trace had expected—any of them. He knew the vampire prince cared for Jason and for Sean, he'd seen that many times over since the boy was born, but the near panic was confusing. Why would a vampire be that worried about a human? They fed on humans. True, the Konstantin Coven didn't kill or torture humans as some covens did, but humans were still food....

"Calm down, Sasha," Jason said as he hopped up and bounded over to him. Jason knelt and then laid his hands over Sasha's. "Sean's fine. Better than fine, really. Just hear Keith out, okay? It's a good thing, what he needs to tell you, promise."

Sasha took a couple of deep breaths, then sat back and nodded. "Sorry, but you know how protective I am of you and Sean."

"I do. Now be a good boy and let Keith finish, 'kay?"

"Yeah." He looked back to Keith. "You were saying?"

Keith shook his head and chuckled. "Thanks for that display of concern, Prince Tolstoi. Not all of my council"—he gestured to Levi, Darla, Neil, Taylor, and Gloria—"believe you will be pleased with the news I have to impart, or that you will see it as a positive thing. I believe your display for Sean's health and welfare should allay their fears some."

The scowl that overtook Sasha's heart-shaped face would have terrified Trace had it been turned on him. The fact he knew it wasn't was the only reason he wasn't trembling as Levi, Darla, and Neil now were. Only Taylor and Gloria seemed immune, but then, they both trusted the vampire and his entourage implicitly. "Why would any here doubt my love for either human?" Sasha ground out, his fangs peeking out between his plump lips.

"Sean isn't human," Taylor said, her voice soft but firm.

"True, but he's not cat enough to count, as he can't shift. When the attack at Keith and Jason's engagement party happened, Jason and the little one with the one human parent were left outside while the full-shifter children were all gathered and protected. So pardon me if I count Sean as human when speaking to shifters."

"And do I tolerate such actions, Prince Tolstoi?" Keith asked, his voice just as hard as Sasha's.

Sasha tore his gaze from Taylor and shook his head. "No. Well, sort of, as it did happen."

"No, the situation in which a human-shifter child and a human mate were left outside during an attack happened. But as you know full well, it wasn't because they are human. The child panicked and ran the wrong way, getting separated from the others. The adults were all punished for losing her. As for Jason, who is right here and can remind you, if you need, he *chose* to run into the attacking shifters to protect the child. He wasn't abandoned. He made a choice, and while I was sick at the thought of losing him, I am, to this day, proud of him for what he did that day.

"I was referring to the practices of my father and those like him. Those who treat humans and those of mixed blood as lesser. The human members of my tribe are no less protected than the lynx shifter members. Any who do so will face me—something they do *not* want to do. Now as for the reason for this meeting: it is because Sean can shift, though we're not sure how."

"Huh?" Sasha flopped back in his chair and stared blankly. "Um, he's your son. Well, he's biologically Taylor and Jason's, but of your bloodline, so yours, but.... But half shifters can't shift. They're too human. It's not like with vampires, where the offspring is whatever the dominant species is, so how?" He suddenly whipped his head around to glare at Jason. "And why am I only just learning of this? I'm his uncle and godfather!"

"Because K-Keith asked m-me to wait s-so he could talk to you f-formally. Why do you th-think this m-meeting was c-called so qu-quickly? P-please don't b-be m-mad." Poor Jason looked like he might cry at any moment. Trace knew Sasha was his best friend whom Jason considered family, though they had no actual blood relation.

"I'm not mad at you, just miffed that I didn't know something so significant about Sean. That's all, hon, so calm down. No need to get all worked up. But are you sure he can shift? I mean, I know you're a Chosen of Baast, Keith, Alpha Skyler, and if he'd been your biological child, I might have even understood, but the lynx half is from your sister, as she was your surrogate."

"You know I can't lie with a female and have a child. No mated shifted can lie with any but their mate, and as mine is male... me having a biological child is out."

"Yes, I do know that, and as I was there for the child's birth, I wasn't questioning the parentage. My question is the how a human-shifter mixed child could shift part."

"We don't know." Keith looked at Trace and he swallowed hard. "Trace?"

"I've already contacted the intertribe council just outside Toronto. So far no one has any ideas how Sean can shift. I want to reach out to a couple of the Chosen in other parts of the world and see if their tribes have any lore that maybe we don't that might help. Also, um...." Trace took a deep breath. "I do have a possible idea or theory, but I don't know if now is the time or place for it."

Everyone in the room turned and stared, even the guards. "What?" Keith, Jason, Sasha, and Taylor all asked at the same time.

"Creepy," Trace grumbled.

"Trace," Keith hissed.

"Yes, Alpha." Trace closed his eyes, took a deep breath, and let it out slowly, then opened his eyes but didn't allow himself to meet anyone's gaze. "While I was out, shifted, before this meeting, I had a thought. Well, I've been thinking, and a few things have been tumbling through my head, but one seemed to fully come together." Well, when he could get his mind off Sasha for two seconds. "You shifted into your Chosen form when you mated Jason, then bit him and bled for him. You fed him your blood on a couple of other occasions thanks to his being injured due to your… well, because of the previous alpha's attacks on him. I wonder if he had or has enough shifter DNA in him because of that, so when he—" He paused, not sure of the word he wanted to use. Jason hadn't mated Taylor, as the impregnation had been done with the help of the vampire doctor. But the concept was the same. "—impregnated Taylor, the child got enough shifter DNA to actually be a lynx, not a human."

"Eww," someone said, though Trace wasn't sure who right away. "That's like suggesting the alpha had a child with his sister."

Trace looked around and found the source of the disgust: Darla.

"No, just that enough of what makes us shifters is present in Jason. Baast blessed their union and blessed them with a child, one who can shift. We are a magically blessed race. You know what happens if a kit happens from true incest?" Trace had seen the outcome from such a union, and it was horrific and tragic. The deformity of body wasn't as bad as the twisting of the mind. The one case he'd personally seen, the poor child's mind was locked in a perpetual state of enraged lynx while the body was twisted, as if stuck between human and lynx—except the child couldn't shift to either form. There was nothing like that in Sean!

Neil shivered. "Darla, that's not what Trace suggested and obviously not what happened. Sean is healthy, happy, and instead of worrying, we need to be preparing to train him properly how to lead, as he is Alpha Keith's heir."

"But I thought Zeke was his heir," Gloria countered.

Trace sighed and sat back, not in the mood to watch the council go at it again. When they were first told of the kit's ability to shift, they'd fought about which child would be the heir, completely ignoring that Keith was the one who chose his successor, not them. Only Taylor, as Zeke's birth mother and Keith's sister, had any sway in the decision. Not even Jason, though he was Keith's mate, would be permitted to speak out in favor of one child over the other.

"Stop!" Keith roared, making Trace smile and the council jump in their seats. He noticed the vampires seemed bored, which only increased his grin. "Both boys will be raised as my heirs, but Sean is my son, so he is my official heir. When the time comes, I will decide based on what's best for the tribe and for the boys. End of discussion."

"Good to know at least one of you has some sense. Now when do I get to see my nephew turn into a kitten?" Sasha asked, his face alight with curiosity.

"But—" Darla started.

"*Urod*, don't you have the sense to know when to shut the hell up?" Sasha snapped, cutting her off. "Neither Alpha," he continued, pointing at Keith, "nor Prince," then moved his finger to point at his own lightly sculpted chest, "has any use for your whining or attempts to sound important. Now shoo." He waved his hand in a swooping, dismissive gesture. "I want to find out more about Sean from those who are actually interested in his future and not in him as a pawn."

It was all Trace could do not to laugh as Darla huffed and flounced out of the room, yelling about horrible vampires and lack of manners as she went.

As soon as she left, Sasha looked back to Jason and Keith. "Now that she's gone, let me say congratulations and offer my doctor and resources in any way I can so we can figure out what truly happened to allow Sean to shift, and what it will mean for him as he gets older."

"Thanks." Keith placed his hand over Jason's but turned to face Trace. "Make sure the doctor the tribe council is sending knows he, or she—I've not been told who it is yet—will be working with a vampire doctor and that's not up for debate."

"Of course. Just...."

"What?" Keith's gaze didn't move.

"Prince Tolstoi's coven doctor having the information is one thing, though the council won't like it, but the information going outside your tribe or the prince's coven will not go well."

"That, Trace, is a given." Sasha smirked. "And I would be disappointed in your council if they didn't think that way. But this tribe has nothing to fear from us, especially not Sean. Now," he said, leaning forward. "When do I get to see him shift? I can't wait. There's nothing cuter than a baby lynx."

CHAPTER THREE

"I STILL can't believe how you talked to Darla," Jason nearly giggled as he and Sasha sat on the back porch of the home Jason shared with Keith. "I thought she was going to keel over, what with the strange shade of red she turned."

"Well, what did you want me to say? I don't know how Keith puts up with her, honestly."

"I usually don't," Keith said from behind them.

Smiling, Jason turned and tugged Keith down into a hug before he settled back against him, wrapped in his arms. Sasha tried, again, not to feel anything at the display of love and companionship between the two men. He didn't begrudge Jason his husband—in fact, Sasha couldn't be happier for Jason—but that didn't change the fact that his heart still wished he had his own lover to cuddle up with. In his opinion it was ridiculous that he was lonely. As the prince of a coven, especially one as strong as his, he could snap his fingers and have company any day or night he wanted it, but he would know they would only be there because he was the prince. The person would also not be Trace, so why bother?

"Earth to Sasha," Jason said and waved a hand in front of Sasha's face.

Sasha swatted at the hand. "You know, with the fact you have felines for a husband and a child, one would think you'd have been broken of that habit."

"Oh, I've tried." Keith shrugged. "I think he likes being swatted, personally."

"TMI, hon. TMI. I so don't want to know about your kinky bedroom life."

Jason chuckled, then snorted. "Oh, puh-leeze. You took me to a BDSM club more than once, and I know for a fact you're into that stuff, at least somewhat."

"He did what?" Keith rumbled.

"Chill, Keith." Sasha waved away the big lynx's worry with the flick of one hand. "Nothing happened. I took him to a couple of theme nights. You know, where they do displays and such, but he was fully clothed and didn't do anything with anyone." Sasha huffed. "Like anyone there could have talked him out of his clothes or into kink. Ha!"

"Then why'd you take him?"

"Because he was curious. I figured if I took him, he'd be safe, and he could find out what he wanted to know in a controlled environment. No danger, no one gets hurt, and he'd be happy."

"You know, I am right here," Jason sulked. "And I'm not *that* vanilla."

"Well, I should hope not, seeing as you're the hubby to a big ol' super alpha kitty." Sasha reached over and petted Keith's bulging biceps. "And I've seen the scars."

"Hey n-now." Jason flushed from hairline to below his collar. "N-no t-touching."

"I don't want your kitty, hon. Don't worry."

"You ever going to claim the lynx you *do* want?" Keith asked, one brow arched as he gazed down at Sasha.

Dammit! The last thing he needed was a meddlesome alpha cat egging on his forever hopeful, softhearted best friend. "I don't know what you're talking about." Sasha held up a hand. "And even if I did, you should be focusing on the little ball of fuzz in the yard playing, not on my love life or on what you're *presuming* is my lack thereof."

"That *ball of fuzz*, as you put it, has a name, thanks, and we all three know you aren't seeing anyone right now. That you haven't seen anyone in quite a while." Jason folded his arms over his chest as he leaned back against Keith, who continued to stare at Sasha. "*Sean* is fine. He's having fun with going back and forth between the human part of the jungle gym we got him and the kitty part Keith and Vance built. I *can* pay attention to my son and to you at the same time. Thanks ever so much, *hon*."

"Fine, Sean is where you should focus, not on my love life."

"Sasha, you might as well give up, and you know it," Keith countered. "I never win when he gets like this. I don't see you winning either."

The sad part was Keith was right. When Jason put his mind to it, no one got away with anything—not human, alpha, or prince. He wished his parents had lived to meet Jason. Sasha was certain his father and mother would have loved the sweet yet ornery human. "True or not, I have no answer for either of you. There is no kitty for me to go claim."

Both men stared at Sasha in blatant disbelief. Jason seemed to recover first. "Sasha, hon, I know you want Trace! And if what I've seen over all this time counts for anything, human though I may be, he certainly seems to *appreciate* an awful lot about you too. I've watched you two dance around each other since he first moved here… over five years ago. What I don't get is why you don't go after him. Is it because he's a lynx and you're a vampire? You didn't seem to think that was a valid reason for me to push Keith away when I first found out what he was, so I don't get it."

"I'm not biased against lynx, Jason. My brother-in-law was a lynx. You know that."

He nodded. "I do. So…."

"I'm not having this conversation. Trace and I are not right for one another. Period." *Besides, he doesn't want me and feels no qualms about sleeping with humans and probably other cats after meeting me, knowing we were supposed to be fated.*

"But—"

"Jason," Keith interrupted. "If Sasha isn't ready for some reason, as long as it isn't prejudice, then we should stay out of it. When he's ready, he'll come to you and tell you what's wrong. Right?" Keith moved his piercing gaze to Sasha, daring him to argue.

"If and when I find someone I want to date, I will share that with you, hon. I've shared that kind of thing with you before, even when I had to swear them to secrecy about their fangs to be allowed around you."

"Still wish you would have been honest about that sooner, but fine. *I* think you two would make a hot couple. But fine, be stubborn."

"I will, thanks."

Before either male could start on anything else dating-related, Sasha hopped up and went out to play with Sean. He was (mostly) confident neither Keith nor Jason would continue to harass him about dating, Trace, or kink/sex with Sean around.

TRACE PACED the hall and living room in his small house on the Glacier Rim Tribe land. After Keith Skyler had defeated his father, the former alpha, he had sold the old tribe lands and moved the tribe to the forests on the opposite side of Seattle. It wasn't where Trace had originally lived when he first moved to Seattle, but he loved his home. The clean lines and uncluttered space was all him—all his. He'd overseen every purchase and placement, and as such there was nothing that didn't comfort and feel like home to him. Nothing of his parents, his siblings, his exes…. Bookshelves lined two of the walls, and an entertainment center with shelving for movies and more took up most of another. He had a few pieces of art that caught his eye on the pale blue walls—except for the wall opposite the entertainment center. It was all rough stone with a fireplace and hearth. His furniture was overstuffed leather, soft and supple, perfect and comfortable, with dark-wood tables and accents. The floors were all hardwood, with throw rugs spread about to pull the leather and color of the walls together in a way that pleased his human and satisfied his lynx.

He stopped in front of the full-length mirror near the front door and turned so he could see his back. He only wore a pair of low-rise gray jogging pants, so his back was completely uncovered—something he didn't usually allow others to see. The marks there were still visible after all this time and would be for as long as he lived. Trace knew that, but he had grown too comfortable and lax in his new home. He'd stripped off his shirt when it became soaked with sweat during a run with Jason and a couple of the other human mates in his adopted tribe.

As the council representative and a friend of Jason's, Trace felt it his place to make sure the nonlynx in the tribe were taken care of and happy. Unfortunately they'd noticed the marks on his back and asked questions. Now he was waiting for Keith—as the tribe's alpha and veterinarian—or his sister Taylor—as a member of the tribe who was a nurse and someone Keith and Jason trusted completely—to stop by and start asking about the damn scars.

He didn't even know what he could say that wouldn't get him into trouble. Withholding health information from the alpha simply wasn't done, he knew that, but he'd never found the right time to talk about his past. He couldn't outright lie to his alpha. Besides, the alpha would smell the lie on him. When they'd made the decision for him to stay long-term, he should have just talked to Keith, and then none of this would be an issue.

The deep lash marks almost hid the bite scarring at his shoulder, but Trace could see it. It was only one of the reasons no lynx would ever accept Trace as a mate. The other marks were part of why Trace could never accept anyone else. Broken matings simply weren't done, nor could he tolerate another touching him that way again.

Stupid! How could he have been so stupid as to have let the humans see his back? Especially Jason!

Even though he knew to expect the knock, when it came, Trace still jumped, his heart racing as he froze at the sound.

"Trace? I know you're there," Keith said through the door. "I can hear you on the other side of the door, you know?"

Trace wondered if Keith would come in if he didn't answer the knock. Keith was the alpha, so he had every right, but he was also huge on respecting the privacy of others. Still....

"Trace. Open the door."

Yeah, he couldn't ignore a direct order like that—though it was said with more kindness than most alphas would afford in the same situation, he imagined. Trying not to sulk, Trace walked over and opened the front door to find Keith standing there. Had he bothered to check, he would have only scented Keith, but he'd been too wound up to think. A dangerous trait, one that had nearly gotten him killed once already. "Yes, Alpha."

Keith stepped inside and closed the door. "Trace, Jason's really worried, but I didn't let him come with me. I hoped you'd be willing to talk to me, though. Would you mind if we sat and discussed what he saw earlier?"

Mind? Yes. Would he refuse? Not specifically.... Drooping as he sighed, Trace replied, "Yes, but I will answer a few questions—to allay Jason's and your concerns. But please understand what caused this is in my past, and I want it to stay there. Please."

"Agreed."

Trace turned, not bothering to hide his back as he led the way to the couch and chairs. The gasp that followed him wasn't encouraging; neither was the hissing growl that followed. When he turned around and sat, he faced a pissed-off looking Keith, though thankfully he still appeared nearly all human. As impressive as Keith's Chosen of Baast form was, Trace really didn't want him going all super Alpha or Alpha King in his living room.

"That had better have been part of you when you first arrived here, Trace," Keith rumbled, his words slightly slurred as he spoke around his fangs. Top and bottom had come out, it seemed, in his agitated state.

Unable to meet Keith's gaze, Trace nodded. "It's part of why I was chosen to be your representative. Why even when they realized how flawed your training was at the hands of your previous alpha, I was left in place instead of them sending in someone specifically trained as a teacher of the alphas and of the old ways."

"I don't understand. The intertribal council sent me a rep and a trainer based on the fact he was abused, not based on qualifications?"

That made Trace's fur bristle even if it wasn't out. "No," he snapped. "I'm fully qualified, thank you oh so *very* fucking much. Have I let you down, or failed you or the Glacier Rim Tribe in any way since I arrived?"

"No, you have not."

"Then don't judge me based on what you saw on my back." Trace closed his eyes and prayed to Baast for patience, and that Keith could understand without his having to go into any real detail. Trace was positive he couldn't handle that. "I was selected because they thought it would give me a clean slate. Let me have a chance at a fresh start where no one would look at me with pity for what I'd been through. Where, in their infinite ignorance, they thought I might find a new mate and still have a chance for a family of my own. Since you're gay, you wouldn't have an issue with me being gay. And this being Seattle, I would be away from those who knew my past and those from it."

"And how you came by those scars, I take it."

It should have been a question, but it wasn't. Trace still replied, "Yes, that too. They are what they are, and as you well know, they won't fade any more than they have."

"You should have died with how bad they are, Trace. Most would have."

He knew that too. Had it not been for who gave them to him and how, he would have. The only reason he'd physically survived, other than having been rescued, was *thanks* to his mate using his blood to help him heal enough to live. Not that Trace wanted to by the end. All Trace could manage was a nod.

"I won't make you tell me the story, but I do have some questions. If they are that old, then there's nothing to be done for them, sadly. I still want to know the health and condition of all my cats, though. And while you technically belong to the council, you are still one of mine."

"I—" Trace cut himself off, knowing it was pointless to argue. Keith was his alpha—plus it was somewhat nice to know his alpha was looking out for him, even if he'd never wanted his new tribe, his new friends, to know of his past. And really, answering questions wasn't too bad, he hoped. "Yes, sir." Trace stood and took a deep breath. He let it out slowly as he stepped closer to Keith before he turned and presented his back to his alpha. "As you can see, they aren't new, so you have nothing to worry about." He stood tall until he felt the lightest of touches where Keith followed the marks down Trace's back. Trace nearly crumpled when

Keith touched the bite on the back of his shoulder and growled, the strange hiss and rumble that only happened when Keith was in his Chosen form. He knew if he turned, he would see Keith's face, but wider and with short hair that matched his lynx fur, his Technicolor-blue eyes would nearly glow, and he would be larger, wider, stronger… but still Keith. And Trace would have to fight his lynx even harder to stay still under Alpha Keith's inspection—no cat wanted its back to such a powerful being.

"Is this one still alive?" Keith asked as he again traced the bite.

"N-no," Trace whispered. "Duncan and his guards tended to…." Trace couldn't say his name. Could. Not. Do it. Even after all this time, it was beyond him. Sadly, his dreams still conjured the monster, his last ex, from time to time. He was certain later that night would be one of those times, unfortunately.

"Good. He doesn't deserve to live for what he did to you."

"It's over, so please…." *Please drop it.*

Keith continued to grumble for another minute or three, but finally allowed Trace to return to his chair and did the same after returning to his fully human form—his clothes a bit overstressed from the partial shift, but not completely destroyed. Trace had no desire to explain that to Jason. When Trace met Keith's gaze, he was startled to see not pity, but concern and remorse. "I must apologize, Trace. I should not have touched the marks, especially the mating bite. That is what the one on your shoulder is, right?"

He tried to speak but couldn't manage anything more than a squeak.

"That was thoughtless of me. I was upset at seeing what someone had done to you and didn't think about what my touch might do. Please forgive me."

"Nothing to forgive, sir."

"There is, but I won't push you. I've done too much of that already in my overzealous need to protect. For now I will smooth things over with Jason and the others for you, as we can all empathize with the concept of an abusive situation."

Trace nodded, unable to vocalize his response. He'd once believed Ford loved him. Oh, how wrong he'd been. He had to lose nearly everything, his life included, to see that. It was one of the reasons he quietly donated to the domestic abuse centers in Seattle and why he pushed for gay and lesbian domestic violence advocacy. If only he'd never….

"Hey, Trace."

"Huh?" What did Keith want, and why the strange tone of voice?

"Don't go there in your head. I've seen it before, so don't look at me with that incredulous face. You were doing the 'if only' routine in your head. You want to live your life, then stop doing that and move forward. You can't undo the past, but you can choose not to let it taint your future."

"What would you know about it? No one ever did that to you. You never let anyone...," Trace choked out, hating that he was discussing this, but now that they were talking, he needed to talk some. Insane but true.

"No, but I've had friends who did. One that we fought hard to get him to see what was happening, to see that the guy he was head over heels in love with was abusive, manipulative, and a lying, cheating asshole." Keith turned away as he continued, "Taylor can tell you about Flynn sometime."

"I've not heard that name before."

"You're not likely to. He was human. One of our few mutual human friends. He didn't make it out. I'm glad you did."

Trace gasped as his stomach both knotted and flipped. "Oh Goddess. He didn't? The guy he was with—"

"Is serving a not nearly long enough sentence in prison right now for murder. When I said I understood and empathized, I do."

CHAPTER FOUR

TRACE LOOKED around the club and wondered, again, what had possessed him to tell Jason that yes, he would babysit the humans. Of course he was sure they would be less than amused with that description, but realistically, that's why he was there. Not that he knew why they needed a chaperone in the first place. Well, he had concerns about what he'd felt and scented in the forest, but the rest of the tribe didn't feel the same, so Jason asking for the guard duty seemed overkill. But as the alpha mate, he knew about things that even Trace didn't at times, so he went along with the "request."

The two women and one man wanted to go out dancing to celebrate something or another. The only human in the tribe he wasn't taking out with them was Jason. He hadn't paid much attention to the why, as he honestly didn't care—Trace'd figured out early on it was just an excuse to go drink and dance. None of their partners wanted to go, or so he'd been told. But Jason asked, so he said yes.

It was the third time in the last month Jason had done this to him. The only time the humans seemed to want to have these inane outings happened to be when their mates weren't available.

At the one before last, Lethe, one of the human mates, had gotten a bit on the tipsy side and decided to hang all over Trace about the time Trace decided it was time to take them all back to the tribe lands. Unfortunately that was when Lethe had caused a slight detour and ran the two of them straight into Prince Sasha. As if taking home a drunk human who smelled of Trace—far too much for his mate's comfort, and damn, was she prone to hissing!—wasn't bad enough, he also had to deal with his stupid hormones going crazy. The entire time Sasha had stood there, Trace's lynx had prowled below the surface, demanding they go claim their *so not a* mate.

But now the bass from the speakers strategically placed around the club beat just under his skin, making his skin crawl instead of driving him out to the masses to dance. He'd loved to writhe and dance once, but it had been many a year since he felt safe enough to manage that. Now the press of bodies, the miasma of hormones, alcohol, and sex bruised his heart and stabbed at his senses. Too much perfume and cologne turned his stomach as well.

"Come on out and dance with us," Mandy said as she slithered off the dance floor and wrapped her arms around Trace's neck. He knew she was completely human, but the way she moved, seemingly without bones at times, often made him wonder if there weren't a touch of lynx in her family tree somewhere.

"I can't very well watch out for you if I'm on the dance floor with you, Mandy, my love," Trace teased as he steadied her when a large man bumped into her from behind. Out there being rubbed up against by who knew how many strangers? No! Not again in this lifetime.

She pouted prettily. "But Trace, you'd look so hot out there dancing with us. Carla and I would protect your virtue." He raised his eyebrows and cocked his head, waiting. Her only response was a throaty giggle.

He couldn't help but laugh. "It's not *my* virtue I'm worried about, love. Though if you come home smelling too much like me, your husband might be a touch miffed. Go have fun, just not too much." He turned her around and nudged her back toward the writhing horde, which quickly swallowed her up. Even with all the humans, Trace could easily still track her and the other two he was there to guard.

Trace shook his head and smiled. As much as he disliked the duty and the environment he found himself in, he did enjoy the company of the others in the tribe, be they lynx or the rare human. It was good to have a family again, one that didn't look at him with pity—even Keith hadn't changed his attitude or tone toward Trace in their few interactions over the last couple of days. Jason still seemed torn about the scars on Trace's back, though he hadn't asked. The slight staring and the aborted questions were enough to tell Trace that Keith had told Jason not to ask, but he had also, apparently, not told Jason what they were from, much to Trace's relief. He didn't want his new friends to look at him differently, nor did he want it getting back to Sasha, and he was certain if Jason were to learn the truth, Sasha would know immediately as well. No way would Jason think not to share that knowledge with his best friend, especially since he had it in his insane head the two of them "belonged together," usually with a stupid sigh following directly after the pronouncement. It wasn't that Jason was a maudlin teen, but he was ever hopeful on behalf of his friend.

As Trace made his way through the crowd toward the bar, hoping he could manage to get a drink without getting groped too many times by male hands—seriously, it wasn't even a gay club!—his thoughts and attention were suddenly arrested by the scent of vampire. Only the fact he was in Seattle stopped him from immediately grabbing his charges and demanding they leave. Still, knowing Prince Sasha didn't allow his members to harm humans or to attack shifters without due cause didn't mean all vampires were safe. What if it was a vamp from outside the Seattle area, or someone who didn't like Sasha's rules? No way would he allow anyone to harm his charges!

Detouring from his intended target, Trace circled the room, looking for the vampire in question. No, the *vampires*—plural—as, once he managed to back out of the crush of bodies, Trace quickly realized there were two distinct vampire scents. Both made his nose twitch and his fur bristle under his skin; there was something nasty at the core of them, though he couldn't put his finger on what. Trace was reaching for his phone when hands slammed against his wrists, trapping them against his sides.

"Wouldn't be doing that if I were you, kitty cat," purred a husky male voice behind him.

Dammit! The vampire had gotten behind him. "Release me now. Prince Sasha won't stand for any hostilities between our peoples, and you know it."

The voice that came next shocked Trace as much as it fascinated, sounding light and airy yet somehow decidedly cruel at the same time. "Aligning with filth such as you? Shameful. And to think his family was once so great. It will be again once we fix this teeny-tiny oversight so he can be bound to Tatiana. But you will have to go." She sounded almost sad at the end, not that any of what she said made sense.

Trace stiffened as he processed the rest of the words. Sasha couldn't be bound to anyone else, much less some hussy vampire named Tatiana! "You're wrong."

"Nope. Papa has had Sasha under surveillance for a while now. Nevertheless, we're to get rid of you and this inane treaty with the filthy animals. So...." The vampire wrenched Trace's arms behind him, and he found himself forcibly led out the back of the club and into the dingy alley.

There was a couple down past the dumpster enjoying each other's company, though they didn't stay long after the female vampire left to chase them off. "Now," she said as she sauntered back. "Where were we?"

"You two were going to let me go and return to your papa without having harmed anyone here."

She chuckled, as did the male still holding Trace in a viselike grip. Dammit! Why did he have to be a trainer and a diplomat type—not that his years as either were coming to use right then—instead of a warrior? Trace continued to struggle, but a single shifter, unskilled in combat against a vampire, had no real chance.

"Why does your papa care who Prince Sasha marries? And who's your papa?" *Really, if he's ordering my death, can't I at least know who beforehand?*

"Why wouldn't he care about who his nephew marries?" The female shrugged. "Now you have to go, so be a good kitty."

"Please don't do this." He didn't want to beg, but he didn't want Sasha hurt, and this *would* hurt Sasha. He knew it would as sure as he knew his own name, even if he refused to acknowledge part of that pain would be from Trace's death, not just from the war this could bring.

"It's nothing personal, kitty-cat boy. Papa just said to kill you first," she said and shrugged, then grasped his head. She pulled his head forward only a moment before Trace felt fangs rip into the flesh of his neck. It wasn't the neat slide like in the movies of the current era, but the violent rending of flesh as in the old horror films, the ones meant to scare the audience and cause blood to flow in vast amounts.

By all the Gods, it hurt! *Baast, please, it hurts....* If he were to die here, he wished he could have seen Sasha once more. To have seen his smile and heard that sultry, carefree laugh of his.

Trace tried to shift, not caring if a human might come out the back door and see him, but he couldn't focus enough to release his lynx. He fought the vampire's grip, but that too was a lost cause. He couldn't bring himself to give up, though, even though his cat couldn't get out and he couldn't get free.

As the world darkened around the edges, he could have sworn he heard Sasha yell his name, but the black swallowed him before he could find a way to tell him it would be okay.

"AGAIN, WHY am I accompanying you out to a club, Jalin?" Sasha asked as he pulled his Hellcat out of his reserved parking spot at the hospital. He looked to his left and noted Summer and Dimka were already in their SUV and ready, as always, to follow along. It was still odd to have them back full-time as his guards after all the years he'd had them taking turns guarding Jason. During that time, he'd only traveled with one of them at any given time, sometimes accompanied by one of their fighters. Still, going to a human club was something they deemed worthy of their watchful eyes.

"Because you need to do more than run the coven and the hospital. You need to do something fun."

"And watching you dance will be fun for me how?" he teased.

"It will get you out without any real responsibility. It's a human club, so no politics required. And you can even heckle me if you really must," Jalin added, sounding a touch put-upon, though Sasha knew he was no such thing. Jalin, in all their years together as servant and served, had never asked Sasha to accompany him somewhere that wasn't appropriate to his station. Sasha knew it was out of concern for him that Jalin did so now. The truth of that worry touched him even as it annoyed him—Jalin should not waste his personal time off trying to cheer Sasha up! That was time for his own life, for his own making, for carving out a family and relaxing and whatever it was Jalin did in his free time.

"But what will it get you? It's your night off," Sasha countered. He wanted to go home and not deal with people. Well, what he really wanted wasn't what was best for him, so that was off the list of choices, so home to read and listen to music, or maybe watch a movie. Were there any good ones out he hadn't already seen?

"A happier liege?" Jalin sounded so hopeful it near broke Sasha's heart. There was nothing to do to fix things the way Jalin wanted, but Sasha couldn't exactly explain that to him. Somehow a conversation of how he wasn't going to get happy because his fated heart was a lynx who didn't want to be mated with him… nor would the coven accept that their prince was bonded to an absentee cat…. Yeah, that wasn't a conversation he wanted to have. Not to mention he had to have an heir at some point. That he couldn't get out of, gay or not. There were some, such as his uncle, who believed he should already have an heir, especially since his parents and his only sister were dead.

"And pointing out that hanging out at a straight club isn't exactly my thing won't do any good, will it?" He could simply refuse, but Jalin had never asked him before, had never shown such concern for his mental well-being before.

"No, sir. I know you'd rather attend an event at one of the BDSM clubs or maybe go dance at one of the many gay nightclubs, but since you refuse to date, refuse even a dalliance, for some reason, those options mean little for you right now. So—"

Sasha jerked forward as his hands convulsed on the steering wheel. He slammed the gearshift into neutral for a moment as he tried to figure out what had just happened. Never in his two-hundred-plus years had his body betrayed him like that. Ever. Trembling, Sasha tried to think, but all he could focus on was an immediate need to get to Trace. Now! Right now!

Fumbling, Sasha put the car back into gear and peeled out of the parking lot, not caring if there were cops or oncoming traffic. He only knew he had to get to Trace.

"Sasha!" Jalin's panicked voice cut in, and the way he said it told Sasha it wasn't the first time he'd said it.

"What?" he snarled as the Hellcat careened around a corner, tires squealing loudly as they gripped the road. Sasha had no idea how, but he knew he was getting close to Trace. He followed the pull he felt, determined to get to his heart as fast as he could—hopefully without hurting anyone in the process.

"What's going on?"

"Trace" was all he managed to force out as he slammed into the parking lot of a club. Sasha didn't even pay attention to which one, just jerked the car into park, threw the door open, and, after nearly strangling himself, managed to get free. He then took off across the parking lot as fast as he could—a fact a tiny voice murmured would get him in trouble if anyone noticed, as he would seem to have simply disappeared. Not that he cared right then.

He could scent Trace and fear, two things that should never be together, as far as Sasha was concerned. Then he heard a female voice say, "Papa just told me to kill you first." Immediately after, the tang of blood flooded the air. Trace's blood!

"No!" he bellowed as he entered the alleyway. Sasha would have gone after the two fleeing vampires but for the crumpled form of Trace bleeding heavily on the filthy, wet ground.

Sasha dropped to his knees beside Trace as he hissed for Jalin to make sure they were safe. He then scooped Trace into his arms. It was difficult to see how bad the damage was, as the blood was so thick in the air it pulled at Sasha—it would any vampire. He was more worried about saving his heart than in tasting the male in his arms, no matter how sweet he smelled.

He ripped his button-down over his head and used it to wipe away as much of the blood as he could to see the actual damage—he just hoped it wasn't as bad as it seemed. Ha!

There were a series of deep puncture wounds made so violently, the edges were little rips and tears in Trace's neck. Sasha was pretty sure there was no way they could be stitched up, nor would they heal on their own. Not unless the lynx could come out, but since Trace was unconscious, that wasn't going to happen. The weird thing was every one of the punctures had missed his carotid artery.

Gods, but how he'd wanted to taste his mate, *but not like this! Never like this!*

He tried applying pressure to the wounds, even though he knew it wouldn't help. How could he heal his heart and not lose it at the same time?

"Unless you're prepared for him to die, you're going to have to seal those wounds, sir," Jalin said as he approached slowly from the opposite side of the alley, hands out, palms turned up. "Not even a shifter can heal all that. He's lost too much blood."

"I know." Sasha swallowed hard, knowing saving his fated heart was likely to cost it as well. There was no way a shifter would be okay with a vampire tasting their blood on the best of days, much less after such an attack. Trace would likely equate him with the monsters who hurt him, but Sasha couldn't let Trace die. "Pull the car around to the access."

He didn't take the time to see what Jalin did or didn't do, or to see if Dimka and Summer had caught up with them yet. Instead he laid Trace across his lap and chest so he could brace him in case he jerked when Sasha healed the wounds. Sasha then bent his head and carefully traced the tip of his tongue along the punctures in Trace's flesh, lapping up the blood there and closing the wound with the chemicals all vampires had in their saliva, which had prevented mortals throughout history from noticing their feedings.

He couldn't help the growl that slipped out, or the fact he was harder than he'd ever been in his life, even with Trace unconscious and hurt, draped across him. Trace tasted…. Gods, he didn't have the words to describe how the lynx tasted or how he affected him. Sasha also knew this would be a hundred times worse on him now, as tasting Trace would start the bond for him, in truth. There would be no one for him for as long as Trace existed, probably not even after. Just that tiny amount, and he knew he was lost to the lynx in his arms. To a male who didn't want him even as a friend, much less as anything more.

Sasha continued to lick the wounds until there wasn't a mark left. He couldn't remove all the blood or the damage inside Trace so easily, he knew, though he would if he could.

Summer stepped into Sasha's line of sight. "My lord, if you'll allow me, I'll carry him to the car."

"No," Sasha snarled.

"We need to get out of here before the cops are called. There's a lot of blood out here."

Sasha looked up then and nodded, but he still didn't release Trace. Instead he carefully maneuvered Trace until he could cradle him, then stood and walked toward the SUV Summer and Dimka drove. Summer followed along beside him but thankfully didn't speak again. When they reached the SUV, Summer opened the back door. Sasha levitated up, still cradling Trace, into the backseat.

Jalin stepped up before the door closed. "I have your keys and will follow you in your car. Are we going back to the coven house or to the lynx lands?"

"Home. Call our doctor." He was too worried about why Trace wasn't waking to get much else out. Was it normal for lynx shifters to stay unconscious when attacked like this? He didn't pay attention as the vehicle started, and then they pulled away from the club.

CHAPTER FIVE

SASHA PACED outside the bedroom Trace was currently in. The doctor and one of his assistants, along with Jalin, were still inside with him. It had taken Dr. Niko throwing Sasha out of the room to get him to let go of Trace. If the others hadn't known there was something more between the two men, they did now. Not that Trace was likely to ever allow Sasha near him after this.

When Dimka and Summer came around the corner together, Sasha stopped and faced them. "What did you find out?" he hissed. "Who were they, and could you track them?"

"Tracking them wasn't hard, sir, which is why what we found is highly suspect." Dimka glanced to Summer before he met Sasha's gaze. "If the hotel room's items are to be believed, your uncle is behind this. However—"

"What!"

"However," he repeated louder but without yelling. "It's all too neat and well laid out for my liking. If they had written a confession and put out a map, it wouldn't have been any simpler to find the room or the information we now have. I don't trust it."

"Nor do I, my lord." Summer worried the cuticle of his right thumb before he continued. "Something isn't right. I have never liked your mother's brother. He's far too power hungry, in my opinion, as you know, but this…." He shook his head, brows drawn together. "Having his children do this also makes no sense to me, as you would simply kill both his heirs and then him. Anyone with sense knows this. Well, had the attack worked and Trace died."

Sasha didn't want to think about Trace dead, so he focused on the rest of the information instead. "Very true. Family or not, I am not known for my patience or kindness when those I care for and protect are attacked. And attacking this particular tribe is doubly insane." The last group of vampires to set upon the Glacier Rim Tribe—specifically against Sasha's sister, Princess Nadia, and her fated heart, Alpha Orin Green—were destroyed to a man. Harming Trace would bring the same once he found out who was truly behind it.

"As for the cat in question" came the doctor's voice from behind Sasha.

Sasha spun around so quickly he nearly overbalanced himself. "What news of Trace?"

"That's what I thought." Dr. Niko stared at Sasha a moment longer before motioning him to enter the room. "Come. We may have a problem, and I'm thinking you are the only one who can fix it, my lord."

"Why? What's wrong with Tr...?" The words died on Sasha's tongue when he entered the room and found Trace. Sasha's worries about why his would-be mate wasn't waking up were over, as Trace was crouched against the far wall of the guest bedroom. He was obviously awake. However, the strange look in Trace's eyes and the quiet hissing coming from him didn't comfort Sasha in the least.

With a loud screech—or what would approximate the lynx version, but with a human voice—Trace launched himself across the room and landed atop Sasha. Too startled to do more than brace himself for the fall, Sasha allowed the shifter to bear him to the floor and kneel above him. Trace then paced around him, snarling and hissing and arching his back if anyone got too close. The only saving grace for his loyal guards was that Trace's fingers were human instead of being their lynx paws—with their razor-sharp claws.

"Back off, everyone. I don't know what's going on with Trace, but he's not harming me in any way, so stay back."

The collective yeses were slow to come and in no way happy sounding.

"Jalin, please call Alpha Keith Skyler. Maybe he will know why Trace is doing this." As soon as Jalin stepped out, Sasha turned his head to search out the doctor. "Any clue what's going on?"

"I don't know enough about shifter psychology, but he seems to think he's protecting you from us. I've never heard of such a thing happening, though."

Nor had Sasha.

"Shifters don't protect vampires, and definitely not from their own servants and guards," Summer insisted. "Well, maybe if there was a coup or something and they were especially close, or had been raised and trained as guards, but that's not the case here."

Sasha nodded as he thought. Sadly, nothing came to mind to explain Trace's odd behavior.

"Trace? Can you talk to me?"

Nothing.

"Why don't you let me sit up and we can talk, hon?"

Hiss....

"Okay, so you don't like that idea either. You could sit beside me instead of menacing my doctor and guards. I promise not to go anywhere."

All that got him was a growl. Instead of feeling indignant, as he was certain he ought to feel, it turned him on, the sound shooting straight to his groin—a fact he would deny to his dying day! He knew this was his fated heart, but still, this was a cat man acting like a literal cat.... That shouldn't be anything but disgusting. And yet....

The longer the strange standoff went on, the more Trace seemed to tune out the others' presence. He did nothing to try to force them out of the room as long as they stayed on their side. Instead he rubbed his face against Sasha's face and chest, purring constantly—driving Sasha crazy at the same time and causing his dick to fill to the point of pain, even with all the strangeness. Having Trace so close and wanting to be in contact with him, weird or not, was doing nothing to help him control his desire for the damnable lynx!

When a knock came some time later, Sasha jumped, causing Trace to snarl and hiss, arching his back as his stance became rigid in front of Sasha again.

Keith walked into the room slowly, followed by Jason. Keith's expression gave nothing away, but Jason looked scared as he looked at Sasha and gasped.

"Trace," Keith said in a deep rumble. His nostrils flared and he immediately tensed. "Think you dumped enough pheromones in here? You know vampires don't respond to them the same way we do, right?"

Trace huffed but didn't move or respond otherwise.

"Move away from Sasha now."

Trace let out a long, plaintive mewl and collapsed on top of Sasha, his fingers biting into Sasha's shoulders.

Keith cocked his head to the side before he shifted into his Chosen of Baast form—*and damn if that isn't just as impressive now as the first time!*

"Are you claiming him, Trace?" Keith growled, his voice harder to understand in that form but still clear enough. He took a deliberate step forward, his aura so imposing that he seemed to take up half the room. While Sasha did want Trace to calm down, now he was conflicted; he didn't want Keith to have to hurt Trace to stop him! "Because unless you are, you have no right to keep him. You know that."

Trace knelt over Sasha and made strange mewling noises that sounded very odd coming from a human body. The pattern seemed almost as if Trace were trying to explain something, but there were no words. Well, no words Sasha could understand.

"What the hell do you mean, *claim*, and why is he doing this?" Sasha snapped.

"Wait your turn, vampire," Keith replied as he continued to stare at Trace.

Trace hissed at Keith. He then huddled over Sasha and again rubbed his face over Sasha's, purring softly as he did.

"Well, I'll be damned." Keith's voice was gravelly but back to human.

Sasha turned his head as best he could with a human cat trying to keep his full attention. "What? You know what's going on? I don't want to forcibly move him to free myself. I could, but Trace would get hurt in the process."

"In more ways than one."

"Meaning? I'm in no mood for kitty doublespeak right now."

"That's Trace, though it's not. Well, to be more precise, that's Trace the lynx, though he's in the human body somehow. What the hell happened tonight?" Keith demanded. "I only know of one thing that can cause the human side to retreat and leave the lynx in charge like this, and I don't want to believe you would have anything to do with something like that."

"We can get to that in a minute. Can you get him to let me up, and what do you mean, claim me?"

"Once you make all the vampires, especially all those unmated, leave your presence, he'll calm down. He sees them as a threat to his claim on you. As for the claim, just get them out of here, and we'll talk."

If this Trace were just the cat side, that might make sense. Instinct not letting the "reasons" for why they couldn't be mated get in the way?

"Doctor, Dimka, Summer, Jalin, please leave and keep everyone out of my suite until otherwise notified."

"But we can't leave you alone with a rogue shifter, sir," Jalin snapped.

"Really, Jalin? You think Keith is going to hurt me?"

"I was more thinking the cat currently sitting on you, actually."

"Thank you for your concern, but you know full well I could remove him if I so chose. I don't wish to harm him, so I'm doing things Alpha Keith's way. However, clear my chambers *now*!"

Once it was only Sasha, Trace, Keith, and Jason, Sasha let out a slow breath. "Trace, hon, can you move a little now? Please?"

Trace huffed but finally let Sasha up. Sasha slowly stood and looked around the room, somehow knowing if he picked anywhere to sit Trace couldn't easily get to him, it would cause issues. Again. With that in mind, he climbed up onto the bed, shoving the pillows to the headboard so he could prop his back against them. Trace immediately draped himself across Sasha so his head was in Sasha's lap, facing outward so he could see Keith and Jason.

Keith pulled chairs up beside the bed for him and Jason.

"Sasha?" Jason swallowed hard. "Are you okay?"

"I'm all right, hon. Trace is having a terrible night, though." Sasha dropped one hand down to pet Trace, enjoying the feel of Trace's hair as he ran it through his fingers. "I didn't want to hurt him by forcing him to back off or to restrain him. I could tell he would have fought me, or the others, had they tried to move him. He's really in no condition for any kind of fighting."

"Explain this to me, please." Keith sat forward, his elbows on his knees. "Why is Trace like this all of a sudden? And why is he here? Oh, and why do I smell his blood?" Keith dipped his gaze to Trace for a moment, then added, "And *you* need to control your emotions. The pheromones are so thick in here that if I'd brought another shifter with me, you would have ended up in a fight."

Trace pushed closer to Sasha but didn't make any more mewling noises.

Sasha sighed, not happy about what little information he had to share. He relayed what he knew: finding Trace, the injuries, the fact Dimka and Summer believed it was a setup, the way he'd found Trace when the doctor called him into the room. "Unfortunately I have no idea what's going on. I don't know who they are, other than they obviously want to cause trouble between your tribe and my coven, me and my uncle, and who knows what else. Plus there's Trace and the literal cat-man issue he's got going on right now."

"Do you know what's wrong with him, Keith?" Jason held Keith's hand tight, but his gaze only left Sasha's to flit to Trace, and then went back to Sasha. "And are you really okay, hon? I know you seem all right, but he knocked you to the floor and all."

"I'm fine. It didn't hurt, even at the time. We vampires are a little more resilient than that. Besides, he wasn't trying to hurt me. Just"—Sasha ran his fingers through Trace's hair again as he looked at the man in his lap—"guard me for some reason. Keith, you ready to explain all that yet?"

"Depends on if you're ready to admit he's your mate yet."

"My what?" Sasha swallowed hard. He couldn't deny a direct challenge of their status. That would be cruel, especially if Trace really were his instinctual lynx right now. "Vampires, occasionally, have fated hearts, not destined mates."

"Fine, he's your *fated heart*, then."

Trace sat up and turned to face Sasha. As he took in the male—cat—beside him, he realized Keith was right. It was the lynx staring out through Trace's human eyes, not the Trace he'd spoken to and lusted after before. He didn't want to answer, especially with the cat staring at him, but he didn't seem to have a choice.

"Yes," he whispered.

"Then why aren't you two bonded?" Jason demanded.

"Because he doesn't want that, and I would never force him to accept me as his mate. We agreed, mutually, to never speak of it and to not bond."

"Is that the only reason?" Keith stared so hard Sasha wondered at the intensity.

"At the time we met, I wasn't in the right place. I needed time to accept the idea of another male in my life, fated or not. Jason can tell you a bit about my last boyfriend, and he only knows the surface of that pain. The fact I'm a prince and that others see my position and power often instead of me the person, vampire or not, means sometimes my relationships end… badly. I wanted time, but he wanted nothing to do with the whole idea. That's never changed. I can't help that we're fated, but I would never force the bond on him. Instead I am perpetually single."

"If you didn't bond, can't you go your own way? Keith said there was a way to break the beginnings of the bond if I'd refused him early on." Poor Jason looked so earnest as he sat forward.

Sasha shook his head. "It doesn't work that way for vampires. Besides, I've tasted his blood now. Even if I could have, the bond's begun for me. As long as he lives, I am tied to a male who wants nothing to do with me and that I cannot have." *One who's spent that last five years having sex with others while I—*

"That's what I was afraid of," Keith muttered, bringing a stop to Sasha's train wreck of a thought. "And his lynx has claimed you, but his human side has rejected you. You began the bond on your side. Do you know if that starts the mating bond on his?"

"Not that I am aware of. I don't remember Nadia mentioning Orin having any effects from her drinking from him. Why?"

"Um, why did she drink from him?" Jason seemed both curious and mildly nauseous.

Unable to help it, Sasha smiled. "Because feeding while having sex is the height of—" Sasha startled as Trace hopped up so he was suddenly straddling him and then began rubbing his face against his again before he wiggled around enough to push his neck against Sasha's mouth.

Trace's hard cock dug into Sasha's abdomen, combining with the scent of blood beneath Trace's skin. Sasha let out a low moan as he grasped Trace's hips and carefully pushed him back as he pulled his head away from temptation. "Trace, *mal'chik*, you can't just do that. Be still."

Trace went rigid, panting slightly before he gave a plaintive cry. He didn't try to fight Sasha's hold on him, though.

"Yeah, that's the other thing I was afraid of."

"Keith, you want to share with me since I'm the one with the overexcited kitty in my lap?" Sasha snapped, not taking his eyes off Trace.

"We're not getting the human side of Trace back until you bond with the side you've got right now."

"I can't do that! That's rape," Sasha hissed, unable to believe Keith would suggest he take away Trace's choice like that—and no, he didn't think letting the lynx make the choice counted. "Besides, I am not having sex with a cat. A shifter that's in human form and human mind is one thing, but human body or no, he's a cat right now! That's… just no!"

"I didn't say have sex with Trace," Keith said with a calm that only served to make Sasha more upset. "I said bond him. The cat side of him needs to know you want him. He's not trying to force you to mate with him. I think he understands that that is something that has to happen between his human side and you, but you can do the vampire equivalent, can't you?"

"But—"

"Or does that require sex too, like ours does?"

Sasha let go of Trace, then pulled him back down so he was again resting in Sasha's lap. He ran his hands over Trace's head and shoulders, down his back, and back up through his hair. He flitted his hands again to Trace's back and stopped. "What's wrong with his back?"

Trace tensed but didn't move from how Sasha put him.

"That's something you will have to ask him once he's back to his usual self. And before you ask, he's not told Jason either, so no, asking him won't help. It's one of those things you will simply have to wait to find out. It's not my story to tell."

Unhappy but not seeing a way around it, not if it was something Trace didn't want others to know, Sasha nodded. "Fine. For now."

Instead he tried to think through what Keith was asking of him, but the idea of completing the fated heart bond with one who didn't truly want him made his heart hurt more than he thought possible. Still, the world was already cold and gray. What difference would this really make?

"Do you know what you're asking me to do? Really?"

"Keith, if it's going to hurt Sasha to do this…," Jason whispered as he leaned against Keith.

"Hurt? If only." Sasha turned away from them both. "As things are now, I will be alone as long as Trace lives, for the two centuries or so he has left. I will then feel the loss and mourn him for who knows how long. What you are asking is that I make it so I have an immortal companion who will never want me, never touch me, never feed me, never love me. You aren't just asking me to save my fated heart; you are asking me to willingly turn what should be a blessing into a curse for the rest of my eternal life.

"But to answer your question, Keith, yes, I can bond him without sex. Though it will mean nothing to him and deny me the energy to function for a while that way. Please leave now. Both of you."

Jason jumped up and started toward Sasha but stopped when Sasha growled. "Get. Out. Of. This. Room. Now!"

CHAPTER SIX

IT HAD been over an hour since Sasha had thrown his best friend and his friend's mate out of the room. He hadn't meant to put so much of his power behind his words, but the thought of Jason touching him or trying to comfort him at that moment was more than he could take. So using the ability to command and persuade that most vampires had, to one degree or another, just happened. He had never used it on Jason before—well, not to that extent—but right then he couldn't bring himself to care.

It had also been over an hour since he'd made his bizarre call to Jalin. Thinking back on that call had him torn between laughter and frustration. He'd pulled out his cell as Trace watched him.

"Jalin."

"Yes, sir. May we come back in?"

"Ha-ha, no," he replied flatly. "Can I trust you with something no one else is to know of? Not even Summer or Dimka."

Jalin's voice was tight when he replied, "Of course, my lord. You are first always."

"Good. Then here's what I need you to do...."

Giving his assistant instructions for how to set up his personal chambers was odd. Sasha had dreamed of taking a fated heart of his own when he was a child, but somehow the entire situation seemed a mockery of his hopes and longing. But if it would save Trace, he would do it. No matter that the cost was to his own soul, it seemed.

Now settled on his king-size bed, Sasha looked down at Trace and wondered what the male inside would think when he managed to resurface. Would he forgive Sasha for what he was about to do? Shifters lived longer, but in comparison, a shifter's life ended before a vampire's barely began. Instead of letting his worries about the future take hold, he focused on the now, and the cat before him.

"Trace?"

Trace perked up and met his gaze.

"Can you understand me? I really need you to know what's going on, even if it's your lynx, not your human side, agreeing."

Trace purred and cuddled close, all tension having left as soon as they were alone. Now that they were in Sasha's bedchamber, Trace seemed even more at ease. He'd prowled around, rubbing against various things, before joining Sasha on the bed. It was a peculiar and somewhat amusing sight, seeing Trace doing these things in his human form, though Sasha could so easily imagine the lynx in his place. He ached to have the lynx there in his home by choice, and Trace, the human side, there with him willingly in bed.

Sasha shook off his wandering thoughts and hoped Trace's actions meant yes. The fact Trace had tried to make Sasha bite him earlier gave him hope the understanding was there, even if the human side wasn't fully. "I need to bite you, bond you, but I won't have sex with you. Not as long as it's you, the kitty, in control."

The disgruntled growl and huff made Sasha smile even if the situation didn't. "Sorry, boy, but I don't have sex with kitty cats. Kitty boys is a whole other topic, but no matter what your body shape, you're still the animal, sorry."

Trace flopped down against Sasha's side hard enough that, had he been a human, Sasha was certain he would have found himself suddenly on the floor looking up. "That's not negotiable. But I can bind you to me as my fated heart without doing anything against what Trace, the human part of you, wants. It won't force the mating and hurt that part of you." *I hope you see it that way when the human side of you wakes up. Keith better damn well know what he's talking about!*

He again found himself with a lapful of Trace and that same tantalizing scent of blood directly under his fangs. *Dammit! Why's he have to push so hard?*

"Your life span will match mine. Can you understand that?"

Trace froze, then pulled back to stare at Sasha. He mewed at Sasha but didn't seem upset, just waiting.

"Can you accept that? Accept me?" *Can the lynx part of you want me that much, even if the human part doesn't?*

Trace again mewled, then pushed his neck against Sasha's face as he had before. "I guess that's as good a yes as I'm going to get." Sasha nudged Trace back and stood again. "Let's get you undressed. I hate that the first time I get to see you like this, it's not really you, though." Trace cocked his head and stood there with his arms at off angles. "I don't know if the human part of you reintegrating with the rest will trigger a shift.

He'll be pissed if we ruin all his clothes. This shirt is a replacement, but the pants aren't, nor are the shoes and such." Sasha continued to divest Trace of his clothing, doing his best to ignore the male before him as he folded, stacked, and set aside the items. When done, he coaxed Trace under the sheet, hoping if he couldn't see all that sexy flesh on display, he might be less tempted. It didn't help much, but the mewl Trace made as Sasha climbed up on top of the sheet did.

The only light in the room was from candles, and there was soft music and light incense burning. Had things been different, this would have been romantic, but as it was, it only served to underscore what he was losing as far as Sasha was concerned. Still, his fated heart would be safe, and he would still be able to lead and protect his coven. That was all that mattered. In time he would find a female to act as a surrogate so he could have children. He would focus on that instead of what he would be without.

Yeah, if only it were that easy.

Refocusing on the here and now, he pulled Trace into his arms. "I know this is strange for you and that this probably makes no sense to you since you're the lynx, not the human Trace, but I need you to be still for me, okay? I need to bite you and take a small bit of your blood after I release something into your bloodstream. It might feel strange for a moment, but it shouldn't hurt. The thing is, because I'm not taking in more of your energy than that, I will collapse after that and won't be able to help you if you pass out and wake up as the human Trace. You'll need to help your human side understand what happened, okay? Can you do that?"

Could the lynx do that? Sasha wasn't sure how much they communicated in a regular shifter, much less one who had somehow done whatever Trace did to retreat into himself. He had to hope it worked, as the covenstead was no place for a lone and panicked shifter to go running around, and only Jalin knew this was happening. He'd had to tell him after having him set up the room to include food for Trace once he was back in his right mind-body combo again. Keith and Jason were still on-site, so Trace would have their help with understanding what just happened, but Jalin knew too much not to be informed, and besides, Jalin would need to know so he could help Trace as time moved forward. Trace might never be truly Sasha's, but that didn't mean Trace would be without the benefits being Sasha's should afford him.

It still took him a few more moments to get his courage up to actually bite. Sasha knew the stories—that your souls merged for a moment, that time stood still, and everything was blended and became one whole, only with two bodies. That he would know Trace, and Trace him, in ways neither could imagine beforehand. The thought of the bonding with someone who didn't want him made him feel like he was five again and hiding under his bed, afraid of the storms. His mother had coaxed him out and shown him storms were beautiful things and not something he should hide from. Unfortunately his mother wasn't here—a death he had never been able to avenge, as no one knew who killed her and his father, or how.

Shaking off the morbid thought, he refocused on Trace and bit, sliding his fangs in carefully. He didn't want what the monster did earlier to be remembered now, nor did he ever want any part of Trace to fear him. Trace whimpered and pushed closer. Sasha released the bonding chemical, then licked at the tiny trails of blood that slid down Trace's throat past his fangs. Once everything had flooded Trace's blood, Sasha took a few good pulls of Trace's rich blood, the vibrancy and spiciness a shock. The bonding had altered its flavor already. As his head swam, he managed one more taste before he knew he had to pull away. He licked the punctures closed.

The last thing he heard as the world spun faster, then went black, was Trace ask, "Sasha? What...?"

TRACE TURNED over, unsure what his sheet was caught on but annoyed just the same. He never slept without something covering him. Not in his human form, at least. He gave a hard tug as he tried not to let the waking world invade his dreams too much. All he wanted was more sleep. The last thing he wanted was to deal with the real world right then, dammit. There was nothing but pain and fear there. When the sheet still wouldn't move, he turned his head and cracked one eye open, hoping it was a simple fix and he could get back to what he'd been doing. Instead he came face-to-face with a sleeping Sasha.

Before he could think better of it, he was out of the bed, across the room, and had let out a scream he was sure they heard all the way back in Toronto. The odd thing was Sasha didn't so much as twitch. Trace knew the human stories said vampires were undead and basically were dead during the day, but that was all crap. Just like the stories about shifters being monsters created by curses or how they murdered people and ate them. However, with how still Sasha was right then and how he didn't even breathe loud enough to be heard even after the yell, Trace might have believed it of him.

The door to the room burst open, drawing another yell as he expected an attack—and dammit, he was naked too!

"Trace, sir?" Sasha's assistant, Jalin, said after he looked around and then retreated to the doorway.

"Um...."

"It's okay, sir." Jalin flicked his gaze to Sasha for a moment, but then quickly back to Trace. "If you'd feel more comfortable, your clothes are right there." He pointed to a plush lounger across the room. "I can wait in the hall until you're dressed and then return to speak with you."

Trace managed a small nod, confused as to where he was and why. The last thing he remembered was.... No, he didn't want to think about that now.

"Just let me know when you're ready, and I can show you where the food and drinks are. The doctor wants to see you, as does your alpha and his mate. But for now get dressed." Jalin immediately stepped outside the room and closed the door.

Trace listened, and when he was as certain as he could be no one else was coming in, he darted over to his clothes and dressed as quickly as his trembling fingers would allow. The shirt wasn't his, but as it would cover his back, he decided not to be picky right then. Even fully dressed, he still felt so cold, though, and naked. He wanted more layers of clothing on and more warmth. It had been years since he'd felt like this and he hated that he did so now, especially knowing he had to deal with vampires and his alpha.

He noticed a warm-looking throw folded across the foot of the bed and decided since he'd been stripped and thrown in here, the least Sasha could do was let him borrow it until he felt better. Trace unfolded it, noting the deep jade color and the edging of tiny cat paw prints, then wrapped it around his shoulders. When he tried to call out to Jalin, he realized he had another problem. No coherent sound came out.

A moment later a soft knock sounded on the door. "Trace? Are you ready?"

Trace tried again, managing a soft, if painful, yes.

Jalin reentered the room and gave a short bow. "Prince Sasha wished me to show you where the food and drink he had brought in for you are. Also, if you need anything, please let me know and I'll arrange for it right away."

"Can—" He cleared his throat and tried again. "Can I leave?"

"After the doctor and your alpha have seen you, Prince Sasha has given you leave to go if you wish, but you must have either Summer, Dimka, or myself with you if you do so. Well, if you're off the tribe's lands, at least for now."

"What?" he managed to yell—well, more of a whispered yell, but he was ignoring that point right then.

"Your alpha can explain it, as Sasha isn't in a position to right now. He, his mate, and the doctor are all waiting to see you. Now let me show you to your nourishment, and I'll let them know you're up and about."

"But...."

"Hmm...?"

"Why is Sasha just lying there through all this?"

Jalin frowned as he glanced at Sasha again. "He will be very cross with me if I answer any such questions, sir."

"I don't want you in trouble, but...." Trace bit his lip. Would Sasha hurt Jalin? He was a servant, not a friend, maybe. Or maybe he was both. Trace had no clue how that worked.

"Please allow your alpha to explain things to you, as I believe he would be best able to do so. At least until Prince Sasha can." He could have sworn he heard Jalin add "if he will" at the end, but wasn't quite sure.

Trace nodded, not sure what else to do. He wanted to leave but didn't at the same time. There was something odd about Sasha not waking, but he didn't know what. The threats the monsters who attacked him had made kept running through his mind. *Does Sasha know his uncle wanted to hurt him? Did someone hurt him? Is that why he's sleeping like that?* No, that didn't make sense. If Sasha were hurt, his assistant wouldn't be so calm.

It didn't take long for Jalin to show him where the minifridge and cabinet of nonperishable foods that Sasha had set aside for him were. Trace couldn't figure out why Sasha had rearranged his bedroom to accommodate him like that since the vampire knew full well Trace wasn't about to stay. They were *not* mates, no matter what Fate thought! Of course, nothing made sense from the point when Jason had asked Trace to escort the humans out to the club. From there forward he hoped was all part of the same nightmare.

As he sat on the lounger eating an energy bar and drinking tons of water, another knock came, this one stronger. The scent with it was all alpha and cat, with a touch of human. Keith and Jason entered a moment later. Jason stopped just inside the room, but Keith strode right up to Trace.

Every muscle tensed, and he bolted before he realized what he'd done, his half-eaten food and open bottle left where he'd been—the water spilling on the expensive rug beneath his feet. Again Trace found himself with his back against the wall, crouched in the corner of the room. It didn't make sense logically; he knew that. His alpha wouldn't hurt him, but for whatever reason, something in him wasn't listening. He didn't want any male near him.

Keith stopped and stared down at the mess Trace had left on the floor. "Um, Trace? What's going on?"

"Please," he croaked out. "Please don't come closer." Yeah, that didn't make him seem nuts at all....

CHAPTER SEVEN

"JASON, PLEASE go get the doctor." Keith's gaze didn't leave Trace's, but he didn't speak again until Jason left the room. "If I sit over here, will that be all right?"

Trace tried to will himself to calm, really he did, but it wasn't working. His skin crawled if any male approached him—at the least— and he wanted people near Sasha when he was sleeping or unconscious or whatever he was even less. "Can you, um, not be so close to Sasha? Please, Alpha?"

"You know I would never hurt Sasha. Jason would never allow it, even if I wanted to."

"My head knows that, but the rest of me seems to not be listening so well. So please?"

"Okay. We need you checked over and we need to talk to you. Can you come out of the corner?" Keith slid down into a squat against the far wall, right inside the room, and slumped his shoulders in what Trace assumed was supposed to be a nonthreatening pose. If he knew why he felt threatened, that might have helped more. "You're in Sasha's personal suite. We could do all of this out in his sitting room instead of his sleeping area."

Trace thought that over, and while it sounded logical, he didn't relish the thought of being out there with others. Letting the doctor *touch* him. The very *male* doctor. But them being in Sasha's room while he wasn't able to defend himself made Trace's skin crawl even worse. No, that wasn't acceptable.

"The sitting room."

"We'll meet you there when you're ready, then." Keith slowly stood and exited the room, leaving the door open behind him.

It took Trace a good fifteen minutes or so to join them. Keith, Jason, and Dr. Niko were there, but thankfully, no one else. He could smell other vampires close by, but not inside the suite. "Hi," he whispered as he stood just inside the doorway.

"Welcome, Trace." Keith motioned to a chair a little way from the others. "I set one close, but I hoped not too close for you. Do you know what's happened or why you're here?"

Trace shook his head. "No." He edged toward his seat, watching the others carefully. "Well, I remember being attacked at the club. Um, I failed to protect the humans I was there for. Were they hurt too?" Was that why he was there? Was Sasha trying to protect him, even though he'd spurned their mating bond?

"They're fine," Jason said, his voice soft, his brows pulled together tight. "They had n-no idea what happened until one of the other vampires under D-Dimka and Summer went inside to g-gather them and return them to the t-tribe after Sasha had left with y-you."

"I don't understand what happened. How am I not dead, and why am I in the vampires' big house instead of our tribe lands? Am I banished for failing you?" Trace bit his lip hard enough to draw blood as he looked at Keith; he could taste the strong tang of copper and knew that hadn't been the smartest thing to do when the doctor's nostrils flared and he snapped his head up. Thankfully the doctor didn't move or speak.

"Of course not!" Keith leaned forward—it took all of Trace's willpower not to skitter away when he did that. "Sasha brought you here when he found you. You'd been badly hurt. They couldn't figure out what was wrong with you, so Jalin called us to come and help."

"I...." He shook his head, trying to make sense of Keith's words. He vaguely remembered Keith and Jason being with him and Sasha, but it was all fuzzy and wrong somehow. Not like how his lynx thought, but something else altogether. Something... clouded. Why couldn't he remember? "I can't remember." He tugged on his short hair. "Why can't I remember?"

"If I could examine you, it might help to find a few of those answers you seek, Trace. The blood loss, I'm sure, isn't helping." Dr. Niko patted a black bag beside him. "I do know more than a little about lynx shifters, so it's not like I'm working in the dark here, if you're worried. Besides, I would never do anything to you that might anger Prince Sasha. I'm opinionated and have an attitude at times, but I'm not so stupid as to deliberately get on his bad side."

That statement didn't make any more sense than how everyone was acting. Why was everyone so worried about how Sasha would react? Trace didn't need some vampire to fight his battles!

"I'm sure that if Alpha Keith says you're okay, then you know what you're doing, just, um—" Baast, but he didn't want anyone touching him!

"You don't want anyone to touch you?"

Trace nodded. "Yeah."

"That's not surprising, really."

"Why? I mean, I never like strangers touching me, but they aren't strangers." He motioned to Keith and Jason. "And I've met you before and know you aren't a danger to me. Not in this situation, at least."

"You were attacked and bled by a vampire, actually two, I believe, and with what I saw on your back, it is little wonder you're having issues. If you were human, you would still be bedridden, so the facts of the trauma would still be easy to see and remember for all here. But as a shifter, you heal outwardly, so it seems as though you should be fine. You're not, not really."

"My back is off-limits." No way was he discussing that with some vampire doctor in earshot of Sasha. "And I am all healed up, so I *am* fine."

"No, you are not. Your body might be better, though I can't determine that without an examination," Dr. Niko added pointedly. "But the fact you nearly bolt when anyone moves tells me quite a bit about how not okay you are."

"Shouldn't you be more worried about why Sasha isn't up or even moving around a little? I'm just a shifter. He's your prince."

"Prince Sasha will be fine once he regains his strength from what he did to help heal you." Dr. Niko shrugged, which was a strange sight. The male seemed old and grumpy—even if vampires never looked old physically, no matter their actual age—yet that motion seemed almost flippant. "Had you had sex with him when he did it, he'd be up and about by now. But since you didn't, he isn't. Now would you please let me examine you so I can figure out if you need anything else?"

Trace was too stunned to do anything when the vampire approached. Had the vampire doctor really just chastised him for *not* putting out for the vampire prince? How the hell did that make sense? Once he managed to get his brain to engage again, he raised his head as he did his best to ignore the doctor's light, impersonal touches, to look at Keith and Jason.

"Can you make what he just said make sense? Or maybe hurry him up before my skin crawls off my body to get away from him?" Trace held on to the edge of his chair as he forced himself not to bolt back into

Sasha's room and throw the lock—and he refused to examine why that seemed like such a safe place right then.

Keith sighed but then nodded. "When you awoke the first time, it wasn't you they found, but your lynx in your human shape. This became more of a problem when you flattened Sasha and proceeded to guard him from the others. That's when I was called." The look his alpha gave him stirred something inside, as did the words, but he still couldn't grasp the memory. "You don't remember any of this, do you?"

"No."

"Did that happen the last time your lynx took over for you?"

"Why would that have happened before?" Jason asked. "And why now?"

"Jason, love, don't interrupt. This is hard enough on Trace as it is."

"S-sorry."

"No, it's okay. I shouldn't have expected to keep this from the alpha couple of my new tribe. I just didn't want the pity or to be seen as something broken."

"You're not broken or to be pitied," Keith growled. "You overcame something no one should have to ever endure. Jason has no idea what we're talking about, and I don't believe Sasha does either unless that bite thing he did to help you showed him."

"I have no idea what you're talking about bites for, but that's good, I guess. I…. Yes, it happened then too. I know what they did to save me then because they told me, not because I remember the final rescue. I had blacked out from the last bit of the final whipping and blood loss. Even with our healing being as strong and fast as it is, we can get infections if we remain at a certain level of loss, and, well… I was." The room started to spin and his vision tunneled slightly, but he forced himself to keep talking, knowing if he didn't get it out now, he likely never would.

"It was over a month before they managed to coax my lynx side into giving up control and me into returning. You would have to ask them how they did it. I never asked. Didn't want to know, honestly. I don't remember most of that time. Even when I'm in my lynx form, I only have blurry memories of that time—nothing that makes sense. I figure it's some kind of self-preservation due to what happened."

Dr. Niko made a strange noise in the back of his throat, making Trace jump. "And whoever hurt you like that is dead now?"

"That's what Keith asked when he saw my back."

"That's not an answer."

"He is."

"Good. The world is a better place for it."

Trace looked over his shoulder at the doctor, confused why the male would care about a shifter so much. "But what difference does it make now?"

"It tells me that you may not be ready to return to the lynx tribe lands yet, Trace. If what we saw was the result of extreme emotional and physical trauma. Even though this time it wasn't long-term, you may need to stay close to Sasha for a while."

"But how is Sasha supposed to help?" They didn't know about... did they?

Dr. Niko looked at Keith and nodded to the door. "Make sure no one but Jalin is within hearing range."

Keith did as asked, and moments later, it was the four of them again, though Trace had caught a brief glimpse of Jalin outside the door before Keith closed it and returned.

"He has Dimka and Summer posted farther out to make sure no one can get too close to the suite, and he said the rooms are vampire-level soundproofed."

"They are, for the most part, but if anyone is within the rooms, things could be overheard. Now to answer you, Trace, he is your, um... I believe you use the term 'true mate' or 'destined mate,' though you've never claimed him."

"What?" he screeched.

The doctor ignored him and kept talking. "That bond the other way will allow Prince Sasha to help soothe you when fear or worry starts getting too much for you. At least until you can work past what happened last night. Also I believe Summer and Dimka need to know if those who attacked you said anything to you. They're trying to find out who is trying to hurt our prince and why."

"But... but we aren't mated! And of course they talked. Idiots and puffed-up lackeys always want to run off at the mouth. His uncle sent them to destroy the alliance between the coven and the tribe. They were to kill me first, then make sure the alliance was destroyed. That way Sasha would bond or marry or whatever some Tatiana chick, make little vamp babies, and be a good little vamp boy under his uncle's thumb."

"Trace, you need to calm down." Dr. Niko put his hand on Trace's shoulder, but that was one touch too many, and it sent him flying across the room and against the wall.

"Don't fuckin' touch me!"

"Mal'chik" came Sasha's soft voice from nearby. Trace slowly turned to where he knew Sasha to be and took in his disheveled appearance—something he couldn't remember seeing before. "You need to calm down before you hurt yourself."

"Please don't let him keep touching me." Trace hated the pleading clear in his voice, but he was certain he would go crazy if another person touched him right then.

"Shh…. Trace. Dr. Niko won't touch you without me with you."

Sasha swayed slightly. Trace darted over and wrapped an arm around his shoulders. "Should you be up? What's wrong with you, anyway?"

A shudder went through Sasha as he leaned into Trace a little more. "I'm fine. Just a little tired."

Dr. Niko looked hard at Sasha and shook his head. "You need to feed."

"I will later. For now did you figure out what you needed to about Trace? Is he better?"

"Eh, physically he seems to be fine. I'd like to examine his back to compare it to how it was when you first brought him in, but otherwise, he's in top shifter health. It's his mental health that concerns me."

Trace cringed and Sasha turned to look up at him. "What do you mean? Trace, what's wrong?"

"Nothing. Shouldn't we be more worried about your uncle and your *bride-to-be*?" He knew he sounded waspish, but the idea of Sasha married to some female, vampire or otherwise, made him ill and angry all at the same time. Just because they weren't going to be mates didn't mean Sasha could go have sex and bond with some… some vampire slut!

"I'm not marrying Tatiana, Trace. But do you think we could have this discussion while sitting? I'm still a little tired."

"Oh! I'm so sorry, Sasha." Trace pulled Sasha over to the chair he'd abandoned only a short time before and practically shoved him down into it. "You sure you don't need something to eat or drink?"

"Normal food and drink won't help him right now, Trace," Dr. Niko said from behind Trace. "He needs to feed."

"Which I will do when there aren't any shifters around, thanks. As for my uncle, I've sent for him. Dimka and Summer believe whoever is behind this is setting him up. I have to agree. While I don't overly care for some of his ideas and attitudes, he would never attack the lynx, not of this particular tribe, at least."

"Um, why?" Keith asked.

Trace didn't know where to sit. All the other chairs were farther away from the one Sasha was now using. And oddly he really didn't want to be away from Sasha.

"Trace, mal'chik, sit on the floor beside me. You can participate in the meeting and I can help keep you calm that way."

He immediately knelt beside Sasha's chair, then relaxed against the side of it and Sasha's leg when Sasha trailed his fingers through Trace's hair.

"My uncle is my mother's brother, and he well remembers what happened to the band of renegades who attacked and killed my sister and her fated heart, the last Chosen of Baast your tribe had. I told you this story before—my father and his people destroyed them. I helped, but I was young, so it was more him and his warriors. I'm not that young boy now, and I am not known for my patience or tolerance when it comes to those I care for or protect being hurt."

"So wh-whoever is doing this is c-counting on you retaliating b-based on what Trace would t-tell you?" Jason asked, the color draining from his face.

"And what was found in their rooms. Yes. If we believed what we found, my uncle would already be in custody awaiting trial and execution. If I didn't kill him outright."

"Are you r-really that r-ruthless, Sasha?" Jason's eyes were huge as he stared at his friend. Trace felt sorry for the human. It had to be hard to reconcile the vampire and the best friend in one.

Sasha sighed and leaned forward, his elbows on his knees. "Hon, don't get me wrong. He would have time to defend himself, to show that he wasn't guilty if he wasn't. But this isn't the human world. You don't really live in that world anymore—you haven't for a long time. Think about it—if Keith hadn't killed the previous alpha when he did, you would be dead, and all those who had joined him would have been killed or at least tortured and brought back in line. The ones with human mates and children would have lost them to the old alpha's abuse and evil nature by now. Do you hold it against Keith that he has to be hard and at times violent?"

"Of course not. He was defending his tribe and his mate. Me."

"Exactly. I have to do the same. The people you see around me here are my tribe, though we use the term coven. They are mine to rule, to protect, to guide. Any that would seek to harm them must be stopped. I can't do that if I'm seen to be soft. I'm not cruel or abusive, though."

"And they did directly attack Trace, Jason," Keith added.

"True."

"I'm not sure how they figured out our connection, but trying to rip out my fated heart's throat is an automatic death sentence when I find them."

Trace whipped his head up to stare at Sasha. They'd agreed never to discuss that, much less in front of others. Why was no one else surprised at his pronouncement of that concept? "What?"

"They know, Trace. Your alpha demanded to know if I was your mate when he figured out it was the feline, not the human side of you in the human body."

"But—"

"Trace?" Keith demanded his attention in tone alone. "It was vital based on how you were acting. Your lynx was trying to claim Sasha. Not sexually, but in every other way. You wouldn't let anyone near him, wouldn't even let him sit up. You were both going to get hurt if we didn't do something to fix the problem."

He slumped his shoulders, but he nodded. "Fine, but that doesn't change anything."

CHAPTER EIGHT

"WELL, IT does and it doesn't." Sasha slid his fingers through Trace's hair again and tugged lightly. Damn, but touching Trace felt good.

"What's that mean?"

"It means Keith determined, after some kind of kitty conference with your lynx, that the way to get you back was for me to bind you to me."

"I told you I'm not taking a mate!" Trace jumped up and stalked across the room, balling his fists at his sides. "It's not…. I won't and that's all there is to it."

Sasha's voice didn't rise. There was an edge and a sadness to it he couldn't withhold, though he tried. "I know, and I'm not asking you to do that. But I did do what he asked of me. It doesn't force the mating on your side. Don't worry. But it did heal your mind so the human side is back in control of the human body."

"Fool prince," Dr. Niko grumbled. "And you've made yourself weak and sick in the process. I understand wanting to help, but I still don't understand doing this for a bond that will only serve to weaken you."

"Shut up, Doctor." Sasha damn well knew the "risks" and consequences of what he'd done. And he'd make the same choice again, even hearing Trace reject their bonding afterward—no matter how much it hurt. "I'll be fine shortly, and as soon as Trace has adjusted fully and he settles back down, he can return to his home, if that is his wish. He will have access to all my homes any time he wishes, permanently, no matter what you or anyone else thinks of my choices or actions. And I will work with the shifters to figure out who wants our people separated and why."

"I still don't understand." Trace huffed even as he tilted his head to glare at Sasha. "What exactly did you do? And why did it weaken you?"

"You said it would only temporarily weaken you, Sasha," Jason added, his voice cracking on Sasha's name.

Sasha inhaled loudly, then held his breath a moment before releasing it slowly. "I will be fine once I feed and have time to properly rest. The side effects for me are my problem to deal with, not something for any of you to be concerned with. The only concern Trace needs to worry about is that his life span will mimic mine now. Otherwise he is free to live his life as he chooses. I swore I would not force a mating on him, and I won't." Sasha turned a cold stare on Trace, determined to make his fated heart hear him even if he didn't want to accept anything about them being bonded. "The only thing I demand is that you not flaunt any males you choose to take in front of me. If that—" He paused and closed his eyes for a moment before he opened them and continued. "—is not adhered to, I will not be held accountable for the outcome."

"What?" Trace squeaked.

"That seems more than fair," Keith said, his voice as level as his gaze on Trace.

"But—" Trace began again.

"You can't really expect me to tolerate that, Trace. I'm not holding you to what our bond ought to be, but don't push me that far. I told you I'm not known for my patience or tolerance. I would never harm you, but a trick? A lover?" Sasha struggled for a moment before he managed to wrap that calm he was known for around himself—a mere facade, at least in this case. "Just don't put him or me in that position, Trace. Respect me that much. Please."

The last word cost Sasha personally to have said in front of the others, but he had to make Trace understand. He had to. He would kill anyone he found with Trace now. It was bad enough before, but now? There was simply no way he would be able to control the impulse to destroy any who would take his heart from him.

"I'm sorry. For all of this. I won't do anything like that to you." Trace sat again, then leaned against Sasha's leg, his warmth seeping into Sasha, soothing and painful at the same time.

"Thank you."

Jason opened his mouth, Sasha assumed to ask something else, but the knock on the door startled Trace and Jason while it drew everyone else's attention.

"Come in, Jalin," Sasha said, his voice still tired. He really needed to feed, and soon. Had he been with Trace and truly fed from him when he released the bonding serum, Sasha would be fine now. Unfortunately Trace gave neither enough blood nor any energy to nourish him during the bonding. Sasha fought the depression that wanted to settle over him as the knowledge that Trace never would again echoed through him.

Jalin stepped into the room, closed the door, and gave a short bow. "I'm sorry to interrupt you, sir. I thought you would like to know that your uncle has sent word that he will be here at the end of the week. He will have Tatiana with him. He seems to be under the impression that you called this meeting as a preliminary to accepting the betrothal."

"That's because I allowed him to believe that. I want to know what's going on, and either he's behind this, she is, or they are both in danger. Pawns, at the very least."

"Makes it look like you're playing the game to whoever is behind this as well." Keith nodded. "Well, other than still having shifters in alliance with you and Trace alive."

"Yes, and that worries me. Why, out of all the shifters in the area they could have gone after, did they pick Trace?"

"Um...." Trace swallowed loudly and stared down at his hands, twisting his fingers together hard enough Sasha was concerned Trace might injure himself.

"Mal'chik, calm your hands. Hurting yourself is not acceptable to anyone here."

Trace froze, not even breathing for a moment, then slowly laid his hands in his lap and exhaled gently. "Sorry."

"It's fine. Now what was it you wanted to say?"

"Well, the one, the male vampire, said they picked me because your uncle had been watching you, that they needed to get rid of me so you would bond or marry that Tatiana chick or something."

Sasha almost smiled at the way Trace said Tatiana. He wondered if Trace realized he nearly spat her name. It didn't matter in the end, as his fated heart still rejected him, but it still felt good to know at least a part of Trace wanted him. Knowing the lynx side of Trace wanted their bonding helped too. More than he wanted to admit, truly. Sadly that wasn't the kind of bond he wanted, as half a bond was still not a true bond. Besides, now that Trace was whole, his mind would be present when in lynx form, so even the lynx side wouldn't show the level of devotion and protectiveness, much less the frustrating parts now.

"Tatiana isn't some 'chick,' Trace. She's the younger princess from one of the other covens—Pennsylvania, to be exact. Not the oldest, obviously, or she wouldn't be the one they are trying to marry off to me, but close."

Trace shifted on the floor but didn't move away or stop leaning against Sasha's leg. "You, um, know her?"

"I do. She's a strange choice, honestly. She doesn't believe in arranged marriages any more than I do. However, she is who they've been trying to marry me off to for…." He looked to Jalin and sighed. "What, two, three years now?"

"About that, yes. They want you to have an heir and a spare, as the last missive said, with a respectable female from a decent bloodline."

Sasha snorted at that. "I still want to know what my uncle gets out of the deal, because I don't believe he cares about the succession of my coven."

"What would happen?" A deep frown marred Jason's typically sweet face.

"If I were to die without an heir?"

"Y-yes."

"You're not usually so morbid, hon." Jason glared at Sasha. Trace gripped Sasha's ankle, drawing Sasha's attention away from his best friend. "What is it?"

"What would happen? He's right. It's a legitimate question. In the tribes there's a very particular set of laws set up for if there is no apparent heir, though it's extremely rare that there would be no family fit to take over if the alpha died and it wasn't a challenge."

"I have a couple of cousins who could take the position as prince or princess, though they would have to fight for the position, both physically and politically, to prove themselves worthy and capable. Neither is powerful enough to do so outright. If my sister were alive, it would go to her and any offspring she had."

"So then you having children is actually imperative. Why haven't you done so yet?"

He couldn't help it. Sasha gaped at Trace. Was the male really going to chastise him for not having sex with and getting some female pregnant? "Children should be raised in love."

"True, but for the sake of your coven, of the vampires you rule and care for, it seems wrong to not ensure your line and your beliefs endure."

Sasha couldn't believe he was having this… conversation?… with Trace. What the hell? "So I should be a single father, a prince, a CEO, be everything alone, and teach my children what love is, what proper relationships are, when they can't see them in action?"

"You know, millions of people are single parents and do just fine. If you show your children love, if you're there for them, that's what's important. Besides, you would have nannies and valets and such to help you, so it's not like you would have to do it all by yourself."

"You'd be a great father," Jason chimed in. "You make an excellent uncle already."

"And I love Sean and Zeke, you know that, but I never wanted to be a single dad. I want to be…." Sasha closed his eyes and fought the nausea that swelled suddenly. "It doesn't matter what I wanted. You're right. I will be a single father because there is no longer a reason to put it off. It's dangerous for my coven and pointless for me." He looked up at Jalin, who still stood before them. "But I will not look for a consort, so don't start that again."

"Yes, sir. Of course. For now you wish the guest wing prepared for the sets of arrivals?"

"If we must. They are to be treated with respect, but they go nowhere unchaperoned. That will include their servants. I know that will be a burden on the staff here, but I will not have anyone using the unseen servant as a spy in my home. Especially not right now."

"Of course." Jalin bowed and a moment later left, securing the door behind him.

Jason smiled after a minute of no one speaking. "So I'm going to be an uncle?"

Sasha rolled his eyes and shook his head. "I only just agreed to this, and you're already plotting outings and how to spoil the royal babies, aren't you?"

"Of course." He grinned wide. "Like you didn't the moment we told you we planned to talk to Taylor about her acting as our surrogate."

"True."

Trace's cell phone vibrated and pinged in his pocket just then. He shifted away from Sasha long enough to pull it out, but much to Sasha's delight, Trace leaned against him again as soon as he had it out. Trace swiped his thumb over the screen in a pattern and then scrolled through something while Sasha continued to run his fingers through Trace's hair. He was determined to soak up every bit of touch Trace would allow before Trace returned to the tribe lands.

"Um, I have good news, and it's fortuitous that both Keith and Sasha are here, as well as the doctor. The tribal rep doctor will arrive in three days. One Dr. Liliana Petronia. She'll need accommodations, which I've already arranged. Access to Sean, Taylor, Jason, and Alpha Keith, of course. And, uh… the e-mail says…. I'm sorry, but I'm instructed to relay that if she's to work with a vampire, he needs to make sure to bring his own lunch. She won't be providing catering."

Sasha and Dr. Niko both laughed at that, though Keith and Jason looked aghast at Trace. "Trace!" Keith snapped.

"I'm sorry. That's what it says I'm to say, and I assure you, I cleaned it up from how it's actually worded."

Dr. Niko smiled and held up a hand. "It's all right, Alpha Keith. I'm honestly amazed that she's willing to work with me. Once upon a time, your tribe and this coven were close, but that's been an age. The council you answer to never actually approved, even with it being due to the last Chosen of Baast's bonding to our princess. And Trace, you can assure her I will not have blood around her. I will, however, have food around her, as we do eat, just smaller portions, as you know."

"I'll remind her when she arrives. Most shifters don't really understand about vampire diets, believing that you only consume blood and that it's always forcibly taken. The council knows that's against the rules of this coven, but that doesn't mean she truly understands or believes it. I don't know her, which means she's being brought in and isn't one that usually resides at the council compound."

"I'm not worried."

"Nor am I." Sasha shifted in his chair but made sure not to dislodge Trace from his leg. "I'm glad they are taking such care with Sean, as long as they don't try anything unethical or harmful."

"That won't be allowed," Keith rumbled as he folded his arms across his wide chest. "No one will harm my son. I don't care who they are or what species."

"Which is as it should be."

"And as important as all this is, I t-think we should g-go for now." Jason gave a shy smile and began to reach toward Sasha but stopped, then dropped his hand back to his lap. "Sasha looks too tired, and Trace does too. I think they b-both need more rest. The doctor and Sasha's problem vamps don't arrive quite y-yet, so...."

"Agreed. We can meet again later." Keith stood, pulling Jason up with him. "Call when you're up for more discussion, please. We need to figure all this out, but you need rest and to feed, as your doc here keeps saying. I don't want to think about that too much, sorry, but it is what it is, so go take care of yourself, and take care of Trace."

"Of course. Take care of Jason and my nephews. Safe journey."

"And Trace, get well, okay? You are not only welcome and free to come home whenever you want, but expected. I know you were afraid I'd banished you, but nothing could be further from the truth. Just let someone escort you back. Someone obviously has decided you are the way to hurt Sasha, so you're a target until we figure all this out."

"Yes, Alpha."

Sasha stroked his hand over Trace's head a few times, then stood. "Stay here a moment." He stepped forward and hugged Jason tight. "Be safe, hon. If they'd go after Trace, they might go after you. You've been under my protection for years, but someone obviously wants to cause trouble."

"I know, but it sounds like it's more in the relationship department, not friendship area, so I should be safe."

"Don't kid yourself, Jason. If someone wants to hurt me, going after you is a known way to do it. So let your big bad kitty make sure you're safe, okay?"

"I will. And you be careful too, please. I don't want anything to happen to you."

"I'll be fine."

Jason huffed and tightened his hold before he let go and stepped back. He glared down at Sasha. "Uh-huh. You're weak, pale even for you, depressed, and your doctor is worried. You've got some nut after you willing to hurt Trace to get to you, no less. Pardon me if I worry, oh great and mighty prince."

The laugh slipped out before Sasha could contain it. "God, but I love you, hon. I promise to go feed, jeesh! I am protected and can take care of myself. Trace will have his own guard from now on, by the way, so relax. Now go home and take your hubby with you."

"Fine, but even vampires need to be cautious, right?"

It didn't take long to get them to all go, other than Trace. He still sat next to Sasha's chair, looking the same: confused, scared, and haunted.

"Trace?"

"Huh? You need me to go too?"

"No, not until you're ready, and only if you want. But I need to rest more."

"You need blood too. Your grumpy doctor said so repeatedly."

It was hard not to yell about the feeding issue, as Sasha didn't want to do that with any but Trace. Unfortunately that wasn't an option. Blood from any other source would be like gruel to a human—able to sustain him but not really what one would call food, much less appetizing or palatable. Still, it was better to endure this and have even this much of Trace, and a healed Trace, than nothing. He would just remind himself of that… a lot.

"You need to rest more as well. Why don't you lie back down, and I'll be back soon? Or do you not feel safe enough yet, even in my chambers, for me to leave? I can have Dimka or Summer stay with you to protect you if that would help."

"Alone, please. I don't want…."

"Anyone else near you. Okay, mal'chik. Then go back and lie down. I'll return shortly."

Trace nodded and wandered back into Sasha's room. He couldn't help the small hope that Trace's clinging and comfort in Sasha's space would one day turn into more between them. Forever was a long time for Trace to spurn him, after all.

CHAPTER NINE

TRACE WANDERED around the lavish comfort of Sasha's bedroom, torn between the desperate need to recharge and the desire to leave. He didn't want to stay, yet he couldn't just leave either. How messed up was that? He was so tired he ached down in his bones. He assumed it was due to the healing from all the damage and whatever it was Sasha did to heal his mind. He feared it meant Sasha was now mated to him, even if he wasn't mated to Sasha—not that he'd figured out how that worked. They'd mentioned that whole fated hearts thing and Sasha had said it wasn't a forced mating, but it still didn't make any sense yet.

Right then, though, he wanted sleep. He couldn't bring himself to climb into Sasha's huge bed, but the thought of hunting up a guest room wasn't any more appealing. Trace looked around the room again, both hoping for a solution to his sleep issue and to try to keep his mind off what Sasha was doing at that moment.

It was ridiculous to be pissed off at Sasha for feeding on some human when Trace wasn't about to let Sasha bite him. Trace knew it was insane to be jealous. Unfortunately logic didn't seem to help any, no matter how many times he reminded himself that Sasha needed blood and was only doing what was appropriate to get his nutritional needs met.

Eventually he gave up and decided to shift into his lynx. Things were always simpler in his feline skin. Once he'd shifted he stretched out each leg, then arched his back before he prowled around, checking out Sasha's room. When satisfied he knew the layout of the room and that there was nothing hiding from him—and he'd rubbed up against enough items—he hopped up onto the lounger at the foot of the bed and settled down to take a bath. He was finishing up his ears and whiskers when Sasha *finally* returned.

Sasha gave a tired chuckle. "I know you're a big wildcat type, being a lynx and all, but that's still adorable."

Trace wrinkled his muzzle and snorted. *Am not.* Just because he wanted to be clean was no reason to be rude. Trace finished, doing his best to ignore Sasha as he gathered a pair of pale blue silky-looking sleep pants and a robe from a cabinet. "I don't wish to offend you, so I will change in my bathroom. Excuse me."

When he returned Sasha's hair was damp and he was clad in only the pants and robe. It seemed odd to Trace that if Sasha had fed, and he could smell the hint of foreign blood from Sasha, he didn't look much better than when he'd left. He hoped it had to do with the interrupted sleep after whatever Sasha did to help him. Sasha would be better in the morning, Trace would feel like himself again, and they could both go back to their lives. Right? Right.

"Are you staying as your lynx, Trace?"

"Reow." *Of course. I'm not curling up in bed with you as my two-legged self!*

"Don't get so offended. I could lead you back to the adjoining room so you could sleep in the bed there, if you'd like."

Yeah, and you so sound like you want to do that. Trace sneezed at Sasha and curled up on the cushion, kneading it with his paws pointedly.

"I'll still have that chamber set up for you tomorrow for any time you're here. You can think it over and let Jalin know how you want it decorated then. Night."

Sasha climbed into the king-size four-poster bed and, once under the covers, moved around until he was on his stomach, and then stopped moving other than to breathe softly. It took a long time for the words Sasha had said to stop ringing in Trace's ears enough for him to drift off to sleep, but eventually the lullaby of Sasha's gentle breaths won out, and sleep finally claimed him.

"I DON'T see why I need to discuss redecorating the other main bedroom in Sasha's suite, and why the hell does this area have two master bedrooms anyway?" Trace kept snapping at Jalin, who didn't deserve his temper, Trace knew that, but Sasha had left the two of them together with instructions to decorate the room for Trace and hadn't returned since. That was over an hour ago.

"This is a very, very old mansion, Trace. At one point that was common. There were two because the master and mistress of the house kept separate bedchambers, though they often connected. The one Prince Sasha ordered set up for you was actually used as the nursery, as his parents didn't like the idea of having their little ones too far away at night."

"So I'm being either given the 'little woman's' room, the concubine's room, or the baby's room? None of which is acceptable. I have a home, thanks." Trace crossed his arms and glared at Jalin, refusing to look at the magazines or tablet the male held.

"You have no idea how many vampires would kill to have what you are belittling," Jalin muttered softly, but not so much that Trace didn't catch the words.

"I didn't ask for this."

"No, you are being gifted this by one of the most powerful vampire princes in the world. One that doesn't flaunt his power, or abuse it, just because he can. You ought to be honored to belong to such a male, but instead you treat him and his gifts like dirt." With that Jalin turned on his heel and stormed out of the room, slamming the door behind him.

As the sound died in the room, Trace stood in the middle of the room, unsure what to do. He didn't want to make Sasha look bad or upset Sasha's people, but he couldn't explain to them why he couldn't *be* Sasha's. Just being in the room with Jalin without Sasha there to mute the effect was hard enough—and he'd really like to know what the hell that was about. With a sigh Trace slumped his shoulders and dipped his head. He turned around slowly, for once truly taking in the space before he thought about what he would want done to the room if it were his. He couldn't imagine staying at the covenstead house, even though that was exactly what he was doing right then. However, if it would make Jalin and Sasha happy, he would let them make him a room.

After a few minutes, he poked his head out and realized Jalin was sitting in one of the chairs in the sitting room area, legs crossed, drumming the fingers of his left hand in a lightning-fast tattoo as he glared out the window. "Jalin?"

Jalin stopped his fingers and turned his head, but his gaze didn't meet Trace's. "Yes, sir?"

"I have a few ideas, if you still want to help...."

BY THE time he left to meet up with the council doctor, Trace was feeling more stable, though he still couldn't deal with others touching him much—a handshake or a very brief hug was about his limit, and only if he knew about it in advance. Sasha hadn't wanted him to leave—citing his safety and the touching issue—but Trace countered that he couldn't let the attack undermine his life or his work. That figuring out why Sean could shift and what it meant for him in the future was too important. In the end Summer escorted Trace back to the tribe lands, and Kelley, one of Keith's best friends and personal guards, was assigned to guard him while outside the reach of the vampires.

Dr. Liliana Petronia's car arrived in the late afternoon of the day Trace returned home. There was a large van following behind it, but Trace had been notified about its presence already—it held her required equipment, as their tribe only had a small clinic and birthing center. Keith also ran an extensive veterinary hospital on the edge of the tribal land. He was a veterinarian, and it served to bring in income for not just himself, but others he employed. Keith also helped out the forestry service part-time, unlike when Trace first moved there—back then Keith worked for the forestry service full-time and the hospital didn't yet exist.

The doctor's driver got out and then opened the back door, letting out two large lynx shifters—obviously her guards. A moment later the doctor herself exited the vehicle. She was about five seven, with silver-streaked brown hair and reddish-brown eyes. She reminded him of grandmothers and fresh cookies. He knew better. She was older, but she was a shifter, and so she was still lethal when needed.

Keith stepped forward and gave a small smile. "Welcome to the Glacier Rim Tribe of Seattle, Washington. I'm Alpha Keith Skyler." He then motioned to each male in turn. "This is my mate and husband, Jason Grant, and you've been in contact with Trace Wilson, our council representative and trainer."

"Thank you, Alpha." She bent her head as was appropriate, then stood straight again. "Are my accommodations and work areas ready?"

"They are." Trace gestured to John and Seth, a couple of the tribe members who were to act as her bellboys, basically. "They will help you unload anything you need moved. The vampire doctor, Dr. Niko, will be here later to give you time to settle in. He's already set up his things at the clinic."

She frowned but nodded. "I'm still not sure about working with one of them," she said, her tone snide. "But if you insist, then can you at least guarantee he won't bite?"

"That attitude will get you sent home faster than anything," Keith snapped. "We don't tolerate bigotry or hate here. Dr. Niko has no interest in nibbling on you or any shifter. He's helped us before. He's even taken care of my human mate once."

She swallowed hard and nodded. "Sorry. It's just... weird to be working with... vampires. I mean, in most places we're at war with them or, at least, an uneasy truce."

"Well, here we have an alliance and Jason is the best friend of Prince Tolstoi, so play nice."

"Yes, Alpha."

"Ma'am, the home right over here is the one you'll be staying in." Trace took over again, hoping to move things away from the vamp-versus-shifter issue and into setting up things for the research and hopefully figuring things out for Sean.

Once they were inside, she looked around the cottage that would be her home for the next while. "It seems clean and neat enough. Are the same rules of etiquette observed here as at the council headquarters, Trace?"

He nodded and smiled. "No one will enter your home without permission. Not even the alpha will do that unless it is deemed necessary, such as someone believes you are in grave danger or are committing a crime of great import. The only possible exception is if one of the kits gets a little too curious and wanders." Trace gestured to the cat door most all the houses had. "We all know how to access and use them, so I would suggest you make sure to secure it from curious little ones. They mean no harm, but you're new," he finished with a shrug. It was the same anywhere that had young ones. Human children were curious enough, but shifter children, especially when in their lynx form, were even more like their feline cousins, and therefore into *every*thing.

"Understood. Now if you will excuse me."

Keith and Jason dismissed Trace, which he was thankful for right then. He wanted to be in his lynx skin, out in the forest. Well, what he actually wanted bugged him, as the feline side of him wanted to be back at the vampire house, curled up near Sasha. Or maybe exploring the grounds there. He hadn't been able to do that. Sasha hadn't felt it was safe—yet—not with Trace having just suffered an attack, and them not yet knowing who was behind it.

Shaking off his idiotic annoyance, Trace hurried inside to strip off his clothes, tending to them carefully before shifting and going out to run and play in the trees. He tried to play, at least, but unfortunately his mind kept wandering to Sasha, and his lynx wanted nothing more than to head right over to his home. That it would require them going through the middle of town to get there didn't faze his feline side one bit. His lynx just wanted Sasha near, a fact Trace was less than amused with.

By the time he made it back, all Trace wanted to do was sleep. Sadly that wasn't to happen yet. Out front was a dark gray Audi of some kind, and there on his doorstep was the vampire Jalin.

Trace padded onto the porch before shifting, ignoring how he was naked while Jalin was fully dressed. He looked around but didn't see Sasha or his car. The SUV his guards tended to drive was missing, and neither Keith nor Jason had mentioned anything about Jalin visiting. "Um…. What are you doing here, and why are you here alone? Do the guards know?"

"Yes, your guards know. I had to be cleared with them before I came onto the property." Jalin fidgeted, an odd, uncertain look clear in his eyes—Trace hadn't even known the vampire was capable of such. "As for why, could we speak privately, please? And maybe you could dress?"

"So much for peace and quiet," he grumbled before pasting on a smile and opening his door. "Come in." And of course he'd dress.

"Thank you."

"Mmm-hmm."

Trace walked past Jalin directly into his bedroom and quickly pulled on a pair of running pants and a T-shirt. He then walked into the living room and flopped down onto his favorite comfy chair.

"Sit and tell me why you're here. I still have to deal with the introduction between the two doctors later. The council one seems to believe the vampire one will want to bite her. Ugh! So whatever you're here about, please tell me it's not that some vampire has also been watching too many human movies and believes all that nonsense too."

Jalin perched on the couch, his hands palms-down on his knees. "Wow, that's a long way to say your doctor has a lot to learn about vampires, though I do understand. Making sure things flow properly is tiring at times."

"Sadly. Now what can I do for you, as I'm certain you didn't leave your prince's side the day before his uncle is to arrive to see if the new doctor is annoying me."

"It's about Prince Sasha."

Trace hopped up without thinking. "What's wrong with Sasha?"

"Calm down, please. Nothing that wasn't wrong when you left." Jalin motioned to the chair. "Please." It took a minute for Trace to calm himself enough to sit, but he managed. Once he did, Jalin continued, "I'm…. I don't know how to explain this, and I'm honestly not sure what he will do to me when he finds out I came to you, but—"

"Why would you be afraid of that?"

"Once you hear why I'm here, you'll understand. I hope." Trace nodded, which seemed to encourage Jalin. "Our prince is very important to us, not simply as our leader, but he is also immensely powerful. Most of the other covens and especially the rogues would never think to come against us merely because of him, forget the power or might of the rest of his people. That's part of why the attack on you was so significant, and why he's putting up with his uncle and Tatiana visiting."

"Right, it's the same with the alpha. He's leader, power, guide, father figure, and more."

"But ours is suffering due to what he did for you."

"I'm still not really certain what he did. He said it makes my life span like his, but that otherwise I'm the same. Then he cut off anyone who wanted more specifics with me in the room."

"You're his fated heart, Trace. It's similar to being a true mate, only the vampire version."

"He said that, but I won't take a mate again. I don't care what the Fates think." He'd made that mistake once. Trace's stomach roiled as he fought back the pain and memories of his past that threatened to bleed into the now.

"It makes no difference what you think or what happened in your past with this previous mate. He still bonded with you. It's incomplete because you didn't mate with him, though. You also didn't feed him or give him your energy like a normal fated heart would have. Because of this he's not gaining the nourishment from normal blood sources that he always has before. He's…. I don't know how he will react when he finds I came to you, but I've done some research, and he will continue to get sicker if this continues."

Trace shook his head. "I can't take him as my mate."

"Can you let him feed from you at least occasionally?" Jalin's voice softened as he continued, "Could you do that much?"

CHAPTER TEN

"Do what now?" *Did he really just ask me to bleed for a vampire?*

"He's starving, Trace. No matter how much or from whom he drinks, he's weakening." Jalin leaned forward, his voice higher than before. His hands were clasped in his lap as if he were trying not to reach out and touch Trace. "Do you really care that little for him?"

"S-starving?" Trace had a vague memory of pushing his neck against Sasha's fangs, trying to get him to bite, but no, that was when his lynx was in control. Right? His thoughts were so fuzzy and vague from that time he couldn't be sure it had actually happened instead of him dreaming of it. Because Trace had had dreams where Sasha did a lot more than just bite….

"Effectively. He can't…." Jalin took a deep breath and let it out slowly. "Dr. Niko explained it to me this way—Sasha can't properly absorb what's in the blood that we, as vampires, need to survive. So no matter how much he drinks, he won't ever be full, won't ever be… not be weakened. Because he's such a strong prince, it will take a long time, and he'll be able to hide it from those who aren't close enough to him on a regular basis to know better. But he could lose control and kill a human or possibly eventually even starve to death. That knowledge doesn't change anything. The only cure is the blood of his fated heart. That's you."

"I won't take a mate." But he couldn't let Sasha suffer, much less die. What the hell! How could Sasha do something so foolish? Did he not know better?

"You don't have to give him the mating bite. Dr. Niko said that if you would agree to feed Sasha at least monthly, and possibly if he's hurt or has to do something major—like this insanity with the attack, his uncle, and the not-a-betrothal—it would protect Sasha and the coven. You have his life span, so it's not a problem for this to continue as long as you are willing to allow him to feed from you."

"Give me a minute to think about this. Shifters don't just up and feed vampires."

"Not usually, no."

Never. Usually, that is. Though to be fair, Sasha's sister, Princess Nadia, probably fed from her Chosen of Baast, Alpha Orin Green, so it's not like it was never done. Of course, he was her mate. Still, Trace was torn between fear, revulsion, and longing. He'd been fascinated with and lusting after Sasha since they first met—the mating pull making it worse—but Trace was certain he would have wanted Sasha even without that. Over the years since they'd met, Trace had come to respect and wish for things to be different the more he watched Sasha interact with Jason, Zeke, Sean, and more. But to allow another male any power over him, sexually especially, was something he had refused since the night of his rescue from his now-dead mate's home. To agree to feed Sasha like this would go against that. However, to not would potentially kill Sasha, if what Jalin said was true. It would also endanger all the vampires in Sasha's coven. And the bond between the coven and the tribe.

Goddess Baast, if you sent him to me, why now when I'm too damaged to accept the gift? What do I do?

The one thing he knew for certain was he couldn't risk Sasha, even if it meant giving up part of himself. Sasha deserved his care, even if Trace could never give him more.

"This won't give him control over me or force me to give him the mating bite, right?"

"No, it won't. He wouldn't do that to anyone, much less to you," Jalin snapped. "Prince Sasha is a good and decent vampire who would never force his heart to be with him, no matter what it cost him to allow that freedom. Now will you help him or not?"

"I will, but I'd rather go in my lynx skin. I'm stronger that way, and not all of you vamps are thrilled to have me 'lurking' about the covenstead."

"Then please shift, and I'll drive us back. I will wait outside to give you your privacy."

"Thank you."

Trace watched Jalin exit his little cottage of a home before he stripped and shifted. He loved the roll of power as it poured over his body, shifting and rearranging him until he settled into his other skin and his lynx self came forward.

After a moment or two to stretch and twist his new body, Trace padded silently through the cat door, only stopping when he reached Jalin. He nudged Jalin's leg with his head, then continued to the car, annoyed when the vampire didn't immediately open the door. Paws were great, he loved his paws, but they weren't the best for opening vehicle doors and such. After letting out a loud hiss, he pawed at the door, careful not to scratch it, then glared at Jalin.

"Sorry. Let me get that for you." Jalin slipped his cell phone into his pocket before he pulled open the car door for Trace. "I was letting Dr. Niko know that you said yes and that you were returning with me now."

Yeah, whatever. Trace didn't overly care who Jalin was playing with the plastic to talk to; he just wanted to get back to Sasha. Now that he was in his lynx skin, the drive to be with Sasha was stronger—as it always was—and his arguments against being with Sasha became even fuzzier and harder to maintain. Even as Trace tried to keep a tight hold on his lynx side.

SASHA DREADED the next day but knew he needed to help his people keep calm with the coming storm. A few had seen Trace brought in the other night, and many more knew about the impending visit of his uncle. Gods, but he didn't want to deal with his mother's brother.

"Will you be taking the princess as your wife?" Liz asked as she stared up at him. She was a tiny little thing, even to Sasha, which was saying something. She was maybe four six, with big gray eyes and hair that always stood up a bit—personally he'd always thought she looked like she belonged in one of those manga he'd seen.

He'd finished speaking with a large group of his people in the ballroom, but he still had to soothe a few of the higher-ranking ones. Sadly, he hadn't caught up with all of them yet. He took a slow breath, trying not to make it look like a sigh, as it wasn't, really—he was just tired, though he ought not be and couldn't let on to anyone he wasn't at top power and form.

"You know better than that, Liz. I know you heard me announce that I found my fated heart and that *he* was under my protection. The fact I forbade you to discuss certain points about him to my uncle or Tatiana is completely beside the point."

"My prince, I understand that you found your heart. I'm happy for you, even if I don't understand what the Gods were thinking giving you one of the two-skinned kind, but you still need an heir. You know that, my prince, as well as I do. That's probably at the root of what your uncle is up to, and until you have at least two children, he will have the leverage to continue this harassment."

"He has no rights as far as this coven goes, and you know it."

"Rights? No. But he will be seen to be only looking out for you and yours as long as you continue not to have heirs so that your family rule is secure. You are the last Tolstoi in this coven, and while I have no love lost for your uncle"—he tended to treat females as though they were less, for the mere fact of their gender—a rather old-fashioned human trait, unfortunately, that had infected many of his generation—"I have to agree that it would be a tragedy to not only lose you, but your line as well."

This time the sigh did escape, not that he'd tried hard to stop it. "Now you sound like Jalin."

"I'm not sure if I should be insulted to be compared to your valet or pleased at being placed in the same category as one that you obviously listen to and value. Either way I would listen to him in this instance. Your fated heart cannot give you heirs, so you still need a consort, my prince. You still need blood children."

"I cannot lie with some female, and you know it." Liz had been a friend since childhood, even though she shifted to more of an adviser of sorts once he ascended to the crown, as it were. Even so, every born vampire knew what a fated heart meant. And what was and was not possible.

She smirked and folded her arms over her ample chest on her small frame. "I'll buy you a turkey baster if you can't figure out how surrogacy works."

"Eww...."

"Oh please"—she flitted her hands to her hips, somehow making her seem taller all of a sudden—"your best friend, the human, Jason, used his husband's sister as a surrogate so he and his alpha mate could have a child. I don't see why the idea is so hard for you to grasp. Sir."

"It's not," Sasha grumbled. "It's the idea of anyone but Trace near any part of me—yes, even with medical intervention." He shook his head and mumbled, "Can't believe you suggested a turkey baster. Really?"

She shrugged. "It got your attention, which was the point. You seriously need to give this consideration. Even without your uncle or the attack on your heart, you need to consider having children. You would make a wonderful father, and there are a few in training who would make excellent nannies and valets."

Yeah, he knew he needed children—he simply didn't want them to be heirs instead of family. Trace didn't want to build a family with him, though, and wasn't likely to change his mind about that anytime soon. "I will consider it, but not with someone my uncle controls."

"No, that makes sense."

"Good. Make sure the others understand that as well. The females in the coven gave up ages ago on trying to seduce me into bonding with them, but every time children are brought up...."

"It starts all over again. I know. I will see what I can do to curb that. I am sorry they see your status as prince over who you are when it comes to such things."

"Such is the position." Sasha had opened his mouth to continue when he felt Trace enter the grounds. *What is he doing back?* The pain and panic of Trace being hurt wasn't present, so that wasn't it. There was no scheduled meeting, so no.... Trace had made it abundantly clear he didn't wish to be near Sasha or at the covenstead, so why would he be on the grounds now?

"What's wrong, Sasha?"

Liz's use of his preferred nickname startled him enough to bring his mind back to the here and now. "You know, it's been years since you've addressed me so informally."

"I'm sorry—"

"Don't apologize. I told you when you took your position on my council not to buy in to the hype, that you could still call me Sasha."

She huffed but smiled. "What startled you?"

"Trace is back."

"Oh." She bounced on her toes, her smile growing. "Then hurry back to your section of the house, and I'll do my best to head off anyone who thinks they need you right now."

"I—"

"You're not really going to argue that you want to stay out here with us when your heart has returned, are you?" How could such a tiny little thing manage such an imperious arch to her brow and her voice all at the same time? And at her prince, no less!

The fact she was right was the only reason he didn't stay to tease her. "Point. So be a good goose and defend me as I go find out what's brought him back so soon." Sasha quickly hugged Liz, chuckling at her startled squeak before he turned and hurried back to his suite. He was confident he would beat Trace there, but he could also feel that was where Trace was headed. Sasha did pause a moment just as he entered his private area when he realized he scented Trace's lynx, not his human.

He had to fight down the panic that something had gone wrong and Trace was once again trapped in his fur. *No, Trace is fine. He's in his fur by choice.* He repeated it a couple of times, hoping he was right, before the door opened and Jalin stepped inside.

"Sir?" Jalin said, his eyes wide as he jumped slightly.

Sasha stood in front of his favorite chair, his hands curled, though he'd managed to stop them from becoming full fists. "Where's Trace?"

He looked at the floor around Jalin's feet but didn't see Trace, though he could feel and smell him. He could even hear his heartbeat—fast, but not more so than normal for his lynx side.

"He wanted me to announce him, oddly enough, before he came in."

"I know he's here. I knew he was close before he fully entered the grounds." *Why the hell do I need my fated heart announced to me?*

"I'm simply doing as he asked. You ordered me to obey him as I would you unless it would endanger him, the coven, or you, or directly counter you. This is his wish."

Sasha sighed but nodded for Jalin to continue. He just wanted to see Trace!

"Trace is here and will explain the conditions of what he's here for himself. Please listen to him, sir," Jalin added, his voice cracking oddly at the end. Sasha had never heard Jalin sound so imploring or afraid, ever.

"What's going on?" Sasha approached Jalin, his hand out. He kept his movements slow, genuinely worried for the first time ever for his servant/assistant. "Why are you afraid?"

"You'll understand once you talk to Trace. Just please, listen to him."

"I always listen to him." *Even when it guts me to do so.*

"Then do what he says."

He was certain his face showed how shocked he felt, but Sasha couldn't remember a time Jalin had ever suggested Sasha blindly follow anyone's word, especially not a nonvampire. Of course, it wasn't blindly…. Jalin knew what was going on.

"I don't appreciate you two managing me. I assume that's what you're attempting to do." Sasha took a step back, crossing his arms over his chest. "How on earth did you get him to even come here?"

"He'll explain why he's here, sir. I was just to tell you he's here in his lynx form and that he has conditions and rules that you have to follow. I don't know what they are, but I implore you to hear him out."

Dumbfounded, Sasha dropped his stance and gaped at Jalin. "You what? You do?"

"Yes, sir. Dimka and Summer are already clearing the area near your chambers and will guard once that's complete. I am, as always, on call and at your service, sir. On your word, I will send in your consort and heart."

Unsure what to make of any of what Jalin said, Sasha nodded. "All right. Send him in, and I promise to listen to everything he has to say."

"Thank you."

Exhausted—he was beyond tired all the time as it was—he decided to sit back down while Jalin went to bring Trace to him. He was thrilled Trace was back, though all the weirdness of Jalin prefacing the visit worried Sasha. Why all the qualifiers? What was Trace there for? And why show up in his fur instead of in his human skin?

A few moments later, Sasha fought down the urge to giggle—a sound his father always thought he should have grown out of. It wasn't manly! Of course, in the more current age, at least the way he tended to act wasn't seen as so odd. Thank the Gods for humans and how their cultures changed and bled into others. Still, the sight of Trace's lynx, with his head held high, stalking into Sasha's morning room, dragging a light silk robe behind him—he held the edge in his teeth—was beyond adorable. Not that he'd use that word, probably.

"Trace? Mal'chik?"

Trace stopped and dropped the robe, then stepped away from it. Sasha watched as Trace shifted to his human self. Damn, but he would never not be impressed by that. He'd seen shifters over his life change, but those in Keith's tribe were faster and stronger than others, Trace even more so than the average of the tribe.

Once he was human again, Trace bent down and retrieved the robe, then slipped it on before he finally looked up and tentatively met Sasha's gaze.

Damn, but the male was beautiful! Sasha also noted that he felt a little better now that Trace was near. No more energy, unfortunately, but he felt as though he could breathe a little better and that his muscles weren't quite as tight. *Huh.*

Sasha fought the urge to reach out and yank Trace into his arms, knowing that wouldn't be appreciated or tolerated, no matter how much Sasha needed to touch, hold, taste.... "Trace?"

CHAPTER ELEVEN

TRACE PADDED into the room, again taking in how luxurious while still homey it seemed. He tried not to focus too hard on Sasha, though that was as futile an effort as ever. He was immediately drawn to the inky-black hair and the pale blue eyes that almost didn't seem to match. Once he was caught in their gaze, he was always reminded of wickedness, power, ice, and warmth all at the same time. The mystique of a vampire prince, yet there was so much more to Sasha.... If only....

"Sasha," he said, his voice softer than he wanted it to be but as loud as he could make it right then.

"I'm always happy to see you, you know that, but why are you here? Is something wrong?" Sasha clutched the arms of the overstuffed leather chair he sat in, as if he were trying to hold himself in place—of course he might be. Trace knew how handsy Sasha tended to be, so the space Trace put between them had to be difficult for Sasha to deal with on a good day. He thought about how it had been before he left the previous morning and figured it was even more so now that he'd allowed Sasha to touch and pet him so much while he was recovering. The fact Trace hadn't been able to handle anyone but Sasha's touch hadn't missed his notice—he just didn't know how to process it yet.

"Yes, but not with me. Jalin came to see me and convinced me to come back and speak with Dr. Niko. Together we discussed your health issues that have to do with me."

"What!" Sasha roared and jumped out of his seat. "How dare they go behind my back."

Trace cowered, dropping into a low crouch, covering his head. He hated showing such weakness but couldn't help it. A mewl slipped out before he could stop it.

A moment later he felt Sasha's presence close, but the anger seemed to be gone. Still, he couldn't uncoil or look up.

"Trace, hon, shhh...." Sasha touched Trace's elbow so gently he wasn't sure it was real at first. After a moment it turned into a light caress up and down that arm. "You have no need to fear me. I could never hurt you. Shhh...."

It took him a few moments, but Trace did manage to unwind and finally meet Sasha's gaze. "S-sorry."

"No, I should never have reacted that way near you. I know better. I'm not happy that you three went behind my back, but I would never attack you. You are under my protection, Trace. That includes from me as well. I will never touch you in any way that you do not wish." Sasha smoothed Trace's hair, then cupped his cheek. "Please come and get comfortable, mal—" Sasha took a deep breath and closed his eyes before opening them and giving a slight smile. "Please have a seat and tell me what it is you three think I need," he said in a soft voice, most of the command missing for once.

Sasha stepped back, giving Trace space, something the few who had seen Trace panic like this never seemed to understand he needed. He stood and took a moment to dust off the robe and retie it, not that it actually needed it, but Trace did. "Thank you. I'll... take you up on that offer of a seat, if you don't mind."

"Of course."

Sasha returned to his chair, and while his gaze never left Trace—he could feel it like a touch, he was certain—Sasha made no other moves toward Trace. Trace took the seat closest. If he were honest, which he had no intention of being right then, he missed sitting on the cushy rug next to Sasha while Sasha played with his hair as they talked. But Trace wasn't like that anymore. He didn't need anyone or bend to anyone except his alpha and the council, and that was a tribal thing, not a sexual one.

"Trace? Unlike the popular fiction of this time, I can't read your mind. I need you to tell me what's going on. Please."

"You're weakening, and even when you feed, it's not nourishing you as it ought."

The sigh that came out of Sasha could have started a tornado, Trace was certain. He flopped back in his seat, the motion reminding Trace more of the young male Sasha appeared to be when he was around Jason or out around other humans than the powerful prince he truly was. "Jalin, the doctor, and I will have words later. They were *not* supposed to drag you in to my little health issue. And it's not as bad as Jalin thinks it is."

"Dr. Niko also believes it's a major issue, and he's someone you have repeatedly pushed on us as being knowledgeable and experienced."

"That doesn't mean he knows everything," Sasha snapped. "I'm not going to die from being a little tired and hungry. Humans deal with it all the time and survive just fine."

"Those who are malnourished die faster and have a host of other health issues in the in-between time. Plus you are not human; you're a vampire prince. One that a large coven is dependent upon." *One I can't stand to see suffer, especially since this is because you healed me.*

"I can't unbond you, Trace." Sasha looked away, his voice drawn and slow. "You can't stand my touch, much less the thought of what nourishing me would actually entail."

"I know you can't, Sasha. Dr. Niko explained that you need my blood." He couldn't stop the slight shiver that raced up his spine. Ever since he'd met Sasha, he'd had dreams and naughty fantasies of letting Sasha bite him, no matter how hard he tried to banish the idea. The more he'd gotten to know him over time, the worse it'd gotten, because he went from fantasy to real person—one he would be honored to belong to if things were only different. "He also…." Trace took a deep gulp of air, then forced out, "He said vampires, especially ones with fated hearts, need touch and to… to…." *Dammit!* He couldn't get the stupid words out.

Sasha cocked his head to the right and stared, unblinking, at Trace. "He told you that it's nourishing with the body, not just the blood?"

"Yes," Trace whispered.

"But only your lynx wants that. Not you. I won't let them guilt you into doing anything with me." Sasha stood and turned away. "That's no different than rape. I won't abuse you or allow them to either." He then strode out of the room toward where Trace knew Sasha's bedroom was.

Trace sat and stared at where Sasha disappeared. He easily saw how tired and worn Sasha was already, and it had only been a few days. Sasha's energy was off too, though Trace doubted anyone but Jalin, maybe Dimka and Summer, and he could tell that, as he thought it was only because of the bite that he could sense that much. He hadn't been able to sense all that before the attack. The others could because they were that close and observant of their friend and prince. But he'd come here to offer his blood, nearly naked. He now knew Sasha really needed at least some form of sex with the blood to truly be in top form—*what a weird sort of mating bond/diet!* He knew that wasn't the norm for vampires, just for those who had fated hearts. But then they got a lot out of the bond, if it were true. Again he lamented that the Gods had waited to bring them together until after he couldn't take a mate.

Still, the noble rejection stung, even if Trace understood it on an intellectual level. Unfortunately for Trace, he did want Sasha. He simply couldn't mate with him or submit to him, and he wasn't sure which part was sadder.

He drummed his fingers on the arm of his chair as he tried to decide what to do. Regrettably, when it came to sexual issues, Trace was never the aggressor. Ever. Still, no way would he allow Sasha to suffer for pride or a misunderstanding. Especially not now that Sasha had bound himself to Trace, knowing what it could cost him.

"Yep, this won't do," he mumbled to himself as he stood. "Not at all." Trace smoothed his hands down the soft material of his robe before he followed the same path Sasha had taken.

When he reached the door to Sasha's bedchamber, he stopped and knocked.

It seemed forever, though he knew it had to be less than a minute before Sasha's voice rang out. "Come in, mal'chik."

Through sheer force of will and a massive dose of worry for Sasha, Trace managed to reach out and open the door. When he stepped inside, he found Sasha sitting on the edge of his opulent four-poster bed, his head in his hands as he leaned forward. He looked almost doll-like sitting there, as if some child had set their toys down and walked away. Shaking off the odd thought, Trace approached Sasha.

"Thought it was my job to run, not yours."

"I wasn't running, Trace." Sasha raised his head, though he didn't meet Trace's gaze. "But I don't see the point in continuing a discussion where they've obviously coerced you. No matter what I want or need, or they think I need, I will have no part of hurting you. Someone has done more than enough of that already. I won't add to it."

"Jalin did implore me to come, but he only asked me to feed you, nothing more. I'm without clothes because I came in my fur, not my skin. I don't have clothes here."

"They're ordered but won't begin to arrive until tomorrow. Sorry."

Trace waved away the apology. It was a silly comment; Sasha ought to know that. Trace hadn't asked for the clothes or the bedchamber or any of the things gifted him, but that was their way now that he was the official prince consort—even though Sasha wasn't holding him to any of the "duties" of a consort. Still....

"But I brought up the other part because the doctor did. And...."

Sasha finally looked at Trace, meeting his eyes as he leaned forward. "Yes? And?"

"And... um...."

"Trace, hon, what else?"

"Um... how susceptible to pheromones are vampires?" he asked, his voice hoarse as he fought his lynx. His lynx had never agreed with them not taking Sasha, or not letting Sasha take them, more like. But now that they knew Sasha needed their blood and, realistically, their energy—best if raised through sex of some form—his cat was nearly beyond his control. That part of him wanted their mate, *thank you oh so fucking much!* It didn't care about all the reasons why *no* was the right answer.

"I can scent them on you easily, but coming from a lynx, they don't control me as they would if I were another lynx. Why?"

Yeah, he was kinda afraid of that. That would make this harder, as Trace couldn't get out the words to ask Sasha to come to him, and he couldn't go and touch Sasha without an invitation or order. He just couldn't. He'd agreed to that much with his lynx. They could mess around with Sasha as long as there was no anal and no mating bite. Oh, and Trace got to leave when he wanted.

He arched his body slightly, stretching his neck and spine as he deliberately released pheromones into the air. Had Sasha been a lynx shifter and Trace's mate, Sasha would have been harder than hell and raging to get his hands on Trace. As it was Sasha's nostrils flared as he took a deep shuddering breath. A small moan slipped out as he closed his eyes.

"Why are you torturing me, Trace? I know you were angry I bonded you to me, but I thought you understood why." He groaned again as he clutched the bedding at his sides. "I don't understand this—you—at all."

"I can't take you as my mate or into my body. I can't serve you as I once would have, but there are other things we...." He gulped, still unable to believe he was doing this. Saying this. "Things we could do. Ways I could nourish you and give to you."

SASHA RAN his hands up and down his legs as he debated if he was actually having this conversation as he fought for control. If Trace didn't stop deliberately dumping his damn pheromones into the air, Sasha wasn't sure he could be held responsible for his actions! The effort to keep his near all-consuming desire bottled up and interact with Trace as he was expected to, as opposed to taking him against the nearest hard surface (repeatedly), had him shaky on the inside on the best of days. Right then....

"Trace," Sasha rumbled. "Pushing my self-control isn't your best idea. What is it you want?" *Gods, please offer yourself and not be doing this as some twisted kind of punishment for bonding you with only your lynx's permission.*

"I... um...."

He cocked his head as he stared at his fated heart, trying to figure out what his beautiful lynx was up to. "Mal'chik—"

"What does that mean? I keep meaning to check."

"Mal'chik?"

Trace shuddered and gave a short nod.

"'Boy.'"

Trace blushed to the tips of his ears and where the pink went below the edge of the robe. "Oh, um, okay."

"As I was saying, mal'chik, do you need a safeword to make you feel more comfortable? I will never do anything to you that you don't approve." Sasha had come to the conclusion a while ago that Trace was a sub, a severely abused and traumatized one, so he hoped the offer might help his heart feel safer.

Trace opened his mouth, then snapped it shut before repeating the action a couple of times. Then he finally nodded. "Um, please?"

"Of course, hon."

"Lemon and cherry?"

"Mmm, those will do nicely. But what, exactly, are you offering me, mal'chik?"

Cherry was an apt description of Trace as he fidgeted, but he finally answered, "No penetration except for your fangs, and no mating bite."

Sasha's breath caught as images of all the things he could do to Trace tumbled at once through his head. He had trouble sorting them out and calming his heart down enough to do more than stare—or possibly pant.

"I want to taste you," he husked. The little tastes he'd had so far only served to make him want more. To make his hunger worse and his need higher for the male before him.

Trace gave the barest of nods at the same time he let out a tiny whimper. Was there a sweeter sound?

Sasha slipped off his bed, then slowly stepped closer to Trace. He held out a hand to Trace. "Why don't you sit on the bed and let me take care of you, hon? I promise not to use my power or strength against you. All right?"

"Oh, okay," Trace murmured as he allowed Sasha to lead him to the large bed.

Once Trace sat on the edge of the bed, Sasha took advantage of the height Trace was at—Trace was already taller than Sasha, but sitting on the tall bed, he hoped, would allow Trace to feel a little more in control and less vulnerable in what he was offering. Sasha still wasn't confident he should accept Trace's offering, but the damn lynx wasn't playing fair, and even a prince had his limits.

Their eyes met even as Sasha's mind whirled and skipped. The thought of what he might now do to Trace, with Trace, what this might mean in their future… that it might mean a future for them—finally—all ran through his head even as he decided where he wanted to begin. The moment the fear and worry shifted into something else, something heated, Sasha knew it was time to move forward with his plan.

He slowly and deliberately straightened to his full five six as he lowered his hands to Trace's knees. He then began caressing up and down Trace's legs, keeping his hands at first on top of the robe, then closer to Trace's core. When Trace finally relaxed into the gentle contact, Sasha moved his hands to touch Trace's silky skin directly. Damn, but he could do that all night. Trace's body was a work of art. Not simply because he was handsome, which he was, but he was so much more than that. Strong and sensual, with silky skin over tight, toned muscles that were more wiry than anything with bulk. He had a light dusting of hair on his legs but nothing too thick, and pale in the extreme. The more Sasha touched him, the more Trace trembled and made those soft little mewling sounds that drove Sasha crazy.

Sasha slid his hands out to Trace's knees and gently but firmly pushed his legs open, then slipped closer.

"Sasha?"

"Lie back. I told you I want to taste you. Unless you'd rather me touch you while I drink from your throat." He didn't believe Trace wanted that, not his human side. Not so soon after the attack, anyways. Not that Sasha was convinced Trace wanted Sasha near his personal bits with his fangs either, but that was because he didn't know any better… a fact Sasha was going to correct shortly. He hoped.

Trace gulped and shook his head. "Um, not really. But, uh, you'll be careful with your fangs down… down there, right?"

CHAPTER TWELVE

"OF COURSE, mal'chik. Now relax and let me show you how much I want you."

Trace slowly lay back, bracing himself on his elbows, though he didn't move his gaze from tracking Sasha. Sasha bent and began kissing his way up Trace's left leg, starting at the knee. He pushed the robe aside more, exposing Trace's groin and hip, nipping the left one before he started the journey all over again back at Trace's right knee. Once both hips were exposed, Sasha slipped the tie from the robe loose and flashed a fanged smile at Trace.

"Fangs," Trace squeaked.

Instead of replying Sasha kissed up Trace's abdomen to his belly button, dipping his tongue into the shallow divot before nipping it, careful not to break the skin. When he finally did, he wanted to be sure nothing but pleasure was connected to the bloodletting in Trace's mind.

He then followed the path back down until he faced the glistening head of Trace's cock as it peeked out of its hood. It wasn't all that thick, but it had a nice length and blood darkened it. The scent of precome and blood was a heady mixture, and Sasha moaned as he nuzzled Trace's member, giving it one long lick from base to tip. He took the time to roll his tongue around the head, gathering the dew that had collected, nibbling on the foreskin gently before going up to the tip and stabbing his tongue into the slit.

The sounds steadily pouring out of Trace drove Sasha's need higher, as well as his hunger. Sasha sucked Trace's cock into his mouth, not stopping until his nose was buried in the neatly trimmed curls at the base. Trace dropped his head down as he let out a long moan and spread his legs wider. Sasha took the invitation and set his pace, bobbing up and down as he used his other hand to caress and tug on Trace's sac, squeezing every few bobs.

When he popped off Trace's length with a loud sucking sound, Trace whined, making Sasha chuckle. Boy didn't want Sasha to be with him? Riiight…. Instead of focusing on why Trace was so skittish, Sasha pulled himself back to the here and now and dove down, licking and mouthing

Trace's sac before sucking in one ball, then the other, licking and rolling it in his mouth as he pulled just enough to heighten the pleasure for his heart. He slipped one hand behind Trace's balls to press and rub along Trace's taint, and he slid the other up until he could reach Trace's nipple. The little nub was already hard and beaded, so Sasha lightly pinched and twisted it, drawing out more mewls and causing Trace to tremble.

Trace's cock swelled a little more as his sounds grew.

"Close," Trace choked out. "Gonna...."

Good!

Sasha dug his hands into Trace's thighs, massaging hard, and on the next up motion, he deliberately nicked the large vein on the underside of Trace's dick. Trace snapped his hips forward, shoving himself down Sasha's throat as he erupted and screamed. Sasha moved off Trace just enough that he could swallow the mixed essences, taking both blood and come into him from his fated heart for the first time. He drank every drop, licking the nick and then the tip of Trace's cock clean before moving backward a little and sinking his fangs into Trace's left thigh, taking gentle pulls of blood only to finish his "meal."

Even as he sank his fangs into Trace's flesh, Trace mewled and his cock twitched, though since he'd only just come hard, it couldn't fill again so soon.

"Oh Gods, Sasha! What...?"

Sasha took one last sip, then pulled away, licking the puncture marks, sealing them before he stood back and met Trace's wide-eyed gaze. "Yes, mal'chik?"

Damn, but Trace looked divine all debauched and spread out on the bed.

"You.... Blood.... Um...." Trace shook his head, then took a series of slow, deliberate breaths before he sat up and resettled the robe, covering himself. "It, um, didn't hurt when you bit me."

At least he stopped saying things as if they were questions. "Of course it didn't. Why would I want it to hurt you? My feeding from you should never be anything but pleasurable." Sasha winked at Trace. "Though how much so is up to you."

Trace swallowed hard, dropping his gaze. "Thank you for not hurting me. I should...." He maneuvered around so he could slip off the bed, going to his knees in front of Sasha. "I should have been the one to service you. Please allow me to make it up to you?" Trace finished, his voice cracking.

Sasha stared down at Trace's beautiful blond hair, his face hidden as he stared at Sasha's feet, confused. He hadn't asked Trace to do anything to or for him other than enjoy, allow, not freak out after. He wanted a real chance for them, and while Sasha was still angry with Jalin and Dr. Niko, if their meddling was what it took to nudge Trace to allow something real to develop between him and Trace, he would accept the gift and be grateful.

"I will never hurt you, mal'chik. Cause you consensual pain, possibly, but never hurt. But why do you believe you need to make anything up to me?" *What the hell is going on in that head of yours?*

"For right now I am acting as your lover, or boy, as you keep calling me." Trace's voice was barely a whisper and he trembled slightly, though in a very different way than he had while on the bed only minutes before. "I should service you, not the other way around. I bend and accept what is done to me, not the other way around. You shouldn't have sullied yourself for me like that. Please let me serve you to make up for it."

"Trace, look at me." When Trace didn't look up, Sasha cupped his cheek and applied gentle pressure until Trace didn't have a choice but to do as requested. "I did exactly what I wished. I wanted to taste you, as I said. You taste wonderful, by the way, and that is something I hope to do again and again."

"But… but why would you want to do that instead of having it done to you? You haven't even gotten off yet!" Trace's voice, coupled with the wide eyes and eyebrows that appeared to want to join with his spiky hair, made Sasha want to laugh—and cry. Had the male never had a lover worth knowing?

"You offered yourself for my nourishment, Trace, not for pure sex. Not that I would have wanted one-sided sex with you either. When we have sex, I want it to be mutual and pleasurable for us both. For you to touch me out of desire and passion, not out of twisted duty or obligation. What you just allowed is questionable enough," Sasha added, turning away, though he did keep his hand on Trace's cheek. "You know I want us, even though you have made it clear you do not. Now that I can think clearly again—thank you, pheromones!—I would not have accepted what you just offered had you not pushed as you did."

"But—"

Sasha turned back to meet Trace's gaze. "Because I don't want you giving me of yourself if you don't wish to. You have reasons not to want our bonding, which are still there. I wish you would allow me the ability to show you that I'm not like the monster who hurt you, to show you that our bonding, our mating, could be a beautiful thing."

Trace stared up at Sasha, blinking hard a few times before he pulled back enough that he could turn his head down again. He shook his head and mumbled, "I don't know if I could ever trust anyone again, much less a Dom."

"A Dom?"

"I know what you are, Sasha. You're a Dom. Not a heavy hitter, as some would say, but a Dom nonetheless. I'm not stupid, nor am I unobservant. Your perfect partner would be your boy twenty-four seven—he would sit at your feet, help you run your coven, be strong of mind and giving of body."

"And sit on the couch and watch movies with me and enjoy popcorn with all kinds of herbs and seasonings. And love shopping. And not be upset that I work outside the covenstead by running one of the hospitals here in Seattle. And… and… and…."

"I don't see your point."

"That I'm so much more than what you're trying to focus on. In fact, I'm not exactly what you're focusing on. Dom? Only sort of. By human standards, yes, and I've acted as such in clubs. I believe that things only work if both parties are getting what they need and are in agreement, though I've never collared a sub or contracted one. It's not seen the same among my kind, the dominant and 'kink' concepts. It's simply something inherent in those of us that are leaders. But that doesn't mean the same thing to everyone. For you it would obviously mean no impact, or at least no whips, belts, et cetera. However, I bet you would love sensation play, orgasm control and denial, maybe wax?"

Trace shivered, a tiny mewl slipping out. "I used to, but that was a long time ago."

"What if instead of focusing on what you don't think you can handle, you let us have a chance and give yourself the ability to find out what you actually can?"

"How?" Trace scrunched his nose and cocked his head to the side. "How do I do that?"

"Date me. Don't worry about the bond or mating bites, just about what to wear out with me to dinner, dancing, movies, and such. We'll do it how the humans do. You can learn about me the old-fashioned way. You have your own space here, plus your home on tribe land, so you don't have to stay in my bed unless you wish to. That's not a right you have to earn, by the way. You are my fated heart, and as I have already bonded you and made that fact public, this entire suite is your residence. That includes my bed. Just no stealing my clothes or footwear. That I'll fight you for," he added with a wink, only half kidding.

"You just said don't worry about the bond, then pointed out the bond."

"Sort of, but only in as much as applies to where you may be in my suite. Now will you give dating a try? Let us work on something other than you debasing yourself for my health, then scurrying back to the tribal land to escape me?" Sasha knew he wasn't playing fair with his wording, but he didn't care. He just wanted his heart!

Trace stared up at Sasha, the intensity more than a bit unnerving. About the time Sasha opened his mouth to ask what Trace was staring at so hard, Trace said, "You know, the dark circles under your eyes are gone and you don't look so pale. Well, you always look a pale olive, but not the sickly pale you were starting to look before."

"Well, yeah, I fed from you, hon. Of course I look better." *Hadn't that been the whole point of Jalin and Niko's intervention?* "Didn't they explain that part?"

"Yeah, but I'm not sure I completely believed them. I mean, how could I be the key to your health? I'm just *me*," he added so softly Sasha almost missed it.

"You're my fated heart, hon. My bonded, fated heart. I didn't bond you to get you to give me your blood or your body, though, and I won't die if you don't, no matter what Jalin says."

"But you will weaken and suffer, all because you used that bonding bite to heal my mind."

Sasha shrugged. "I accepted that when I agreed to bite you. Your lynx agreed to the bite, which, since it didn't require sex like the mating bite does, was good enough for me."

"Yeah, he and I aren't always in agreement."

"Noted." Sasha pulled Trace up to standing, then curled a hand around Trace's right hip. "Would you like to go out with me, not tomorrow night, but the night after? I have to welcome my uncle and Tatiana tomorrow, or I would take you out then."

"Don't like that they're gonna think you're available. Damn Tatiana chick," Trace grumbled so low Sasha almost didn't hear him. He wouldn't have if he weren't a vampire, he was positive.

"Hon, Tatiana knows I'm not available, that I'm bonded to you. It's my uncle who's delusional still, and he's of no import to us. Now please answer the question."

"Wait, what?"

"Goddess, but you distract easily." Sasha sighed and shook his head. "What am I to do with you?"

"Sorry. Um...." Trace took a deep breath, held it, then let it out slowly. "Please don't make me regret this."

Sasha smiled, putting as much of his hope for their future in it as he could manage. "That's a yes."

"Yes, that's a yes."

"Good. Now why don't you rest while I arrange a light meal for you? You're not used to feeding me, so you'll feel a little weak. And mal'chik?" When Trace met his gaze, he quickly leaned in and pecked him on the cheek. "Thank you."

"Uh...."

Thankfully Trace was too dazed, or so it seemed, to argue as Sasha manhandled him up onto the bed and under the covers. Damn, but the male looked good there. Now to hope Trace stayed put and didn't freak out. They both still had things they needed to do, and that was on top of Sasha needing to deal with his wayward assistant and doctor. Those two he was going to strangle, then thank. In that order.

"Rest, Trace," Sasha murmured as he stroked Trace's hair. "I know this is all a bit much for you, but you'll feel better once you've eaten, and thank you for saying yes."

"Just for a few." Trace closed his eyes, his breaths a little fast but not so much it worried Sasha. This all had to be a bit much and beyond confusing to his poor heart.

As Sasha exited the room, he swore he would do a better job of easing Trace into his life, especially now that Trace had agreed to give them a chance. A crack in Trace's walls was all he needed, he was sure of it. The lynx had fascinated him, inflamed him, impressed him for five years. Now to figure out how to get the rest of the way in.

TRACE LAY in Sasha's bed, breathing in the scent of his still-not-a-mate, trying his best to quell the shakes that had started in his hands even before Sasha exited the room. *What the hell have I done?* He groaned and rubbed his trembling hands over his face, unsure what to do next. The plan was to come and offer his blood so Sasha would be strong and healthy, so he could deal with his uncle and the threat against the coven and the tribe. His own want of Sasha had allowed those two vampires to tempt him into offering Sasha more, but while it had made sense at the time....

The longer he lay there, his thoughts spinning, the more out of control they became, the faster his breathing came. He couldn't do this. He had let Sasha touch him. Have control over his body. Agreed to date him, for Gods' sake!

His vision narrowed in, the edges becoming darker and spotty, and he couldn't seem to catch his breath no matter what he did to slow it.

Away. He needed away. Away from the male who would claim him. From anyone who would try to own him.

Never again. He couldn't do this again!

Trace shifted into his lynx skin but didn't fully give his lynx side control. He couldn't... not just yet. Soon. He clawed his way out from under the sheet, shredding the 1,200 thread count, not caring about anything but getting away.

Hide.

Safety.

Mine.

Trace scanned his surroundings, found the door, and bolted, not stopping until he was in his own chambers. Sasha had promised he would be safe here when he was at the covenstead. This was his territory, right? The open space wasn't defensible, though, not in his current size. Trace looked around, poking his nose into corners and climbing up onto everything he could as quickly as possible.

In the end, just before the panic completely overwhelmed him and his lynx pushed him fully aside, he leaped and caught the top edge of the closet shelf with his claws. Trace then shoved the few boxes aside, backing into the corner before the world sucked all the air from his lungs finally and went black.

CHAPTER THIRTEEN

SASHA DIDN'T find Jalin until he fully exited his wing. Jalin stood half behind Summer, the fear scent in the air almost thick enough to choke him. "Come out from behind Summer. Now."

"Sir," Summer began but stopped when Sasha glared at him.

"I would suggest you don't, as I'm in no mood for Jalin's attempt to hide behind you right now, Summer. Now, Jalin."

Jalin gulped but stepped around Summer and came forward before he dropped to a knee. "I'm sorry, sir. I only did what I thought necessary."

"I am well aware of what you did, and even why. I will not have this conversation out here, however. Send someone to gather appropriate food for Trace and then follow me back to my sitting room."

"Y-yes, sir." Jalin jumped up and scurried away, calling out orders immediately, the action almost enough to make Sasha smile.

Summer looked over his shoulder to where Jalin disappeared, then back to Sasha. He folded his arms over his wide chest and frowned slightly. "You're not really going to kill him, are you?"

"Not sure why I would tell you the answer to that, especially with him still within earshot."

Summer huffed but didn't ask again.

"For now make sure things are ready for the visit tomorrow. Are you or Dimka riding out with the *good* doctor tonight?"

"Dimka and Dr. Niko already left."

"I just bet they did," he mumbled.

"Huh?"

Sasha waved Summer away as Jalin came back into view. "Don't worry about it. Dr. Niko is just doing what Jalin wishes he could do right now. Hiding from me. Now"—Sasha turned to stare at Jalin—"where is Trace's food, and are you ready? I wish they hadn't left yet, as I know Trace had wanted to be the one to introduce the two doctors." *Hopefully Trace won't be too put out that the doctor's cowardice wound up with him left behind.*

"His alpha called while you were busy. It seems the female is extremely jittery and wanted their Chosen Alpha, as she put it, to be there. Something about his being powerful enough to protect her."

"Seriously?" He gaped at Jalin, unable to wrap his mind around her continued prejudice and stupidity. The joint project seemed less and less likely to succeed the more he heard about her. "Never mind, of course you are. Let's hope Dr. Niko and Keith can find a way to get through to her. Sean is too important for her stupidity to get in the way."

"They will." Summer gave a small smile as he walked with Sasha, Jalin trailing behind. Just before they reached the entry door to Sasha's suite, one of the kitchen staff hurried up with a rolling cart, the top heavy with covered dishes.

"For the royal consort, sir." The young male bowed low, then scampered off before Sasha could say anything to him.

"Do I want to know what you said to have the poor boy running like that from me? I've never treated the kitchen help badly."

Sasha stepped through the doorway and waited for Jalin to enter before he nodded to Summer to close the door behind them. Summer stayed on the outside of the doors, as Sasha knew he would.

"Everyone knows you are not in the best of moods lately, and my nerves may have transferred to the others. I will smooth things over with them later, sir. What with your uncle's visit, the attack on your consort, and the fact your uncle is bringing someone he's trying to force you to marry, no one wishes to tempt your patience."

"And yet you coerced my fated heart to come to me, got the doctor in on it, bullied him into thinking he needed to offer not only his blood, but his body, or I might die!" he roared at the end. "And you claim that no one wants to try my patience? Seems you do, very much so."

"I—" he croaked.

"Yes, you. You're just lucky that I like you and that Trace told me what you'd done. Had I found out afterward…."

Jalin shifted back a couple of steps, his eyes round as saucers.

"Don't even try that look on me. It didn't work on you when I was a little boy; it won't on me now to save you. How would you have felt if someone had guilted your mother or sister into having sex with someone they didn't choose? Coercion is still assault, and he's been abused enough already!"

"But you could die, and he *does* want you. He's merely confused."

"Tired isn't d—" A soft thump from Trace's chambers drew Sasha's attention from Jalin. No one should be in there. Trace was in Sasha's bed, or had been when last he looked. Without giving his assistant another thought, Sasha turned and hurried to his bedroom door, which stood ajar. When he peered inside, his concern grew exponentially. The sheets were shredded and Trace was gone, though his clothing was there.

"Where the hell is Trace?" he yelled as he snatched up Trace's ripped shirt. Sasha turned the material over even as he took a deep breath. "No blood, though there is the heavy stench of fear."

"No one could have penetrated your chambers and have taken him, sir." Jalin stood in the doorway wringing his hands, his voice firm. "Summer or his guards would have caught anyone foolish enough to try."

"No one thinks Trace was taken. I need to find him." Sasha stilled, focusing on that place within where a part of Trace lived, and flinched. "Dammit! He panicked again. I never should have left him alone so soon. I knew he handled this all too well."

"Where could…."

There was probably more to what Jalin said, but Sasha was too busy following the trail of fear Trace had left behind. When his fated heart was in a better place mentally, they really needed to discuss Trace's habit of scent-dumping into the air like this. In the wild or out and about town with rogue vampires around, it could lead to his being attacked or possibly even killed. Neither was acceptable!

Across the bathing area lay one of the access doors to Trace's bedchambers, and unsurprisingly, that entrance also stood open.

"Aha. Not gone, just a room over," he mumbled as he let their connection pull him toward his heart.

"Sir. You promised not to enter without an invitation. Sasha—"

"Oh, do shut up. Would you have me leave him in the middle of a panic attack, then? No? Didn't think so. I will go help him, leave him his meal, then give him his space, if that's what he chooses. If he wanted me to stay out, he shouldn't have left the shreds, scent, and doors as they are. Now do stay out of his area unless invited, Jalin."

Jalin grumbled, but Sasha didn't take the time or energy to bother finding out what was said. Instead he went in search of Trace. Unfortunately the scent of his fear was so strong in there Sasha had trouble pinpointing where it came from. Not wanting to take the time to sort through all the input, he began a manual search, trying to think of where a lynx would fit. The bed was more than tall enough to allow him to fit under, and with the long bed-skirt, Sasha hoped, but no, Trace hadn't gone for anything that easy.

Sasha kept looking but then thought about the thump he'd heard, changing to look for things that had been knocked over or down. In the large walk-in closet, he found a couple of boxes in the middle of the floor, their lids knocked to the side at odd angles. *Ahh... finally.* Sasha raised his head to peer up at the top shelf, noting the gouges in the polished wood. Thinking of the fit Jalin would throw pulled a small smile from him, even as he wondered how bad Trace was to not have even poked his head out or made a sound yet. Now that he was here, it was easy to discern that, yes, Trace was close. He was also still in his fur.

"Trace, kitty, will you come down for me, hon?" He hoped the fact Trace's lynx liked him and recognized their bond, even when Trace fought against it, might help some.

Reow! Followed by a soft hiss.

"Okay, not sure what that means, hon. You know I can't speak lynx."

That only received a soft mewl but still no movement.

"Would it be all right if I came up to you, then?"

This time the sound was more curious than anything, so he took that for an invitation and used his power to rise until he could see above the edge of the shelf. What he saw then nearly broke his heart. Trace had wedged himself into the corner and shook just enough that even the ends of his fur quivered. His claws were out, his tufted ears back, and his little fangs bared.

To anyone else, coming face-to-face with a cornered lynx would be a terrifying thing. Even though they were one of the "small" wildcats, they were still lethal animals and nothing to play around with; however, given this was Trace, the only danger came from the fact Trace was still obviously on edge thanks to the panic attack he'd suffered. No true mate would ever hurt their mate—and no matter that Trace still refused to claim him, his lynx recognized Sasha.

"Should I call you *mal'chik* or *Trace* like this, huh? I know you like *mal'chik* as your human side, even though you don't exactly admit it. But since you're a handsome lynx, I guess *boy* isn't exactly right now. Oh well, guess I'll just have to stick to *Trace* and *hon* for your furry side." As he rambled Sasha slowly stretched out one arm, reaching until he could almost touch Trace. He stopped about half a foot shy and waited, hand hovering. "I brought you food, but it's all prepared how you like it when you're in your human skin. I can have the kitchen send something for you in your lynx form, or you could shift. Whichever you'd like, but hon, you can't eat up here. And I promise we don't have any mice loose in the mansion, so staying up here will be a boring and hunger-inducing problem."

Trace stretched his neck out and nudged Sasha's hand with his nose.

"I'd really rather you came down and just ate with me, though, either as human or lynx, I don't care. But we need to decide what you want to do for the night and tomorrow, hon. My uncle and Tatiana are coming, and I'm pretty sure that if you choose to meet them, you'll want to do so as your human self."

Trace wiggled forward until his head was completely under Sasha's hand. He then bumped his head up into Sasha's hand a couple of times, giving a light mewl.

Sasha scratched behind Trace's ears before he began smoothing his hand down Trace's head and shoulders repeatedly.

"My uncle will still likely refer to you as my pet, for which I do apologize, but Tatiana—" This time when Sasha said her name, Trace raised his head and hissed before lowering it to rest on his paws. The imperious glare he gave Sasha made him chuckle. "—Tatiana," he emphasized and got another hiss for his trouble, "—will be interested in you on a more personal level. She's not like my uncle."

That got Trace's attention. Finally. He raised his head, tilting it to one side as he gave off a series of mewls, clicks, hisses, and soft yowls Sasha had no clue how to interpret. They didn't sound exactly angry, nor did they hold the panic that sent Trace up there in the first place. Still…. "I have no idea what you're saying or asking. Shift and use people words, please."

Without proper warning Trace lunged at Sasha, catching him off guard. Sasha threw up his arms, wrapping them around Trace, holding him tight as he lowered them to the ground before letting him go. "Dammit! Don't do that! What if I hadn't managed to catch you and you'd fallen?"

Trace shifted to his human self and stood, stretching his long limbs as he turned to face Sasha. "No farther up than we were? Ha! I would have landed on my paws and been fine. Um…." Trace stopped and stared, wide-eyed. "How were you up there?" He looked around at Sasha's feet. "There's no ladder."

"Of course not. Why would I need one?"

"Because you're only five and a half feet tall," Trace replied, deadpan, his brows drawn so tight together he almost had a unibrow.

"Same way I move any object I want, except in this case, I moved me." Why was he asking stupid questions when he ought to be worrying about the fact he could have gotten himself seriously hurt! "Telekinesis."

"That doesn't explain you being up in the air."

"I can move me too, as I said."

"So you can fly? Like in the movies? Vampires fly?"

"No, I can only go up and then back down, left and right is very limited, and distance is pretty much out. Why?"

"So levitation, then."

"Ugh! I suppose. I just know that I chose to move me and it worked. I choose to move the door—" The closet door closed with a soft *thush*. "—and it moves. Few vampires can do it, though some princes and princesses I know can." Sasha wondered if he should point out Trace was standing there naked with his hands on his perfect narrow hips.

"That's… impressive as hell, Sasha, yet you look bored as you explain it."

"Sorry, but it's something I've been able to do since I was little. Got me in a ton of trouble when I was a boy, actually."

"But—"

"Hon, shifting isn't something that overly impresses you, is it? I mean, it's normal to you. It just is. Well, to me this is one of those things that just is. Your shifting is impressive, not my ability to move up to find you." Sasha paused, unsure if he really wanted to draw attention to the issue that drove Trace up there in the first place, but needing to at the same time. "But would you mind telling me what happened to you? I mean, I thought you were going to take a short nap while I arranged a snack for you, but when I returned, you were gone."

Trace dropped his gaze to his feet, at which point he seemed to realize he was without clothes, finally, and turned bright red from midchest to his hairline. He spun around, presenting Sasha with his backside—which was just as mouthwatering as his front—and squeaked, "Robe? Please."

"Of course, mal'chik."

With a chuckle Sasha stepped away to retrieve one of the soft robes in the armoire in the main bedchamber, left from when Trace stayed as he'd recovered. His clothing would begin to arrive in the morning, but he had a few things there already, mainly robes and the like. Nothing fit for Trace to work in, not yet, at least, or for him to attend to his consort duties. That thought almost made Sasha cringe, but he shook off the thought and returned to Trace. He draped the robe over Trace's shoulders and turned to give him some privacy. They'd had sex—oral, but it still counted!—but Trace was more than a bit off and embarrassed right then, so Sasha didn't want to push any more than necessary.

"Thank you," Trace said softly. He brushed Sasha's arm briefly with one hand, there and gone.

Sasha turned and smiled. "Of course. Now would you like that snack? We have things to discuss, and you're awaiting a call from your alpha."

"I… am?"

"Yes. Dimka took the doctor out to meet with your council doc already. She decided she needed the big bad alpha to be there instead of you. Something about protection," Sasha added with a negligent wave. "It's asinine, but she's so prejudiced she can't seem to see the damage she ought to be causing. The fact I could care less about her stupidity is her only saving grace. I can't think of another prince that would allow such disrespect. Honestly if she had done this in front of any but Jalin, Summer, and Dimka, I would have to address her behavior directly, not merely leave it to your alpha."

"I know, and I appreciate your patience. I will make a full report to the council about her actions and about your leniency, citing how you tolerated her because you are more interested in what's best for your godson than in punishing her. I will, however, stress that your patience is growing thin. The council will act to help rein her in, as they want this alliance to work."

"Don't they realize that Jason is my best friend, Sean is my godson, and you are my fated heart? There isn't a doubt that it will 'work out.'"

Chapter Fourteen

"Um... they don't know about that part," Trace mumbled as he looked away, unwilling and unable to meet Sasha's gaze.

Sasha nodded as if he knew that already, though he had to. There was no reason for him to believe otherwise, was there? Sure, Trace could have spoken with Duncan, and unless he had sworn Duncan to secrecy, he would have told the others on the council about the current mating issue, but he hadn't. Trace hadn't really even managed to talk to his alpha, which he should have done first thing—especially considering the relationship between Sasha and Jason. Still....

"Trace?"

"Huh?"

"You're off in your head again, and your breathing is picking up in a way I'm not sure is healthy for you. Think you can share with me? Maybe while you eat."

Did he want to? Not really, but things weren't going to go how he wanted, obviously. "Maybe." At Sasha's raised eyebrow, he added, "Look, I'm not trying to be difficult, but this isn't easy for me to discuss, and being alone with you adds to that."

"Would you feel safer if we asked someone to sit in with us? I'm not sure who you'd find to be appropriate company here since everyone here is loyal to me, but we can put this discussion on hold until we send for someone from your tribe, if that would be better."

That only made him feel worse. The only person he truly felt safe with, stupidly, was Sasha. That was the issue—Sasha had left and what they'd done had crashed in on him. The possible ramifications and his past and... and... and....

"That won't help, and I don't want more people knowing about my messed-up past than already do. Alpha Keith and Jason already have enough to deal with anyway."

"Okay, then come eat and talk. I promise to listen to anything you have to say, and nothing you tell me will change things for me. For us."

"We'll see," he muttered but followed along until he was back in the sitting room, where they found Jalin standing just inside the dining nook. A rolling tray stand sat beside the table and held covered dishes and two large thermoses. "Please tell me that's coffee."

"Actually there's cinnamon vanilla chai in one and hazelnut praline coffee in the other. I have cream, honey, and raw sugar as well."

"Bless you." Trace made a beeline for the coffee and poured some, to which he added a large dose of cream and a little sugar. Once he stirred his coffee, he took a tentative sip, then sighed happily.

"I take it it's to your liking?" Sasha asked through soft laughter.

"It is," Trace replied primly. "Good coffee is nothing to laugh about. I have a Keurig and one of the K-cup trees with various coffees and teas on it in my home and in my office so that both are available at any given time."

Jalin pointed to the bar set up in the corner. "I had one added already, though the K-cup holder is under the counter. Would you like your food now, or should I take it back to the kitchen and return later?"

"No, now is fine."

"We're going to talk for a bit, Jalin, so please let Summer know that our area is off-limits to any but the three of you without my express permission. Not even the maids. Am I understood?"

"Of course, sir." Jalin set various small dishes around the place setting where Trace had chosen to sit. He wasn't used to being served, except when he went out to dinner, but he also knew this was part of what Jalin did, and to not allow the male to do his job would be a great insult—to both him and Sasha. When he was done, Trace thanked him, even managing to give Jalin a small smile.

"You're welcome, sir. Please let me know if there's anything else you need." Jalin then turned and faced Sasha.

"You may go. Just remember what I said earlier. Oh, and while things need to be ready for tomorrow, don't make my uncle too comfortable. He won't be staying long."

"I have them both in the royal wing but as far from you as possible. Though the princess is closer, as she's much less likely to wear on your nerves."

Trace ground his teeth, trying not to react like the jealous asshat he felt like. How could he be upset about her coming here when he'd refused to mate Sasha for over five years? And Sasha had already said he wasn't taking her as his bride. But what if he changed his mind? What if—

"Mal'chik, calm down" came Sasha's soothing voice, breaking through the fog of anger and confusion. "Tatiana is no threat to you or to your place here. Shh…." He trailed his fingers up and down Trace's arm, leaving goose bumps in their wake.

"Sorry. Not my business." Gods, was that his voice? He sounded like he'd been gargling glass.

"It is, but you have other things you need to focus on, not a female who has no interest in challenging you, nor any ability to do so."

"Yes, I need to focus on eating." With that he picked up a finger sandwich and bit it in half. Huh, cucumber and cream cheese. Not bad.

"True, but also on why you panicked or on why you keep running from us. Perhaps on what happened to you that caused those scars down your back."

Trace froze, not even daring to breathe as he tried to decide what to do and say. He knew things couldn't keep going how they had been. That was painfully obvious. And just plain painful. His lynx constantly prowled under his skin, driving him crazy on top of everything else.

He slowly let out a breath and nodded to himself. "Just don't demand I look at you, please."

"My only demand is that whatever you say be the truth, Trace. You may look wherever you need."

"Thanks." To give himself something to do, as what appetite he'd had was gone, he nibbled on another of the little sandwiches. That one was turkey. While his stomach wasn't interested, it was actually pretty good. "Um, Gods, I don't know what to say."

"Let's start with why you were up on the top shelf."

"Most defensible place and it was my space, my territory."

Sasha nodded. "Makes sense, though this entire suite is yours now as much as it is mine. You could have stayed in where you were and still have been in your territory."

Trace shook his head. "No, that's your room. The other is mine. Even my lynx sees the difference, and so he went where it was his. It's the only place here that is."

The deep sigh and frown tugged at Trace's heart, but he stood by his reasoning. That was what he'd thought—well, what little thought he'd managed while panicking.

"When I gave you your own room, it was to give you space, to make it so you didn't feel so pressured by our bonding. It wasn't so you'd section the suite into his and his." Sasha slumped in his chair. "Especially not after what we'd shared."

"That's just it. I've not shared, as you put it, in so long, much less with anyone of importance, that I freaked out. Letting you feed from me was one thing, giving you power over me a whole other."

"I don't understand the power issue exactly. We talked it through beforehand. You had ways to stop things at any given point you needed. And I thought you trusted me enough to know I wouldn't deliberately hurt you."

"I know that." Trace sighed and rubbed his hands over his face. "Look," he mumbled into his hands before dropping them into his lap. "I don't know how to make this make sense to you, but I do know that, but I don't all at the same time. Logically I believe you wouldn't deliberately abuse me or my trust that way, but… but…."

"But you can't trust me not to change and abuse you somehow if you give me what you perceive as power over you." It should have been a question. Sasha seemed to do that too often, stating things that ought to be an inquiry. How could he know that?

Trace wasn't certain how to respond, hating how his past was showing—as usual when he dealt with Sasha. He tried to, though, but nothing came out.

"I have never done the things you fear, Trace. I know my stating that doesn't help you believe, but there is no history of abuse in my past."

"You are a Dom."

Sasha took a deep breath, letting it out slowly. "I already went over that. It's not quite the same thing as the human concept of Dom, but yes, I am. I don't know a ruling member of vampire royalty who isn't. It's a part of us, but that doesn't mean we're cruel or abusive any more than it does in the mortal side of things."

"I've been owned by one who claimed that position before!" Trace jumped up from the table, his vision blurring at the edges as it darkened. His heart beat so loud and fast Jalin and Summer probably heard it. Turning around, he slipped his robe so Sasha could see the marks on his back and hissed, "This is what being owned and loved gets me! I won't go through that again." He raised his robe back into place, spun on his heel, then fled back to his room, not caring the tears he'd struggled not to let fall streamed down his face despite his efforts.

Sasha sat in the chair opposite Trace's, head tilted to one side as he continued to stare after his fated heart, confused not by what had been said, but by what had been seen. Seeing Trace's back before had made Sasha angry and concerned; this time it had made him confused. The scars didn't look the same. Well, from what he could see in that short flash of skin versus the previous time... but Sasha had also followed the lines through Trace's clothes with his fingertips while Trace was recovering, and he was positive the scars seemed much lighter and fewer in number.

He was so caught up in his thoughts about the scars he barely noted Trace's actual leaving until Trace's door slammed. The sound managed to snap him out of his swirling thoughts, though, and back to what was going on now. Sasha jumped up and hurried after Trace, determined not to allow his heart to retreat or overlay the actions of the bastard who hurt him before onto their present and future.

Once again he stood before Trace's door. Gods, but he was getting tired of this! Before he knocked he pulled out his cell and sent a short text to Keith. He hated going around Trace, but it was getting ridiculous: this and the scars changing thing needed answers. For that he needed a doctor, probably, and shifter and vampire ones alike were all on the shifter land.

That done, he raised his hand, only hovering for a moment before he rapped lightly on the solid wood.

"I don't wish to speak to you, Sasha," Trace grumbled through the door.

"You are a grown male, not a child, Trace. Hiding is beneath you."

"Ha! You call me 'boy' all the time."

He counted to thirty, as ten and twenty weren't enough, before he tried again. "Point, but that's meant as an endearment, not as a behavior expectation. I tend to call people—especially Jason—'hon' too, which is short for honey. Do you honestly think I expect them all to turn into a sticky liquid that bees make?" *Cannot believe I just asked that!*

The door flew open to reveal Trace, mouth agape and eyes wide. "What the hell? You did not seriously just ask me that?"

Sasha smoothed his hands down his shirt until they rested at the top of his thighs. "I did. It's just as illogical as what you asked."

"What you just…. No, that's…. Have you lost your mind? That was—"

"Willfully ignorant? Not at all what you meant? Yes, mal'chik, I am well aware what you meant, just as you are of what I meant. But you running from me, from being honest with me, won't help either of us."

Trace wrapped his arms around his abdomen, tight, and shook his head slightly. "My past isn't any of your business."

"Everything about you is now. Just as my past is your business, as you put it."

"I did not take you as my mate!"

The pain that lanced through Sasha's heart along with those words drew a gasp from him, both from the physical pain and from the shock of it. He looked down at his chest and rubbed it with one hand, the other curled around the doorway. Sasha wasn't even sure when he'd grabbed the jamb, but as that was the only reason he still stood, he shrugged it off and focused on the shock he'd just suffered.

"Sasha?" Trace grasped Sasha around the middle and quickly led him inside and to the comfy chair by the window. He lowered Sasha into it, then knelt in front of him, never taking his hands off him.

Sasha looked up into Trace's wet gaze. "What was that?"

"What happened, hon? You cried out and clutched the doorjamb and your chest."

"I…." Sasha shook his head and looked down at his chest again. The pain was gone, though there was a faint ghosting of it. Not painful, but almost as though his chest remembered the pain separately from his mind—not that that made any sense to him at all. "I have no idea." *But I'd like to never experience it again, if possible! Thanks.*

"I'll call for your doctor," Trace said as he started to stand.

Sasha put one hand on Trace's shoulder and Trace froze. "He's gone to the tribe lands, remember? He's not here for you to send for. Just as there's no lynx doctor here for me to send for for you, though I'd like to."

Trace slowly raised his head as he stared at where Sasha touched him, though he did nothing to make Sasha move his hand. Eventually he turned his head back so he could meet Sasha's gaze. "Why do you think I need a doctor?" Trace shook his head, then continued, "I can call and have Dr. Niko return for you. Yes, what he's doing is important, but so is your health. You can't do whatever that was in front of some princess, or worse, your uncle. You can't show any weakness in front of anyone whose loyalty might be questionable, much less an enemy. You know that."

And he did. Whatever just happened couldn't happen around his uncle or any he brought who were loyal to him, or who were in on the attack on Trace. Didn't mean he wanted to be poked and prodded by the doctor.

"I want your scars examined" was all Sasha replied. There was no point in arguing the rest, as they both knew Trace was right. A prince did not show weakness, and Trace, considering his training and position, damn well knew that—just from a shifter point of view.

"Wait, what? What about my scars? Duncan's doctor treated me and tended to things back then. I'm fine now."

Sasha nodded. He still hadn't moved his hand, and Trace still half stood, curled over Sasha. It was an odd position, but as Trace would only move away if Sasha released him, Sasha didn't.

"I believe they've changed since I bound you. I merely want you checked over for your health's sake."

"Dr. Niko just did that before I left. Yesterday." Trace finally stood the rest of the way, Sasha's hand falling to his lap. He hated losing the connection but understood how hard things were for Trace. Or he was trying to, at least. "But my scars are old, so even if they've faded a little, it's nothing to worry about. You having sudden and sharp pain is."

He frowned, not appreciating the fact Trace was right. "Fine, I will have Jalin contact Dr. Niko." Sasha took out his cell and fired off a quick text to Jalin as he continued. "I doubt he is planning to stay long this evening, as today was mostly to meet the other doctor and to see about setting up the blended research area."

"I can call him, or you can. You don't need to have Jalin do it for you."

"So you would have me do everything myself and deny him his position? Take away who and what he is to me and to the coven?" Trace needed to understand and not say such things. If Jalin thought Trace wanted Sasha to replace him, it would devastate the male.

"No, but you can call the doctor just as easily as he can."

"He's my valet and assistant, Trace. Think about that carefully before you say another word."

Trace snapped his mouth shut and stared down at their feet.

"Besides, I can't call Dr. Niko and talk to you at the same time."

"I didn't mean to devalue his position. My apologies. It just seemed…."

"Pompous?" When Trace nodded, Sasha smiled. "I'm a prince, mal'chik, or did you forget? Yes, when I go and hang out with Jason, we cook together, I help him do the cleanup, we goof off and have fun, all of which you've seen me do. However, that is not who I am all the time, nor how I live my life. I am Aleksandr Tolstoi, Prince of the Konstantin Coven, and as such, I have things, people, servants, homes, cars, and more that others do not, will never have. I will not apologize for that either. Just as I will not for the fact I'm five six or that I'm Domish, as you put it. This is me. As you are my fated heart. That also means you have access to all this as well, and all the protection that comes with it."

"So I'm going to end up with my own valet/assistant?"

"Wow, you don't like staying on any topic, especially if it focuses on you."

Trace sniffed and turned away. "Not... not really."

CHAPTER FIFTEEN

SASHA SAT at his desk, staring at a small stack of papers, though he didn't see any of the words he was certain were written on them. He couldn't focus on anything other than Trace. Finally touching his fated heart had been… he couldn't come up with any words that could encompass how he'd felt, or how terrified he'd been shortly after when Trace panicked. But the biggest issue right then was Trace had gone back to his home on the tribe lands. Sasha knew it was stupid to let that bug him so much. It did, though. Especially with the ones who attacked him still out there somewhere.

Trace had protection, so he was safe. Unfortunately that didn't help either. He wanted his heart with him!

"Sir?"

The sound of Jalin's voice broke Sasha's spiraling thoughts apart enough for him to look up. "Yes?"

"You have a visitor."

Sasha blinked a few times before he looked over to the window. The sky was a deep inky black, so he knew it was extremely late to any other race. It had to be one of his own, then. "Who wishes an audience?"

Jalin stood perfectly still, his hands behind his back, his arms folded formally. *Odd.* "High Councilman Greer, my liege."

"I know I've told you to call me si— Wait, what?"

"High Councilman Duncan Greer," Jalin repeated carefully, adding in the lynx's first name, "is here to see you. He has only two of his guards with him, as well as Kelley, Alpha Keith's friend and guard. He wishes a private audience with you."

It took a moment for everything Jalin said to make sense, and then for his brain to catch up enough for Sasha to speak. Well, enough sense to form a reply, as it didn't actually make any sense that the head of the lynx shifter council would be at his door. "The lynx council has never directly contacted me before. Even sending Trace as their representative was to Keith, not to me." Sasha thought for a moment but couldn't think of a reason unless it had to do with their doctor being there to work with Niko on Sean and his shifting. They hadn't ever formally contacted his coven, even when Alpha Orin and Nadia, Sasha's sister, were killed. "Did he say why?"

"That he was here in an adoptive parental capacity. That's all he would say. I didn't understand, but I came immediately upon notification of his arrival."

Adoptive parental capacity? "I have no idea what that means."

"Nor do I, sir, but that was all he would tell me. I did not think it wise to leave him outside, considering, so I have him in one of the receiving rooms downstairs. Summer is with him, as are a few of his men."

"Timing could be better." Sasha rubbed his hands over his face and sighed. "Have him escorted up here to my sitting room, as I have no interest in having anything said be possibly overheard. Nor do I want a strange set of lynx visible for any longer than needed right now."

"Very good, sir." Jalin turned and stepped to the door. He stopped, hand on the knob. His voice soft, he said, "You might want to freshen up, sir. You appear...."

"*Stressed* is the word you're looking for, Jalin."

"Probably. Either way it wouldn't be good for the head of their council to see you at less than your usual powerful, in-command self, sir." With that Jalin quietly slipped from the room.

No, it wouldn't do. Not at all. Sasha quickly entered his room and stripped off his rumpled shirt and pants. He still had them on from earlier when Trace was with him, so they carried Trace's scent. That was the reason he hadn't taken them off already, as he hated being in messy clothes.

Five minutes later he was in a dark gray suit with a light blue shirt and dark blue-and-gray tie, his hair tidied, and highly polished ankle boots on his feet. His rings and bracelets back in place, he almost felt himself again. Sasha took his customary seat just before the knock came at the door.

Jalin stepped inside a moment later. "Sir, High Councilman Duncan Greer to see you."

"Thank you." Sasha stood as Duncan stepped through the doorway. "High Councilman," Sasha said as he gave a slight nod toward Duncan. The shifter wasn't all that tall, probably only a couple inches taller than Sasha, with light tan skin, hazel eyes, and gray-streaked light brown hair. He radiated strength and carried himself as though used to being deferred to—which made sense, given his position.

"Prince Tolstoi," Duncan replied.

Jalin closed the door once all four guards entered.

Duncan frowned as he took in the largish group. "I wish to speak to you privately, if possible. Even my men do not know why I'm here." From the tic of one male's cheek, it seemed they weren't happy about that fact either. "Would it be possible to thin out the numbers some?"

"I'm not concerned, and Kelley here knows I'm no threat to the shifters here." He nodded to Kelley, who stood beside Duncan. The shifter gave him a small smile. "So it's up to your guards if they are willing to wait outside. Summer and Dimka will return to their post outside my suite, and Jalin is only here to escort you." No shifter alone was a match for a vampire prince, and the shifters all knew it.

"Leave us" was all Duncan said. He looked from one guard to the other, steel in his gaze. Neither was happy, but both allowed Kelley to guide them out, Dimka and Summer following behind. Jalin only stayed long enough to offer refreshments, then left as well.

"Thank you for seeing me on such short notice." Duncan sat across from Sasha in a matching overstuffed leather chair, looking relaxed and cool. Only his elevated heart rate gave him away.

"I'm always happy to speak with one of the open-minded shifters." Though the timing could have been better. The last thing he needed was his uncle's entourage showing up while Duncan was still visiting. "What brought you here so late?"

"Trace."

Sasha sat forward quickly. "What's wrong with Trace?"

"Nothing specifically. Relax. I came to speak to you about him. Well, about you and him, to be more exact."

Sasha frowned as he sat back, not liking the way that was worded. "What about us?" No one outside a select few of the lynx knew he'd bonded Trace as his fated heart. The coven all knew Trace was his, but he couldn't imagine how that would have become knowledge to the council.

"As I told your man, I'm not here as High Councilman Greer, but rather as Trace's… pseudoadoptive father, I guess you could say. You have claimed him, or so I've been told, and as the only parental figure he has, there are certain things that then fall to me to do."

Blinking, Sasha fought not to stare. Father—pseudoadoptive or otherwise—was not someone he'd considered having to deal with. Trace was grown and did not live in a feudal society as Sasha did, so what the hell?

"Are you here to demand a marriage contract or some such? He's not taking me as a mate—" A sharp pain spiked through his heart again, though not as severe as when Trace had said that before. Sasha fought not to show the pain outwardly as he continued, "—and I cannot imagine he has asked you to intercede on his behalf, so I'm at a loss here."

Duncan chuckled and smiled slightly as he shook his head. "No, he doesn't know I'm here yet, though he does know I'm on my way. I'm supposed to be coming to deal with the illustrious Dr. Petronia. I knew sending her would be a problem, but she's the best. I had hoped she would be better behaved considering she knows she's under the hospitality and observation of the Chosen of Baast and our council rep, Trace. Regrettably, that has not proven true."

"I don't mean to be rude, and normally I wouldn't overly care if you thought I was, but what is it you want? He won't take a mate, so your concern about me is invalid." Maybe. Probably. Ugh! He didn't know anymore. Did what happened earlier portend a possible future for them or not? His stupid self hoped, but he tried not to let that seed grow too much. "Though your help with the doctor would be appreciated, from what I understand."

"Of course Trace won't," Duncan said, ignoring the comment about the doctor completely. "That abusive asshole, Ford, messed him up too much. He still hasn't gotten over so much of what happened, and you being a vampire won't help that problem."

"Um…." Sasha stared at Duncan, unsure what to say or do. "As you pointed out, I'm a vampire, a vampire prince, no less, and I'm pretty sure him mating a vampire is frowned upon. And don't get me started on that—" He cut himself off as his temper rose, not wishing to completely lose it in front of the lynx. Sasha forced himself to uncurl his fingers from the armrest of the chair, vaguely noting there were small tears in the leather—dammit!—then smoothed his hands down his slacks. He focused on the texture of the material as he fought for the calm he needed and usually had no trouble finding. "I don't wish to discuss Trace's ex, thank you."

"Well, as much as we would both like to not discuss Ford, he is who we need to talk about." Duncan smirked. "As for lynx and vampire matings, your sister mated with a lynx, so the fact your mate is also a lynx isn't that odd to me."

"She did, as we both know, but why do I need to discuss the monster who damaged Trace? Were he still alive, it would be a short-lived status."

"There are things about Trace that he will not be able to explain to you. Some he probably doesn't have the ability to know on a conscious level, even now. If you are his true mate, as I've been led to believe you are, and you've bonded him as your fated heart, then things must change for him, or you are both at risk. I won't have him lost because he's still too afraid of history repeating itself."

"Who told you he's my fated heart and that I'm his true mate?" Sasha hissed. That wasn't information that should have been passed up to the council. Not yet, at least. Not all shifters would accept their relationship as a positive thing, and might seek to harm Trace for "tainting" himself. Or worse. And there were obviously some in the vampire world willing to hurt Trace to get to Sasha.

"An anonymous tip."

"And on someone's hearsay, you traveled all the way from Toronto, Ontario, in Canada, to Seattle, Washington, in the US to discuss my intentions with your... pseudoadoptive son? And what the hell kind of term distinction is 'pseudoadoptive,' anyway?"

"Trace's parents are still alive, and he's a grown male, so I can't actually adopt him. I would if I could, though, and I do consider him mine. I don't have a better term to explain our relationship. As for the other part of your question, no, I didn't travel all this way on just that tip. I contacted Alpha Keith and his mate, Jason, first—"

"No!" No way did Jason betray such a confidence to the lynx council. He knew Trace wasn't ready! Keith might have thought he was doing the right thing, maybe... but Jason wouldn't have done that. And if he knew Keith told them, he would have warned Trace and Sasha. Jason was his best friend. He couldn't believe Jason would withhold such as this from him.

"Yes. I contacted them. Instead of getting either of them on the phone, though, I got one of their tribe's council members. This person let me know about the bond you gave Trace after the attack." Duncan's lips turned down and his eyes clouded over. "He should have told me he'd been attacked. But then Alpha Keith should have done that as well, as Trace is still our representative, not technically his tribe member. I would have been here sooner, had I known."

Okay, so not Jason or Keith. That's... that was good. Sasha didn't like that someone had betrayed Trace's situation to Duncan, but it wasn't them, so he could handle things. He just needed to figure out the best path for information control and how to best protect Trace. "And how is the council taking this?"

"Mmm…? Had it been any other vampire prince, most would have been ready to intercede on Trace's behalf and try to find a way to separate you from him through any means possible. However, being it was the Tolstoi prince, I hoped that would not be necessary. I would normally have spoken to Keith about the situation, but as his mate considers you not only a close personal friend, but a member of his family, I believed coming to you direct would be best."

A growl slipped out despite Sasha's intentions. Separate Trace from him? Never! "The only way to do that would be to kill me, and I'm not about to allow that to happen."

"Or to convince you that you were causing him harm. True harm," Duncan replied, his voice calm and his face placid.

"I am not." No way was this cat going to con him into leaving his fated heart! Not happening. Ever.

"Of that I have no doubt. Keith would never allow you to abuse Trace, nor do I actually believe Trace would let you close enough to do so. Not yet, at least. But that's part of the problem. Trace has healed in so many ways, champions many battered spouse and partner programs, has sheltered battered runaways himself, but he has never truly faced his own past and moved forward."

"And you expect speaking to me behind his back to do what?" If Trace were really this closeted about his past abuse, he would be horrified with the both of them.

"I expect you to be the male he needs you to be, whether he knows it or not." Duncan sighed and for once looked as tired and worn as Sasha felt. "Look, I could tell you all about the abuse itself, the wounds he suffered when we rescued him, how close to death he was, but none of that will help you. It would only hurt you more than you already are. What you need to know is that Trace honestly doesn't remember parts of the abuse. His lynx took over, and our animals don't process quite the same as our human sides—thankfully in this case. Also I believe that, at least in part, it's a deliberate thing on his lynx's part. That side of him is trying to protect them from the pain. But no matter what causes the memory loss, the issue is the same—Trace doesn't trust men not to hurt him. Not to abuse him. Especially if they are someone that he's attracted to. The fact he's shunned you, run from you, as I've been told he has, tells me he does care. The fact you're supposedly his true mate means it's a given that he will fall for you if he'll just let himself."

"The tribe council shouldn't know about the true mate issue. That's something that only Keith and Jason were told." Sasha didn't want to discuss the rest of what Duncan said. Not yet. Could it be that simple, though it wasn't simple at all? But could all of Trace's actions mean he did care but was merely afraid? Not that he didn't want Sasha, didn't want *them*?

"Let's just say that there is someone on the tribal council who is not only for your mating with Trace, but has a way to know more than the rest of the council."

Sasha thought about that a moment before it struck him. "Taylor! That little sneaky—"

"Now, now, now. She's on your side, so no speaking ill of her."

"I knew having the alpha's sister on the council was a bad idea." He'd had no such reservations. In truth he thought it a brilliant idea. Built-in spy of sorts, and someone who would make sure the council actually listened to those it ought. But Keith and Jason never thought much of speaking with her near, as they trusted her implicitly. Still.... "Cannot believe she would betray a trust like this."

"She hasn't betrayed Trace. She's trying to make sure Trace is taken care of. You know she and Keith lost a human friend to an abusive partner, correct?" Sasha nodded. He'd never heard the whole story, but after more than two centuries, he'd heard far too many stories along those lines not to know the basics. "Over the last five years, she's also gotten to know me. Since she became a member of the tribe's council, she took it upon herself to learn what she could about the intertribal council, and so we've spoken many times. She knew she could trust me with this information."

"And all this has what to do with Trace and me?"

"You are his fated mate, Prince Sasha. You've begun the bonding. If you don't move things along, it will only hurt you both, and I won't allow Trace to be hurt anymore, not even by himself."

Sasha thought that over, not liking the implications. "You would suggest what, then? Trace is not thrilled with my bonding him or what it now means for him. He chafes at what it gives him, even, the silly cat."

"Simply put him in a situation where his nature will demand he claim you. He already trusts you, or he would have run—mate or not."

He couldn't help but stare. That was the great lynx's high council leader's recommendation? Make him jealous? "That's… insane. Trace jealous is not a pretty thing. He's unstable and prone to hissing and pouncing on me, and not in a fun way."

Duncan's grin grew as his eyes brightened, and Sasha swore they twinkled. "Really? Oh, that's purrrfect! Now we simply need to find the right trigger…."

CHAPTER SIXTEEN

TRACE STOOD in the hallway, clad in form-hugging dress slacks and a slim-fitting button-down shirt that faded from silver to pale green, which made his jade-green eyes stand out, especially with the kohl edging them. He wore the special bangles and bracelets Sasha had had made for him, all silver, of course, and his almost white-blond hair was spiked to perfection. Not a hair was out of place, not a thread was loose or off on any of his clothing. Even his chunky little boots, accented with silver buckles, were perfectly polished, as were his buffed and trimmed nails.

There was something about Trace's appearance that brought to mind a prissy cat, though Sasha couldn't quite put his finger on what or why. Still, it was sexy as hell, yet confusing. He hadn't expected Trace back so soon, so his appearance was a little surprising right then. Sasha's uncle and Princess Tatiana were due to arrive within the hour, however, so he really didn't have time to placate Trace's worries.

"Trace, what can I do for you?" Sasha gave Trace a smile, as always, hating that he still needed to restrain his natural desire to touch.

"It's almost time for your visitors to arrive, is it not?" Trace asked, his tone cool, almost bored. He looked around the entry area, his gaze bounding from person to item to person in quick succession, never staying for more than a moment.

"It is, but I didn't expect you to attend their arrival." Sasha wrapped one hand around Trace's biceps and pulled him aside. "You've shown no interest," he added softly.

Trace sniffed and raised his chin, showing no sign Sasha had touched him, much less pulled him away. "It would be rude of the royal consort not to attend the arrival of his bonded one's family and honored guests."

What on earth did Duncan or Jason say to get you so riled up? Sasha smiled as he trailed his fingers down Trace's cheek and neck, stopping when the pad of one finger was directly over Trace's pulse point. It fluttered, calling to him, but he ignored the pull, instead enjoying the heat, the scent that was unique to his fated heart. "You know you have nothing to worry about, my heart." He leaned in, going up on his toes to nuzzle Trace's throat. "She is of no threat to you."

"As if I would worry about something like that."

The haughty tone fired Sasha's blood, driving his libido and turning off his brain a bit. He gave Trace's neck a nip, hard enough to mark the skin, but not enough to break through and allow him access to the life-giving nectar below. "Haughty kitty."

Sasha nipped the soft flesh again, sucking up a little mark before letting the flesh go. A soft moan met Sasha's ears, the sound sweeter than any he'd heard before. It wasn't the sound he'd heard from his fated heart before, of a male fighting himself to find pleasure; this was true pleasure for the sake of pleasure, and it startled Sasha enough that he drew back and stared at Trace, unsure what had brought it on.

"Don't stop, please...."

Oh Gods! Sasha immediately dove back in to mark his heart's beautiful pale throat again. Just as he pulled back to admire the mark, he heard Jalin clear his throat—loudly.

"Sir. Prince Sasha!"

Sasha tore himself away from Trace, who moaned, then coiled up around Sasha. "What, Jalin? This better be important."

"Sir, your uncle and his entourage are here," Jalin said, an apology clear in his eyes and tone.

"And?"

"Bloodletting your bonded one is, um... maybe not the best thing to do as a welcome-to-the-covenstead greeting."

Dammit! He hated it when Jalin was right, and right then, the male was right. And just when Trace had finally let him touch him like he ought. "Fine." Sasha pulled back enough to get a good grip on Trace and force him to stand properly. "Mal'chik, we have guests. We have to play nice with the visitors for a bit." Though the Gods knew he didn't want to. All he wanted at that moment was to drag Trace to their chambers and find out how far this new sexy, submissive kitty went.

Trace stood up, shoulders back, and his eyes flashed with green fire. "You would turn this"—he gestured down at himself—"down to go play with an uncle you don't like and some strumpet vamp?"

Okay, so maybe not so submissive, Sasha thought as he fought a grin. "No, I would put what we were doing on pause so that we can try to get to the bottom of the attack on you. So you can be safe, mal'chik.

Keeping you safe and healthy is worth a great deal to me, even putting up with my mother's brother and his inane betrothal attempts."

"I won't share," Trace hissed.

"Nor will I, hon. Now be a good kitty and smile when they come in. You know how to play the diplomat. Keeping him on the right side of things is important, as he's rather influential, sadly."

"And the princess?"

"She's merely a friend, Trace. You'll see if you give her a chance. I haven't spoken to her recently, but we have known each other since we were children. But I assure you, she is well aware I am gay and has no illusions of becoming my bride."

"Better not," Trace muttered, but he plastered on a bright smile that would have fooled Sasha if Sasha hadn't known better. *Interesting... and a little alarming that he can do that so convincingly.* Sasha wondered if he'd learned that as part of his diplomacy training or because of the years of abuse and all the covering for his abuser, lying about how he got injured, why he couldn't do x, y, or z.... He shook off that train wreck of a thought and focused on how Trace quickly smoothed every hair back into place as if he'd had a mirror and an hour, instead of doing it in a minute by feel. Sasha chalked it up to it being a lynx thing and merely shook his head as he motioned Trace to stand beside him at the top of the stairs as the guards opened the doors to the entryway.

Sasha paid no mind to the servants and lesser members of the party, though he knew he probably ought to at some point, but when Vlad stepped inside Sasha noted everything about the damned male. Vlad was just over seven hundred, though he probably only looked to be in his forties to Trace—as he would for the next however many centuries he lived, as long as he didn't begin to tire. Those who looked to be actually "old" were either well over three millennia or had battled the wasting and not fared well. He wore a well-tailored black three-piece suit with a red tie. His hair was close-cropped and he still bore the scar over his right eye from the honor battle he fought in his youth. While he had won, he had been injured with a weapon made from a shifter's claw that was inscribed and blessed. Vlad also tended to always keep his fangs out, refusing to retract them unless around humans—very fanged mafia. Ugh!

Behind him was the ethereal beauty Princess Tatiana. How she'd gotten caught up in Vlad's insanity was anyone's guess, as far as Sasha was concerned. She stood tall—about five ten—draped in lavender silk and pearls. She was elegance defined but did nothing for him—as always.

"Uncle Vlad. Princess Tatiana. Welcome to our home."

"Yes, yes, yes, boy. I'm not interested in your formal greeting nonsense or in your posturing. Come down here and welcome us proper and have your people show ours where our things go. It's been a long trip. I'm tired and would like a rest before I have a look around." Vlad's voice was rough and hard around the edges. It still bore much of the tone and flavor of where he was born and raised in Russia. He scanned the room but stopped, his eyes going wide when his gaze landed on Trace. "What the hell is *that* doing here?" he bellowed.

Trace started and shifted closer, curling one arm around Sasha, clutching the back of Sasha's shirt with his hand.

"I would suggest you control your tone, Uncle," Sasha snapped. He wrapped the closer arm around Trace, pulling him against his side. "This is Trace Wilson, my fated heart and royal consort."

"Your *what?*"

"My fated heart and my royal consort." Sasha hoped pushing the point would both nudge Trace that last bit over the line and help drive the point home to his uncle that, no, he was never going to marry Sasha off to anyone for any political points, no matter what. Yes, Sasha would have children—sooner than he'd thought, most likely, with all the pushing he'd received recently—but it would never come via his uncle's maneuvering.

"Not possible. You are to wed Princess Tatiana and produce heirs like a proper prince. It's time you did your duty and stopped endangering your coven and your line! This... this... mangy creature cannot provide your heirs; therefore, it must go. Now."

"Restrain yourself. Any threat made against a royal consort, especially a fated heart, is a crime punishable by death, as you well know." Ignoring his uncle's sputtering and huffing, Sasha turned to Jalin. "Please see that both *Vlad*"—because there was no way he would give the asshat either the title of uncle or prince right then—"and Princess Tatiana are settled into their respective areas." He then turned to Tatiana and motioned her close. She more floated up the steps than walked, but was quickly to them. "It's wonderful to see you again, my dear. I'm only sad it's under such strained circumstances."

"It's a pleasure to see you again, Sasha." Her voice was as gentle and silky as her dress, a fact Trace didn't miss, if the added tension in his body was anything to go by. "Might I properly be introduced to your partner? He's lovely, but I'm sure, if he's yours, there's a wicked mind to go along with that handsome face of his."

Trace huffed but didn't say anything. He also didn't let go—a fact Sasha thrilled in. Duncan had said Trace needed to be pushed to properly "claim" Sasha as his mate. Gods, but he hoped this situation would work to their advantage. He released Trace and smoothed one hand down his back. Trace stood tall and gave a slight smile that managed to be both welcoming and firm at the same time—Sasha filed the question of how he did that for another time.

"Princess Tatiana Mirovich, may I present Trace Wilson, my consort and fated heart. Trace, this is Princess Tatiana, an old friend and my uncle's most recent attempt to settle me down."

"You don't need settling down," Trace muttered to Sasha. He turned up the wattage on his smile as he faced Tatiana. "Welcome. It's always nice to meet one of Sasha's friends."

"Liar," she countered, her voice soft and playful. "But you're sweet for saying so. I can see you're diplomatically trained. Are you one of the shifter's council?"

Trace looked at Sasha, one brow raised. "Um...."

"Come, walk with us, as my uncle is busy yelling at his servants, and if I watch too much longer I'm liable to do something he will regret." Sasha turned and slipped Trace's right arm through his crooked left. He then took Tatiana's left hand, which she rested on his right arm. Once they were down the hall a ways, Sasha said, "As for your question, Tatiana, Trace is a lynx, and he is a trainer and diplomat for their high council."

"That has to be hard on a relationship between the two of you. I can't imagine allowing my heart, had I one, to traipse around the continents, unchaperoned, with those who usually seek to destroy us. He *is* lovely, though."

"And right here," Trace countered, a slight nip of annoyance slipping into his voice, though not as much as Sasha knew was there. No one liked to be spoken of as if they were not there, especially not by one you considered competition—ridiculous though that idea may be.

"So you are." She smiled, her fangs just peeking over her plump lip. "And how will you deal with living among our kind, dear lynx? With helping to raise royal vampire heirs, with the challenges and challengers you will face in time?"

"Don't harass him, hon. This is all very new to him."

Trace dug his nails into Sasha's arm slightly, the tiny sting sending a thrill up his spine and bringing a smile to his face—something that did not seem to amuse Trace in the least.

"This will be your suite, my dear. I wish it was under better circumstances, but I am glad of your visit. Do try not to allow my uncle to ruin your time with us. You have permission to look around the grounds as you wish."

"Thank you, Sasha." She leaned in and kissed each of his cheeks, then stepped back. "Sleep well, Master Wilson. I hope to speak with you again."

The grinding of Trace's teeth was loud enough for Sasha to hear them over the swishing of Tatiana's silk skirt as she left them. Once her doors were closed, Sasha tugged on Trace's arm to get him moving again. "Let's go make sure my uncle is settling in; then you can relax some before I have to go deal with him." He closed his eyes and counted to forty in Russian when he heard his uncle's bellow from down the hall. "Or perhaps I should go deal with him now before he upsets too many of my people or hurts someone."

"Is that likely?" Trace's eyes were wide and his voice trembled slightly.

"Eh, it has happened once or twice in the past. It's one of the reasons I don't often welcome him here. He's a violent brute at times, and I have no patience for him. I cannot do anything against him, as he is family, and he never provokes me quite enough to justify my well-earned reputation."

"Oh. Um...."

"Don't worry, you're safe from him. You will have someone guarding you while he's here, as I'm not as convinced that he isn't a party to those who attacked you before. Or that one of his servants isn't." Sasha soothed his hands up and down Trace's arms. "You are safe here, mal'chik. I swear this. Any that try to harm you will not live to see the next moonrise. You are my heart, my mal'chik, my love. But for now why don't you retire to our suite. Okay?"

Trace stared at Sasha but slowly nodded. He had no idea what was going on in his fated heart's mind, but he didn't have the time to sort it out just then. So instead he led Trace to their rooms, and once Trace was settled in one of the plush chairs, Sasha made sure Dimka was posted outside, then went in search of his idiot uncle.

Before he reached Vlad's rooms, Tatiana stepped into the wide hall, a wicked smile on her beatific face. "Ah, good, you're alone."

"I am for now. What do you need? I'm on my way to deal with the loudmouthed viper down the hall."

"Two things. First to congratulate you on finding your heart. Your little kitty truly is a handsome male, you lucky, lucky boy. Though…."

"Though what, Tatiana?" *Get to the point, female!*

"He needs to loosen up a bit. I thought he was going to challenge me for you. Your uncle's insanity is bad enough, but your fated heart ought to know better."

"It's a long story, but if he were to challenge you, that would actually be a good thing. As long as it wasn't a formal challenge." Another series of bellows came from Vlad's suite, causing them both to wince. "What was the other issue?"

"I wish to ask…." She looked around before she snagged the edge of his suit sleeve and pulled him close. "I wished to ask if I could stay with your coven after he leaves. I know you have no need of a wife— you're gay, even if he can't seem to grasp that—but I can't return to my home. I will explain it all later, if you wish, but please consider allowing me to stay."

Sasha stared at Tatiana, dumbfounded. "You're asking me for asylum?"

"Effectively, yes."

CHAPTER SEVENTEEN

A LOUD crash reverberated down the hall, drawing Sasha's stunned gaze from Tatiana. "I need to go deal with Vlad. We will speak later, but you have to know I will help you however I can." With that he hurried down the corridor, leaving Tatiana behind. He couldn't help wondering what was so bad that she wished to hide with him, but he forced his attention away from her and those questions, knowing he had to keep his mind focused—especially with his uncle and the threat to Trace and the tribe.

Sasha didn't bother knocking as he usually would; he merely threw open the door and entered, just in time to catch a young male vampire before he hit the wall. "Stop!" he thundered, going to that still, deadly calm place inside that no one wanted him to go.

Everyone froze, the boy in his arms curled against his chest barely breathing even as he continued to cry, his tears hot as they soaked through Sasha's dress shirt. Vlad slowly rose to his full height and glared down his multiply broken nose at Sasha—while it didn't show, Sasha had broken it more than once himself when he lost patience with the abusive, narcissistic asshat. "That boy is my property. Release him now."

"I will do no such thing. You may get away with such behavior other places, but you know the rules and laws here, *Uncle*. You will either live within them or I will have you arrested and you can find out how accommodating the dungeon is."

"I'm not interested in your perversions, boy."

"Summer!" A moment later Summer stepped through the still-open doorway. "Please have the boy checked over, as I have no idea how long he's been abused."

"Abused?" Vlad sputtered, but Sasha ignored him. No one else in the room moved. They watched as Sasha gently handed over the battered youth, smoothed his hands down his jacket, straightened his cuffs, and then walked to where Vlad still stood in a slow, measured step, hoping that would help him not kill the monster in front of him when he got there.

"Yes, abused. I have never understood how you and my mother could be related. You are nothing alike. Now, I invited you here to hear your side of things, as you have been accused of some very serious crimes. I would suggest you shut the hell up, sit your ass down, and answer all questions posed to you—correctly—if you wish to survive this visit."

"I'm here to deal with you and your lack of marriage and offspring, not some stupid nonsense about lies from your pets."

"I would suggest—" Sasha lashed out, inflicting more power and chill into his voice as he wrapped one hand around Vlad's throat faster than the male could raise his arms to block. "—that you watch what you say about my fated heart and his tribe, dear uncle, and that you learn to listen instead of subjecting us to your diarrhea of the mouth so much."

As he spoke he tightened his hold until there was no way for his uncle to respond with more than a squeak, which he did, along with struggling. One thing his uncle never seemed to remember was that Sasha's small stature—especially in comparison to many of the other princes, who were bigger and more powerfully built—was no limitation on the power he held within. He also had more control than many others he knew—it was one of the reasons none of the other covens would raise fang to him or his. Early on a few had tried. All had failed. A young upstart tried every few decades to challenge him. Most died in the process, and a few were now loyal to him. But all underestimated him at the beginning because of his attitude, his dress, his size, and his love for humans and his "odd interest" in shifters.

Sasha walked forward, forcing Vlad to back up until he was slammed down into one of the chairs by the fireplace. He leaned over him, squeezed harder for a moment, then released his hold and stepped back and took the other chair. "Now can you behave, or do we need to do this with you in chains?" He waved one hand negligently. "I don't really care which."

"How dare you treat me this way," Vlad croaked.

Sasha turned to one of the servants closer to him and smiled. "He doesn't really deserve it, hon, but if I have to hear him, I'd really rather not have to put up with that nasty grating sound. Would you be a dear and get him something to soothe his throat? He seems to have done something to it."

"Ye-yes, milord. Right away." The young female curtsied, then scurried away. That seemed to break the charm on the others, and everyone began scurrying around, setting things to rights quickly, wide-eyed glances thrown their way, but only for a moment as each person hurried about their tasks.

"They are not yours to command. Those are my servants."

"I did not command anyone; I merely made a request. One that will benefit you." He flicked a piece of imaginary lint off his trousers and sighed. "If you would rather have this discussion without anything to drink, that can be arranged." Sasha waited, brows raised.

"No."

"Then shut it and drink your tea."

It didn't take long before said tea was served. Jalin returned with the girl, whose name was Leanne, and they served them tea—Sasha from a separate pot, as he would not share with someone he did not respect.

Sasha crossed one leg over the other as he blew steam from the surface of his chamomile and lavender tea, annoyed this entire situation was happening. He wanted to be in his chambers with Trace, not in his uncle's chambers dealing with his abusive nonsense and possible threats. "So would you like to restart this entire meeting, Uncle? I believe it would be in your best interest to do so."

Vlad took a large gulp of his tea and rubbed at his neck, which had a rather impressive bruise already that matched Sasha's hand perfectly. A fact that gave him an odd sort of satisfaction. "I would like to know what nonsense you have in your head that made you attack me and spout off about accusations against me. Yes. And how dare you threaten me with your dungeon? I'm a prince!"

"You are not the ruling prince of any coven. The coven you were born to wants nothing to do with you because of the very behavior I walked in on. You are linked to this coven through the bond of your sister, my mother, but I want nothing to do with you, so you travel from coven to coven, plying your abuse where you can, currying favors and building political power when you can. But you have no power here, and you know it."

The venomous look Vlad gave reminded Sasha of a viper more than a vampire, though both had fangs—the idea actually made him smile slightly, though Vlad frowned in response.

"I want to know what accusations, boy. Now."

"You know, demanding things like that isn't your best move, especially not when here in my covenstead. My people are loyal to me, and many do not like you. I would remember that, were I you."

"Fine." Vlad took a deep breath, letting it out slowly. "What are the accusations against me? I only came here at your invitation after I had written you, again, about your betrothal to Princess Tatiana. I am here at your request, not as part of some attack or infiltration."

"True, though there will be no betrothal to Tatiana or any other. As I said when you arrived, I have found my fated heart. We haven't had the formal ceremony"—an oversight he hoped to fix soon, as soon as Trace would allow them to be a real couple. The coven would begin to demand it soon, and the other covens would wonder why it wasn't announced and no invitations went out.... *Focus!*—"but he is bound to me in all other ways, so it is done."

Vlad's lips twisted down, his nose crinkled, and he leaned back in his chair until he couldn't go any farther. "How could you bond that creature to you? It's a filthy animal! Not fit to be one of us. You can't turn him!"

"No one said a thing about turning him." Sasha put both feet on the floor and sat forward, his tone as lethal as his fangs. "He stays as is. He will be a forever lynx shifter, my consort, and it's done. Not you, nor anyone else, has a say."

"But... but... but he can't give you heirs!"

"True," he said as he returned to his lighter, bordering on bored pose and voice. "But that can be dealt with via a surrogate when we're ready. It's how it's been done since before recorded time. Now as to the accusations—"

"But it's an animal!"

"No, *he* is a lynx shifter. Just as my sister took the Chosen of Baast, Alpha Orin Green, as her fated heart, I have Trace Wilson as mine. The Fates and Gods are determined that there be a link between us, and I, for one, am honored to have Trace as my heart. *Now* to the issue that brought you here...."

"Fine, what are these idiotic allegations?"

"Two vampires, one male, one female, attacked Trace, nearly killing him." Sasha steepled his fingers, his elbows resting on the arms of the chair. "They claimed it was under your orders, that you wanted him out of the way so that I would marry Tatiana, and that it would also break the pact I have with the shifters at the same time or some such. It wouldn't have, but they didn't seem to know that. They also claimed that you were their father."

"Wait, my children?"

"Mmm, yes."

"But... even if I were to do something so foolish—and trying to cause a rift between your coven and that particular tribe of cats would be suicidal, as history has proven—why would I send my own blood to do it? You don't keep prisoners. Ever."

"See, that's what I wondered as well. Dimka and Summer don't think it was you, but rather someone trying to get me to kill you while trying to start a war between my coven and the tribe at the same time. Me, I'm not so sure. Any idea who might want a war and you dead all at the same time?"

"I...." The question seemed to stump Vlad, as he paused, his forehead crinkling as he stared down at his empty cup. "Someone who wants to take over your coven? They might think I'm in line for your throne since I'm your uncle and you have no heirs," he finally replied, the last sounding more like a question than it ought.

"Seems like an awfully roundabout way to start a takeover. And you would never be in line for my coven."

"I know that! I was trying to think of reasons. Wait, you said something about Tatiana too."

"Yes, you wanted Trace gone so I would marry Tatiana and have heirs like a good little boy. I didn't hear it, and Trace can't give us everything that was said word for word, as he was bitten and nearly bled to death during the rant." Sasha had to take a moment to calm down, as even relaying the events had his blood pounding and his vision tinting red. His breathing ramped up and his fangs dropped without thought. *Trace is fine and in our rooms. Trace is fine and in our rooms.* He chanted it in his head until he returned to normal, though when he opened his eyes, his uncle stared at him with wide, blown eyes.

"Wha-what just happened?"

"Even talking about what happened to Trace is hard for me. I was forcibly drawn to him during the attack and found him just as the one bit into him. It was a savage bite meant to rip and cause him to bleed out, not one for nourishment."

"You were drawn and you saw?" What color Vlad had to his pale Slavic skin washed out suddenly. "He really is your fated heart, then?"

"That is what I said, yes?"

Vlad nodded and swallowed hard enough his throat made an odd clicking sound. "It.... I... um...."

"You were supposed to be concentrating on who would do this, not on my fated heart, Uncle."

"R-right, um, well…. Tatiana's brother was rather eager to have you betrothed to her. The younger brother, Yuri, not the one set to inherit, Karl."

"I always did think it was too bad she was second born. She's the only one of the three with a heart and a brain."

"And beauty to match," Vlad added.

"That too. Still, I can't believe that Yuri would try this. He has to know he would lose. The boy doesn't have anywhere near the political or physical power needed to try anything against me."

"There might be one of the old families back in Russia or one of the other old countries that might see you as a possible weak point to take over to move on. You're a *goluboi*."

Sasha stared at Vlad for a moment, trying to gather his thoughts and find the right words. "You think that because I'm an openly gay prince—and seriously, who uses the word *goluboi* like that anymore?— that some idiot wannabe sees me as prey? That's insane."

"No, that's reality. You think it's only humans and shifters who have an issue with your kind? Think again."

"Oh, I know how you feel about gay men, though you don't have the same issue with bi and lesbian women. But your ignorance isn't my problem; this wannabe's is. Unless you're backing this idiot." Sasha leaned forward. "Are you?"

"No! Of course not." Vlad shifted in his seat and looked down. "I'm not stupid, nor would I dishonor my sister that way. You're her son, so like how you do things or not, I would never go against you."

"Just try to forcibly marry me off, knowing I have no interest in women."

"You have a duty to produce at least two heirs!"

"Children. When I have *children*, they will be raised as Nadia and I were, with love, not merely as tools and as heirs."

"Your mother spoiled you and indulged you too much."

"My mother and father took the time to always be there for the both of us, no matter what was going on in the coven or the world, right up until they couldn't because they weren't here any longer. I would warn you not to ever speak ill of either of them in my presence again."

"I was not—"

"Stick to the topic, as my very limited patience is wearing thin, Uncle. Don't make me forget who you are to me and treat you as I ought. Who else? Why else? Any other ideas? I already have people looking for answers, but I'm giving you a chance. Oh, and I would remember your manners when dealing with Trace. He is my royal consort, which puts him above you. Dimka and Summer will not tolerate any actions against Trace any more than I will. Nor will any others here. My coven is happy for me, even the ones who are confused." Not 100 percent honest, as some of Sasha's exes were less than thrilled, and one or two who had set their sights on him recently were unhappy at his status of permanently off the market, especially to a nonvampire. But for the most part, it was true, so.... "He also has a guard of either vampire or shifters, depending on where he is, so don't think of depriving me of my fated heart to further your political agendas."

"I wouldn't," Vlad snapped, head raised, eyes narrowed. "I don't approve, but I would never knowingly come between a true heart bond. That's blasphemous!"

So is abusing your servants and killing your human meals, but you seem to think that's just fine. "We aren't here to debate your beliefs, but to deal with this threat to my heart and his tribe. Any who wants the pact destroyed obviously wants harm to come to the tribe, though I'm not sure why yet. This tribe has lived in harmony with us since Father and his men avenged Nadia and Orin. Before then, really. We just didn't have a formal pact until five and half years ago or so."

Vlad sat back, drumming his fingers on the arm of the chair. "Hmm.... That does seem odd. Have they had any other threats? Has he?"

"No. I'm close to the alpha's mate and am on the tribe lands regularly, so I would hear anything like that." *The only odd thing there is Sean... but only Dimka, Summer, and I know about Sean. Well, and the doctor, as far as vampires. No outsiders. And the timing isn't right.*

"You thought of something?"

"No, I was trying to, but I can't. I could have Trace join us, but I'm not sure I want to subject him to you and your brand of politeness."

He puffed up his chest and huffed, "No need to be rude."

"That's funny. For now I'm going to do a little more digging. I will assume you are telling the truth and not the one behind things. You had better hope your children aren't. A parent should never outlive their children." With that Sasha stood, turned, and exited the room.

CHAPTER EIGHTEEN

TRACE PACED the sitting room, not taking in anything. He'd done this in his human form, but it hadn't helped, and he liked the fact he was in his weaker skin even less than he liked the yelling he'd heard before the doors shut out the sounds from the rest of the royal wing. He still had trouble wrapping his head around that. "Royal wing." Unreal.

Now, however, he paced and prowled in his lynx form, enjoying the pad of his paws better than the slap of his shoes. He also preferred his claws and fangs to his blunt nails and teeth. How long did it take to settle in the princess and the uncle? Surely Sasha would wait on the inquisition until they had time to settle in and rest up a bit at least. Right?

Ugh!

He had no idea how long it took for him to lose his patience completely, as his lynx didn't have the same sense of time his human did, but eventually he prowled over to the heavy wood doors and yowled at them as loudly as he could. It was one of the times he honestly wished he had a full roar like lions and panthers did. A moment later Dimka opened one of the doors and looked down at Trace.

"Yes, sir?"

Trace mewled at him as he stepped out into the hall.

"Um, Trace. You know Prince Sasha wanted you to stay in the suite, yes? If you go out into the covenstead, you have to allow me to go with you. It's not safe otherwise."

Trace huffed but nodded. He rubbed against Dimka's legs, twining between them once before he raised his head and sniffed. He twitched his tufted ears as he sought his mate, not happy Sasha had been gone so long and with only one of his guards. What if something happened to him?

"What are you doing?"

Trace turned his head to stare up at Dimka a moment before he turned and sniffed the air again, looking for Sasha's unique scent mixed with the cologne he always wore. It was woodsy and crisp, clean yet musky. It was damn sexy, that's what it was. He really wished his human side would stop delaying and get on with the claiming. He was tired of not having his mate! Being incomplete made thinking harder at times, and it hurt, deep inside, to not be whole. Why couldn't his human side accept Sasha wasn't like the monster who hurt them and accept the mating?

Pushing aside the deep need to bond was hard, but he did it. Again. Right then Trace needed to find his mate. He needed to be close and protect his mate. That female was here, the one the other male wanted Sasha to marry and have kittens with. No, not kittens, full-blood vampires. Trace couldn't give Sasha heirs. Maybe that was why Sasha hadn't wanted the mating at first? But he'd changed his mind and, in the end, he'd bonded Trace, dammit.

Now where was he!

Trace took off down the hall the way he knew the uncle and the princess were to be housed. As he walked he caught Sasha's scent, which did get stronger, but it wasn't recent. He hadn't been by recently. Trace growled low, not liking that Sasha still had to be in one of the chambers down the way. He stopped at the main door to Tatiana's room, but while Sasha had been there, his scent kept going. *Good!*

"Are you looking for Sasha?"

Trace nodded as he continued down the hall.

"He's in with his uncle still. See where Summer is standing guard?"

Right. Should have thought of that! Trace picked up his pace and ran the rest of the way, skidding on the polished wood in front of Summer, who smiled at Trace.

"Hi, Trace. Looking for your mate?" At Trace's chirp, he continued, "He's still in with his uncle. They're discussing the issue of your attack. Well, they are now that Sasha put that… now that he reminded Prince Vlad whose house he's in and who holds the power here. Would you like me to announce you?"

Trace sat on his haunches and stared at the doors, head held high as he waited for them to open.

Dimka chuckled from behind him. "I believe that would be a yes."

Just as Summer went to knock on one of the doors, it opened and Sasha sashayed out, all attitude and power in his wake. Trace hopped to his paws, mewled once, and fell in step with Sasha.

"Hello, hon. I was just going to come and get you."

Trace mewed at him, leaning as he walked so he could rub against Sasha's leg.

"You know I can't understand you in your lynx form, hon, beautiful though you may be."

Trace huffed, though he did strut a little at being called beautiful.

Sasha bent down to stroke his ears. "You know you're a handsome lynx. You don't need me to tell you that. But why were you looking for me? Is something wrong?"

Trace stopped and shook his head. He had just needed to be near his mate, but how did he tell Sasha that when he knew his human side wouldn't tell his mate that?

"Oh, hon. You look so frustrated. Is it something that your human side can explain to me?"

Trace shook his head again. Well, he could, but he wouldn't. Not unless he accepted that Sasha was his mate, dammit!

Just then the door beside them opened and Tatiana stepped out. She was dressed less lavishly this time, though no less beautifully. She wore a simple blue silky-looking wrap dress and matching sling-back heels. "Oh good, you're still out and about. I'd hoped to—" She gasped and a wide smile bloomed across her face. "Oh, he's marvelous. Is he tame? I mean, you have him inside like this, so he must be, right?" She continued to coo over Trace as if he were a regular Canadian lynx, not a lynx shifter who could understand her every word.

He turned his head to stare at Sasha and yowled softly, waiting for what he wanted him to do about the idiot female. Seriously? She knew Sasha was mated to a lynx shifter, but she just up and assumed the cat beside him was a "normal" animal? Stupid!

"Tatiana?"

"Yeah?"

"I'd like to reintroduce you to my consort and fated heart, Trace."

A series of emotions flitted across her face so fast Trace couldn't grasp them to catalog them. "So can he understand me when he's like this?"

"Yes," Sasha replied through a chuckle. "His thoughts are more cat than human when he's in his lynx skin—he is a lynx right now, after all—but he understands everything you say and will remember it all when he shifts to human."

She turned a lovely shade of pink. Her natural pale skin kept her from being a true red, but it was a close thing. "Oh no. I'm so sorry." She drooped her shoulders and dipped her head as she spoke. She didn't look at Trace or Sasha as she continued. "It honestly didn't occur to me. I've never interacted with a shifter when they've been in their animal form. I've never been near a shifter that didn't flee due to my being a vampire, thanks to how my home coven is."

Trace didn't like how sad her voice turned or the way her body seemed to have the weight of ten people bound to it. He didn't know what was wrong with her, why she was so miserable, but there had to be more to it than never having the chance to interact with a shifter before. He also didn't like how she shivered when she mentioned her home coven. Something wasn't right there either. He mewled and stepped away from Sasha and over to Tatiana.

Unsure how she would take his presence, he moved slow, making sure she could see and move away if she so chose. She didn't. He coiled around her ankles, then bumped her legs, pushing her to return to her rooms. He herded her to one of her chairs, only stopping long enough to mewl and chirp at Sasha to make sure he was following.

"I've never been herded by a cat before."

"Count yourself blessed. He doesn't do this for just anyone. He's obviously worried about you." Sasha squatted and looked straight at Trace. "Hon, I still can't understand you in your lynx form. What do you want now? You have her sitting, but now what?"

Seriously need to teach them how to understand me! Something.

"How about if I go get you something simple to wear and you shift?"

That would solve part of the problem but…. Trace narrowed his eyes and glanced at the chair across from Tatiana, then down to the floor beside it. The floor there wouldn't be as comfortable for his human side as it was in their suite. He went over and padded in a circle a few times before he stopped and kneaded at the area again. After one more circuit, he huffed and flopped down in disgust.

"He doesn't seem to like that spot, even though he's lying there," Tatiana said, her voice as confused as Sasha's face.

Then suddenly Sasha's confusion seemed to clear. "No, he wants a cushion brought in with the clothes. Right, hon?"

Trace hopped up and went over to nuzzle Sasha before he licked Sasha from chin to temple. Sasha chuckled even as he pulled back and wiped his face. "Ugh, eww. That's…. I really prefer your human kisses, hon. But thanks. Be right back."

A moment later he returned with a pair of sweats, a T-shirt, thick socks, underwear, and a large pillow—which he set on the floor next to the chair. Tatiana stepped into one of the other rooms after insisting her retainers and such do the same. Trace shifted and dressed quickly, then arranged himself on the cushion. "Sit, please, Sasha."

"Of course, mal'chik. Let me just tell Tatiana that it's okay to come back in." A moment or two later, Sasha sat in the chair next to Trace, and right after that, Tatiana joined them. Sasha dropped his hand down to Trace's hair and began threading his fingers through the strands.

"I am so sorry, Trace. I didn't mean to be so rude to you," Tatiana said once she'd settled in her seat.

"I can tell. It's all right because you didn't know. Now that you do, though, I expect you to treat me as me when you see me as my lynx self."

"Of course. Are there any other lynx that are shifters around the covenstead? Actually, are there any other lynx here, period, shifter or other?"

"That you are likely to see in their fur here?" Sasha interjected. "Um… there's Trace. Sean or Zeke might visit, but they're both boys, so it would be easy to tell the difference—even their lynx are smaller. Other than that, not really. Keith doesn't usually shift when he's here other than the couple of times he's taken his Chosen of Baast form. So if you see a lynx here on the covenstead grounds, yes, it ought to be Trace. Over time you will learn to tell the difference. Each lynx is unique."

"Why will she do so over time?" Trace looked up, caught in Sasha's pale blue gaze. He fought not to fidget, but it was a close thing between all the questions swirling in his mind, his lynx fighting him, and his body's need driving him to do more with Sasha than his head thought was reasonable.

"Princess Tatiana has asked for asylum with us, mal'chik."

He twisted to look at Tatiana so fast he made himself dizzy. "What? Why?" *She's staying around?* He wasn't sure he liked the sound of that. He knew something was wrong and she was sad—his lynx wanted to help her—but have her stay there? With them? Um…. Where she and others could keep trying to put her and Sasha together? His stomach knotted and his gorge rose. *Yeah, no. No, no, no, no.*

"She hasn't told us yet. Have you, Tatiana?"

"No, I haven't had the chance. You want me to discuss it with Trace here?" she asked, and drew her brows together as her voice rose in pitch.

"He's my consort, Tatiana. If you are to stay, it's as much his decision as it is mine. Especially considering your position and with him perceiving you as a threat."

"I never said—"

"Hush, mal'chik." Sasha tugged Trace's hair hard enough to force him to look at him, but not enough to actually cause pain. Nor did he hold on or control Trace's head movements once he had his attention—thankfully. "We both know that's how you see her. She needs to know what she's up against if she wants to win us over with her petition. Yes?"

Trace thought over the words carefully, not wanting to agree merely out of duty but not wanting to fight him out of mere pique either. "My apologies, and agreed." He turned to face Tatiana again. "I don't mean to be a problem, but your presence is a threat, especially to my lynx, though he also wants to take care of you. It's an odd mix of feelings, actually. I'm honestly not sure what to make of him at the moment."

"It's strange to hear you speak of yourself in the third person like that, but it's fascinating as well."

"Stay on topic, Tatiana. Please." Sasha sat back and resumed his... petting? Whatever it was, Trace loved sitting at his feet and having Sasha play with his hair like that. It was comforting to both parts of Trace, though he refused to acknowledge or investigate that fact right then.

"My apologies to you both. As I stated before, I've never been allowed near any shifters, though I've known they weren't the mindless monsters Father and my brothers claimed. Nadia would never have bonded to something like that, nor would Sasha have befriended or dated the likes." Trace tensed as he fought his lynx at the reminder of Sasha's past with another shifter. A wolf, no less! *Calm. It doesn't matter.*

The hell it doesn't. He's ours, not some wolf's! No one touches our mate!

He's an unclaimed male and that was ages ago. He didn't even know us then. He didn't even know Jason back then. Calm down!

He's our mate! You not biting him doesn't change that.

Trace sighed, hating how often he fought with his lynx. He never used to. Damn vampire. *Behave, please. We need to listen to the female, not go hunt down some wolf.*

His lynx grumbled but settled down, alert but quiet. Trace turned his attention back to Tatiana.

"I can't go home. Father is determined to marry me off, and he'd prefer it be to you, for whatever reason. As would my idiot of a younger brother. I'm not allowed into meetings or in on decisions. I was sent to all the same schools, had all the same training and tutors as my brothers, but I'm to be eye candy while they are the brains and the brawn of the coven. Mother is a virtual prisoner there. I'm no better, really, though I'm allowed out on trips such as these."

"Chaperoned with the likes of my uncle to be married off to another prince? That's no way to live," Sasha snapped and leaned forward. "So you want asylum based on wanting your freedom from an overbearing patriarchal ruler?"

"Yes and no. It's more than that. It's the killing and the pain and…." She turned pleading eyes to Sasha. "Papa wants to eradicate all bondings that are not pure blood. He's already started by killing the mates of those of higher rank if he finds out."

"Oh my Goddess. You came not to possibly fulfill his wishes but to flee. He killed your lover?" Trace blinked and gasped. What his lynx was so worried about her for finally clicked in his mind. "You… you're pregnant." It wasn't a question. That was what his lynx had picked up about her. It wasn't just the sadness; it was the presence of another wrapped within her. No wonder he wanted to help her so badly.

Sasha was up and out of his chair before Trace finished speaking. He had Tatiana in his arms as she lost her composure and began to cry. He sat, curling her up in his lap, soothing her with his voice and touch. Trace crawled over, petted down her back with one hand, and held one of her hands with his other.

It took Trace some time to work through his thoughts and feelings, not that Tatiana seemed to notice anything other than their petting of her as her sounds softened. Eventually he looked at Sasha and forced out, "We have to keep her here, Sasha. She can't return to those that would do this to her. Especially not once they find out you won't marry her. I don't want to even imagine what they might do to her or her child," he added with a shiver.

"Of course she stays. The coven has a princess again. I'm not sure how to word it yet, though I have a few ideas about certain things, but later. For now I think she's fallen asleep." Sasha maneuvered her around a little, and all she did was softly sniff and shift in his arms. "Let's turn her over to her maids and let her rest. I can hear them fretting in the next room."

"As can I." Trace hurried to let in one of the lady's maids while Sasha stood and brought Tatiana to them. It didn't take long for Sasha and Trace to be alone in their rooms again, both stunned and quiet for once.

CHAPTER NINETEEN

TRACE STARED down at the box of insanity neatly situated on his passenger seat and shook his head. The voice of his mentor, savior, and would-be father came through his Bluetooth. "Did you get everything I suggested?"

"Yes, Duncan, though I can't believe I'm being ordered to take donuts to a princess, a vampire princess, by the head of the lynx shifter council. This is insane. You do realize that, right?"

"Yes and no. She's pregnant, and you are trying to be nice to her. You have little experience with females, especially pregnant ones, so I'm advising you," he added with a chuckle. "Sugar is always a good way to go. Trust me. Besides, you want to have her on your side, Trace. You are in a very unusual position and situation."

"Trying to play nice with a pregnant vamp princess?" Trace knew full well that wasn't what Duncan was trying to get at, but he still didn't want to deal with the idea, or reality, of what mating with Sasha could mean. Even if Duncan thought Trace ought to give Sasha the bite and finish the bond.

"Feigning ignorance doesn't suit you in the least, son. You are Sasha's consort. His husband, as it were." A shiver ran up Trace's spine, leaving him almost light-headed. "I—"

"That is how the vampires see you, no matter how you view it."

Yeah, he knew that, though he didn't approve. If he were to be a husband, he ought to get a wedding and everything. A groom—that he accepted, dammit!—and all the fun bits too. *Hell, at least proposed to,* he thought. He knew he was pouting and didn't care, even if the people coming out of Voodoo Doughnut could see him as he sat in his BMW E39.

"It doesn't matter right now." He groaned internally as he ticked off in his head all he had to do. "Today I need to spend some time getting to know Tatiana a little. Then I need to force Sasha to see his doctor, as I don't like that heart pain thing that happened before. Oh, and hopefully help keep that asshat of an uncle away from the princess while Sasha and his guards try to find out more about who is trying to cause trouble and use me as a catalyst."

"And I will be dealing with Dr. Petronia. Lili will learn to deal with Dr. Niko, even if it kills her. I want them to figure things out with Sean before something happens."

Trace wanted that too. He couldn't shake the worry he held about the little one. Human-shifter mixed children never shifted, though Sean did regularly now. The security on the tribe lands had increased, and Sean went nowhere—no matter who he was with—without a guard detail, just to make sure no one outside decided to take him on their own to find out why he was so different. No one ought to know about him, but one never knew what might be known, leaked, sought, et cetera.

"Agreed. Let me get back to the covenstead"—as if that weren't the strangest thing he'd ever said—"and you go play with the vampiphobic doc."

"I'm not sure which of us will have the more trying day."

"Nor am I," Trace mumbled as he clicked off the call and headed back to the vampire house. By the time he made it back, Summer following behind in his black SUV, Trace had mostly shaken off his sullen mood.

"THE GROUNDS really are quite lovely, though the amusing snack you've brought me has to be the highlight of the morning, Trace." Tatiana smiled as she looked again from the various colors and types of roses around them in the secluded garden area where they sat, back down into the box he'd brought for her from Voodoo Doughnut. "I hadn't expected you to bring me food gifts."

Trace shrugged. "I heard that you might like chocolate, meat, sugar, and something fun. These fulfill all those and then some pretty much at the same time." He winked. "And with that one"—he motioned to the voodoo doll donut—"you can destroy your enemies and then eat the evidence."

She giggled, quickly bringing a hand up to cover her mouth. "You're horrible, you naughty boy. They do look delightful, though. I've never seen such strange donuts before."

Of course she hadn't. Nor had Trace before he moved to Seattle, as there were few places with Voodoo Doughnuts, but he thought they were insanely good—if a bit on the odd side. "It's one of the wonders of your new home."

The edges of her lips curled up, and her gaze went soft. "Thank you, Trace. I know this can't be easy on you."

"What difference does it make if it is or not," boomed Vlad as he rounded the corner into their quiet little haven. "He's of no importance—mangy cat doesn't belong here—but you are. Have you secured your place here with my idiot nephew yet?"

Trace fought not to lash out at the male before him, both because he was Sasha's uncle and because, shifter or not, elder vampire versus lynx... the vampire would win. Out of the corner of his eye, Trace caught when Summer stepped forward enough to be available but not enough to interfere yet. "Prince Sasha is not someone you should speak so callously or carelessly of, sir. His people are beyond loyal, as are his guards."

"His vampires are soft, barely deserving of their fangs. Many don't even feed on humans other than the amount required to keep one sane! And every single one I've spoken to so far actually believes this nonsense about you being his fated heart. Fairy tales and bedtime stories are no excuse for lying with the likes of you, nor of trying to shirk his duty to his position or his coven."

Trace hopped up and sauntered toward Vlad, making sure to put himself between the asshat and Tatiana. He still wasn't thrilled there was a female there who others wanted to pair Sasha with, one who by station was "more appropriate," nor was he interested right then in poking his whiskers into why he was so worried about who was with Sasha. He then smiled his most winsome smile. "Oh! I'm so sorry. Where are my manners? Would you like to join us for a little chat and for a light snack?"

"No, I would not. What I want is for you to leave so Sasha can forget this nonsense and do what's right. He needs heirs, not fleas."

The urge to rake his claws across Vlad's snarling face was almost stronger than Trace's wish to be "the bigger man." Almost. Instead of doing what he wished, and ignoring both Summer and Tatiana, Trace blinked at Vlad, tipped his head to the side a tiny bit—not enough it could be misconstrued as baring his throat by vampire or shifter of any kind—and pasted on a smile. "You would wish me to hurt your nephew, the one you claim to care about and only want the best for? That seems an odd wish for you to make. It seems even stranger to do so in clear hearing of a great many of his people. The same ones you just insulted by accusing them of not deserving their fangs."

He could see more than a few of Sasha's vampires, many of whom he didn't know but had seen around the mansion or at an event here and there, approach slowly. The fact Vlad was too busy trying to run Trace off was his own failing. You never failed to take into consideration who might be listening when in a public area—that was true with shifters, but even more so with vampires. Even being in a private place, that could hold true if one didn't take precautions.

"He'll bond with Tatiana or some other princess once you leave," Vlad snarled.

"It doesn't work that way, and you know it. I'm his fated heart, and he's already bonded me." When Vlad started to brush that off again, something broke inside him and he growled, "He's my mate, and he will never bond with anyone else."

Trace froze for a moment as what he'd said sank in.

A soft touch to his elbow distracted him from his internal shock. He turned to see, not Tatiana as he'd expected, but Sasha. "You don't have to justify why you're here, mal'chik. He's a guest here, one that I'm losing what little patience I have with."

"You are still my nephew, and as such, I'm still one of your elders. You owe—"

"I owe you nothing," Sasha hissed. "I've put up with you all these years out of respect for the fact you are my mother's brother. That is the only reason. However, you've overstepped one too many times when you chose to go after my consort."

Vlad stepped back, but Trace's hope the idiot would leave so he could deal with what he'd just said in front of Sasha… and other vampires… outside his head… evaporated when Vlad squared his shoulders and rose to his full height and sneered down at Sasha. "If he's your precious consort, your *fated* heart, then why haven't you announced it to the other covens? Why no ritual yet?"

"Same reason Father took the time to woo Mother even though they were fated—because we want more than the part of the bond Fate gives us. When Trace is ready to accept my suit, we will do all the formal parts. However, you know as well as I that all that is a formality, not a requirement for the bond to be real and lasting."

"He has no coven. No standing. No power. He brings nothing to the coven!"

"And you wonder why you've never managed to keep a wife, even with all your money." Sasha gave a harsh laugh. "Stay away from Trace and Tatiana. You're no longer welcome near either of them."

Trace turned to where Tatiana had been and realized she no longer sat behind him. He looked around, not wanting anything to have happened to her while he was torn between the mess in his head and what was going on in front of him. "Where'd she go?"

Sasha wrapped an arm around Trace's waist. "Dimka escorted her away so she didn't have to deal with *him*."

Vlad barked, "Hey!" but they both ignored him.

"Summer is still here with you, don't worry. As am I."

"I'm not worried about me. I didn't want him upsetting her or to have him continue to run you down how he was."

"I was speaking, you... you—" Vlad snapped again.

"And I was ignoring you," Sasha countered as he looked over to where Vlad stood, fists clenched. "You have no power or standing here other than what I allow you. As of now that is nothing. You may keep your rooms, but any vitriol, abuse, et cetera will be dealt with the same as it would if you were nothing but a commoner. And you no longer have my protection."

"You can't do that! I'm a prince!"

"And I'm the royal prince. The ruling prince. You don't like it? Leave. But not until we've figured out if you had anything to do with the attack on Trace."

Sasha pulled Trace along with him, Vlad sputtering behind them, though Summer didn't allow him to follow—thankfully.

Trace couldn't make much sense of his own thoughts as they made their way back to their suite. The fact he'd publicly claimed Sasha in such a way still shocked him. For the first time, it didn't feel like something he was fighting or saying out of jealousy—not that he would ever admit to that feeling aloud. Still, he couldn't wrap his head around what he'd said. Done. And at least part of the vampires had heard him. More importantly Sasha had heard him.

The door closed behind them about the time his mind caught on something Sasha said earlier. "Wait, what ritual? And what do you mean 'woo'?"

"To woo you, to court you, though I haven't had much luck as of yet."

"I know what 'woo' means, Sasha." He put one hand on his hip and stepped to the side as he stared at Sasha. "But I don't remember being wooed, and I want to know what ritual you two were talking about." Trace didn't know much about vampire rituals, but he didn't like the idea of one he was to participate in without his agreeing first, much less without his knowledge.

Sasha sighed as he stepped back into Trace's space and lightly touched Trace's lower back. "Come and sit down. I'll try to explain it, but you have to promise to hear me out before you start hissing or ranting."

"I do not hiss." Trace crossed his arms over his chest and glared at Sasha, who proceeded to ignore him. He then stepped around him and sat in his preferred chair.

"Right, and I don't bite." Sasha flicked one long-fingered hand negligently. "Now if you want answers, you have to be willing to listen."

"Fine." Trace sat across from Sasha, needing space between them if he had any hope of keeping his focus and wits about him.

"Thank you, hon. The ritual he referred to is the bonding ceremony. It's similar to a wedding or mating ritual, only due to my being the royal prince, there's a bit more... formality and pomp to it."

Well, that made sense, and it was lovely Sasha wasn't trying to bully him into doing that to save face with the other covens. Still…. "I haven't agreed to that."

"I believe I said as much to my uncle a few minutes ago. When you are ready, then we can discuss such things. Not before then."

TRACE SAT still, staring at nothing as far as Sasha could tell for a short time before he moved again. When he finally did, he had that same deer-in-the-headlights look as when he realized he'd said Sasha was his mate earlier—something Sasha still couldn't believe he'd heard, yet wanted to hear again. And again…. "Did I really say you were my mate in front of your idiot of an uncle and the others?"

He couldn't help the small smile he knew curled his lips as he replied, "Yes, mal'chik, you did."

"But… I didn't…. I mean, I didn't mean to say that to him. But how can another vampire be so callous toward your claim on me as your bonded, fated heart? Doesn't he care about what sending me away could do to you?"

Yeah, that again. I still may kill Jalin for meddling! "He doesn't believe in the bond. Or doesn't want to, at least. You're a shifter, so I think he feels that makes it less likely to count, as if that makes sense. He barely recognizes fated hearts, even with his sister having had one, but…." None of that was what they needed to focus on, though he figured Trace knew that as well as he did. "What it really comes down to is you don't fit into his political games, so he's not happy. Not that it matters. He has no say in the matter." Sasha leaned forward and rested his elbows on his knees. "But hon, did you mean that you finally accept me as your mate, or were you only saying that to spite Vlad?"

"Spite never entered my mind. I was just so sick of being told you should mate with someone else, that I wasn't good enough, that you would get tired of me and put me aside. We haven't even really been together, so how could I expect you to want to stay? I've pushed you away constantly, but…."

Oh Gods, could Trace finally be accepting? Was it Vlad who had provided the push Duncan said Trace needed? Sasha had planned to talk to Tatiana to ask her to help him nudge Trace a little, but then she'd asked for help and Vlad had started his nonsense. He thought quickly about how Trace had been, the things Duncan said, and about how he would normally date someone he intended to keep, then scrapped his ideas and tried to think of what his mother would suggest he do in the situation with his heart. "Would you accept my invitation to dinner and a moonlight walk with me tonight?"

Trace twitched, then slowly raised his head. "Uh, y-yes?"

"Thank you, Trace."

"Will we still be followed around by Dimka and Summer? I mean, it's on the coven grounds, and I'd be with you. Do I really need a guard?"

Did that mean he wanted to be alone with Sasha on a date? They were alone in their suite, but that was different, as this would be their first "date," and they both knew it. "They will keep their distance, but we still don't know who is behind the attack, and with Vlad being here, I don't want to risk it. They won't see or hear anything, I assure you."

"Too loyal and well trained for that, I know. Still, not used to being chaperoned like this. It's weird."

"It's only for a little longer. I just want you safe. Besides, they're always twitchy when Vlad's around, so it's not only about you. They don't think he's behind the attack, but they also don't trust him. It drove them both crazy the few times he visited while they were charged with Jason's safety. One would be with Jason and the other with me."

The edges of Trace's lips twitched a couple of times before he lost the fight and not only smiled, but laughed. "I can see that. I wouldn't want you near that… your uncle either without someone to protect you, even knowing that you're probably the most dangerous being here. But you, of course, wouldn't let them leave Jason unguarded."

"Of course not. Jason's the one who actually needed the protection. Besides, not making them have to work together is good for them once in a while. Though they don't believe me."

A knock interrupted the chuckling. A moment later Jalin stepped inside. "Dr. Niko is here to check on you, sir."

Sasha blinked a couple of times as he tried to think of why the doctor would be there to see him instead of at the tribe research center. "And did he say why?"

"I'm here at the request of your consort to examine you," Dr. Niko said as he pushed past Jalin.

CHAPTER TWENTY

SASHA SAT in his favorite chair, staring at Dr. Niko, dumbfounded as to why he was there and why his arrival coincided with Jalin collecting Trace for Alpha Keith. He suspected Jalin and Trace had planned whatever was going on, but as Trace hadn't seemed completely at ease when he left, Sasha decided to go along with whatever his fated heart wanted. Still, why did he need to see the doctor?

"Doctor, what can I do for you?"

"I'm here to examine you, as I said. Though"—Dr. Niko glanced to the closed main door—"I had expected Trace to want to stay since it was him who wanted your heart checked."

"My heart?" *Why would I need my heart...?* "Did he say why?"

"Mm… he did. Said you got sharp pains every time either of you said something about you not being his mate, or some such nonsense. We all know you're his mate and he's your fated heart, so that doesn't make sense why you'd say such a fool thing. But he was upset, so I agreed to see you. I need to get back to the cat's research center, though, so could you hurry up and cooperate?"

"Grumpy," Sasha mumbled as he tried to make sense of what Niko had said. "I did have pain a couple of times. It was about the same time I said that what I'd done… that I hadn't taken Trace as my mate—" A shooting pain tore through Sasha, beginning in his heart but spreading down his body and through his arms and legs until he spasmed and slid to the floor. It only lasted a moment, but that was a lifetime too long, as far as he was concerned.

"Prince Sasha! Sasha! Son, what the hell just happened?" Niko was suddenly bent over Sasha, cradling his head in his lap as he touched his throat gently. Sasha couldn't piece together how Niko had gotten down there with him.

Dimka was suddenly in the room, looming over Sasha and Niko. "Prince Sasha, what's wrong?"

Sasha tried to focus, though it took more effort than it ought. The pain was gone, but it left a wake of soreness and shock throughout his body and mind. "I have no idea. It was worse that time, and I didn't even mean it! I was only explaining what I'd said previously. I'd explained that concept to Trace before and since, though not in those same words. What the hell?"

Niko and Dimka helped Sasha back into his chair before Dimka returned to his post outside the doors. He didn't look happy, but Sasha didn't want anyone getting too close to his suite, especially right then.

"It's only when you deny the mating, not if you say that the bond isn't the same as the mating, right?"

He had to think about it, but yes, that seemed right. But something was still off about it. "Yes, but I'd said that the bond didn't trigger the other and such before, using the M-word, since Trace came back to himself. Why is it now causing so much pain, and why only with that word as the trigger?"

"Possibly because Trace hasn't accepted you as his mate, not fully, and you increased the bond on your side when you fed from him. I think. Since the situation with Trace became something I was aware of, I've researched what I could, contacting other covens if I knew they had records or lore of vampire-shifter bondings. What little I found suggested that if one denies the other, it can cause pain, injury, and even death if it goes on too long. But we thought that had to do with the lack of being able to feed properly, not literal heart pains."

"Don't get me started on what you told Trace. It won't be healthy for you or Jalin."

"Protecting our prince and trying to get Trace past his fears to accept his mate is not a bad thing," Niko grumbled as he pulled out a stethoscope from his ever-present bag. "Now I want to examine you properly. I would really like to take you in to the clinic and get a full workup, but I know you won't agree to that."

"You're right, I won't. Vampires don't have heart attacks. I'll just be more careful of my words. Besides, Trace agreed to a date tonight, and he told Vlad he was my mate. Loudly. So whatever this is might be moot shortly anyway."

"Perhaps. Still...."

Dr. Niko demanded Sasha remove his shirt, then placed the cold device against his chest, back, and abdomen in various places as he told him to breathe deep, slow, normal, et cetera. Sasha thought they were done, but when Niko pulled away, he then insisted on putting Sasha through a series of exercises where he would stop him at various points to listen again or take his pulse or do things Sasha didn't understand. Not that Sasha understood the need for the stethoscope—vampire hearing negated such things.

Finally, *finally* they were done, and Dr. Niko handed Sasha back his shirt. "Get dressed, sir. As far as I can tell, the pain hasn't done any actual damage to you, though it probably didn't feel that way at the time."

"Even if it had, Niko, you know it would have healed by now."

"Still, I would warn you to be very cautious of your words until you have secured your fated heart's affections and bite. Once you have his bite, you should be all right, if I understand correctly. Oh, and work on the bond on your side as well. That should help you both."

"In what way? I won't force him to do things he's not ready for. What feeding we did I only consented to because he pushed." *And it was awkward as hell!*

"I've never seen you not be able to bat those pretty blue eyes and get whomever you wanted into bed. Don't let Trace be the first. As your doctor, I'm telling you, you need to seduce your lover." Sasha stared at Niko. *Seriously, who gets told to go have sex by their doctor?* "As one of your loyal coven members, I'm asking you to make sure you and your consort are strong and stable so our coven stays that way. We need you to be the prince you've always been, especially with whatever's going on with the attack and with your uncle."

"I'm working on the situation with Trace, thank you very much." Sasha sniffed, not liking having his intentions toward Trace questioned. He would win Trace over, and they would be a real couple. True, not that long ago, he hadn't thought that possible, but he knew better now, and so Trace would be his. Period.

"Good."

"Oh, is there any progress with the whole shifting situation with Sean? I know I'm not either of his fathers, but I am his godfather, and I don't want anything to happen to him. I've never heard of this happening. Not that it never has—few shifter groups even allow us to know much about them—but still."

Niko sighed as he shook his head. "We'd get farther, I believe, if that infernal female would get over my fangs and focus on the actual research. But she's so biased it makes it difficult." Yeah, Sasha'd been afraid of that. "Thankfully her councilman's intervention is helping. As for the whys and such? I'm leaning to work more with Trace's idea, honestly. She's against it, determined it has no scientific or logical value or basis. I'm not so lost in my test tubes that I've forgotten that they are a magically created race, so...." He shook his head and quirked his lips on one side. "We shall see in the end. All that matters is we figure out what's needed to protect the boy. So far all his tests show he's stable, as are his cells. So stop worrying and focus on your fated heart."

"Keep me up to date."

"Of course, my liege."

"Now there's something I want you to do for Trace, and yes, he's likely to not want to cooperate."

"Joy. What?" Dr. Niko asked, his tone wary, his body partly turned away, and his eyes not quite meeting Sasha's gaze.

"I want you to check his scars. Something is off about them since I fed on him. I think. I haven't wanted to push to see his back myself, as that's an intimate thing if it's me. He's not quite ready for that, I don't believe. However, it's clinical if it's you. Not at all the same thing."

"He was fussing about his shoulder itching when he spoke to me earlier. Hmm...." Niko stared at his bag for a moment before he jerked upright, then snapped it closed. "I will see about Trace, but I need to get back to the tribe center. Besides, that's where he is right now, so it should be easier to catch him. But it's up to him if he consents to the exam."

"Love how it's up to him, but for me, no," Sasha grumbled, dragging the *o* out for at least the worth of five or six words. "Fine, agreed. Go help Sean. I have a criminal vamp or two to find and deal with."

Dr. Niko smiled wide, his fangs showing. "Good. I want to see whoever is behind this dealt with. No one touches those that are ours, and Trace is one of us, even if his fangs are kitty ones and not proper vampire ones. I just hope you find who is doing this before they find a way to get at Trace again."

"He's well-guarded. And if anyone hurts him, they will die."

"Oh, I know they will," Niko said so matter-of-factly it brought a smile to Sasha's face. It was good to have his people believe in him and believe in the bond he had with Trace.

TRACE PROWLED around the woods near his home on the tribe lands. Jalin had gotten him out of Sasha's area and off the coven grounds without Sasha getting upset, though he knew he would be when Dr. Niko started his poking and prodding. Yet even in his lynx form, Trace knew the doctor was important for Sasha to see.

When he'd first arrived at the tribe lands, he'd tried talking with Dr. Liliana—for all the good it had done him. Gods' fur, that female irritated him. He'd knocked politely on the door and waited, only entering when he'd heard a muffled call of some form.

It took a couple minutes to find her, as she was curled up—in her human skin—in a back sitting room under a light throw, looking out the window. When he looked out the same, he noted only the forest, so she wasn't watching anyone in particular. Huh.

"Excuse me, Doctor."

She turned slowly, her brows pulled together and down until they were more dark slash marks above dark flashing eyes. "What do you want?" she snapped.

"I stopped by to see how the research is coming about Sean. And to see if you needed anything extra brought in. Equipment, materials, chemicals, et cetera."

Her expression of irritation mixed with, well, if he didn't know better, he'd say loathing, didn't lessen. And he did know better—right? "If I have need, I will send my requests to Duncan. I'm not in the mood to deal with one of ours that has decided he's now a vampire pet."

"I am no one's pet. However, I am the council's representative, which means those requests go through me. Push me and everything will go through me... for you. Dr. Niko, however, only has to contact his prince directly. Who has the ear of the alpha mate. Of course, so do I. Have the ear of all three. You might consider getting over yourself and actually focusing on your job. You are a doctor, which means you are to heal. You are a research doctor, which means you are to study and find ways to help, new ways to heal, to find out what's wrong, or what's not, when something is worried over and it's actually a worry. What it isn't is to judge, to harm, or to let your assumptions get in the way of doing your actual job." He took a deep breath and let it out slowly. "Now, if you will excuse me, I have things to do before my appointment with Duncan. Good day, Doctor. I hope to see that list of needs soon."

Not giving her time to respond, though she was sputtering behind him, he walked out, leaving her behind. There was no way he could stay and not want to strangle her. It had taken all he had not to wrap his fingers around her scrawny neck as it was. But that wouldn't help Sean...

and if he kept repeating it, she'd stay healthy and they would get their answer soon.

He climbed his favorite tree, tried hunting some, ran from tree to tree, but nothing he did helped settle his nerves or made him forget the fact he wasn't near Sasha. He wanted to be back with Sasha, even if the covenstead didn't have a good forest to play in. But his human side needed time away from their mate, and their mate needed time to work on his hunt of the one who had tried to kill them. Still....

A strange scent caught his attention as he leaped to a new tree. He hadn't been out this far in a long while, though he knew he was still on tribe land. Why couldn't he place the scent? It wasn't quite right. A bird but not. Owl, maybe... but that wasn't right either. Not exactly....

Hating not knowing what he was scenting, Trace set about following the trail, faint as it was. He kept going, even though he strayed farther and farther from the tribe center. Annoyingly the trail didn't get stronger that he could tell. *What the hell?*

"Trace!"

Trace came to a sudden stop, freezing at the sound of his name in Duncan's strong voice. His very human voice. Why was he out there, and why did he sound so irritated? He twitched his ears as he turned his head to look at the ground far below him. With a frustrated mew, he waited for Duncan to either explain what the issue was or join him.

"You were supposed to see me almost an hour ago, Trace. I should not have to come find you, much less so far out without your guards with you."

Trace cocked his head as he tried to remember why he needed to see Duncan. Oh, right, the human half of him was supposed to discuss the mating issue again. Duncan wanted to push Trace to finally mate Sasha, he thought. He was all for that! But the not-a-bird scent....

"Now, Trace! Come down here. We can talk as we walk back, and by then it will be time for you to return for your date with the prince."

Letting out a disgruntled huff, Trace bounded from branch to branch, making noise and raining leaves and needles on Duncan every chance he got as he descended.

"You're a brat." Duncan brushed the detritus off his head and arms as he grumbled.

When Trace finally landed on the forest floor near Duncan, he noticed a bag that smelled like himself—his human clothes, he assumed. He only took a moment to sniff them and rub against the bag before he shifted. He snatched up the bag and went about getting dressed even as he commented, "I was following something, you know."

"What? Something that was more important than a conference and your date?"

"I have no idea, but this is the second time I've found the scent of something that isn't quite right, and it's not an animal I can place. The first time no one else could even find it. This time I'm marking where it was so I can show the others." He looked in the bag, but no, his cell wasn't in there, dammit. Hmm.... "You have your phone on you?"

"Of course. Why?" Duncan asked even as he pulled out his smartphone and handed it over.

"Thanks."

Trace quickly tapped in the numbers he needed and waited as it rang twice before he heard the deep hello.

"Hey, Van? Can you come out to where I am right now? Duncan is insisting I return to the main area with him, but there's something here that I think needs to be checked out."

Vance's rumbling chuckle made Trace smile even as he awaited his response. "If you feel it's important, I'll come out. I trust your instincts, man. But I don't know where you are and this isn't your cell, so I can't just pull up the app and find you like I normally could."

"Damn, didn't think of that. Hold on. Let me see if Duncan has a GPS locater app." Trace pulled the cell away from his face and went to tap the central app button, but Duncan pushed his hand away.

"I have one. Here."

An app popped up, and a moment later, Trace read the coordinates to Van. "It smells like bird but not. Almost like an owl, but that's not right either. My lynx is not happy at being interrupted, but not like he was hunting. I can't explain it right. Still, something was odd. So since I have to go back and I don't have my guards," he grumbled, "can you investigate for me?"

"I'll head out now. Thanks for letting me know."

He clicked off and returned the phone to Duncan. "Thanks. I know it probably seems like a weird worry, but this is the second time I've found something that doesn't belong here. Something that I've never scented before. I just hope Vance can find it this time. Last time no one else could."

"Wonder if it could be one of the snowy shifters? They're so rare, and I don't know of any in this region. The regular snowy owls, sure, but not the shifter kind."

"Huh. Didn't think of that. I've never met one, so maybe. I'll leave it to Vance to figure out. If he finds a stray shifter, he won't hurt them, so I'm not worried. Do you want to take me back or help me follow the trail?" His lynx was all for following, though he knew Duncan wouldn't be. Plus he'd agreed to the date with Sasha, so he had to show up. The side of him that had spent all these years with the intertribal council sided with his lynx, though—the possibility of meeting a bird shifter was tempting.

"Nice try, son. Let Vance do his job. Neither of us ought to be out here alone. You even less so."

"I'm so sick of the guards."

"I know, and I understand, but it's needed for now. I have people looking into what's going on as well, but unfortunately, those responsible haven't left any trails other than what you've already been told about."

They weaved their way back through the forest, the walk slower as humans than it was in their lynx skin. "I can't figure out the endgame. I could have died, and Sasha would have been hurt, but that wouldn't have destroyed his ability to rule his coven. It might have damaged his relationship with the tribe, maybe, but with his being family with Jason, even that's not likely given that it wasn't one of his who attacked me. They left too much proof that it was linked to Sasha's uncle to make it believable that it was Sasha's fault, unless the tribe was to blame vampires as a whole." Trace shook his head as he climbed over a fallen tree instead of walking around. "I don't get it at all."

"Does make one wonder how well they know Prince Sasha, the tribe, and the coven. I would say not well to not at all. As for endgame, causing war seems most likely but not realistic. Removal of the prince, perhaps."

"On what grounds?" Trace snapped, stopping to face Duncan, hands flying around as his temper flared.

"Not that way, son. Ousting him. If he's too distraught and gets hurts fighting, it would make him easier to attack and take out or capture so someone else could take over. That's the logic behind thinking it's his uncle, right? That and the claim it was his children."

"Well, yes." Trace thought about it for a moment, dropping his hands to his hips. "But the coven would never follow him. From what I've seen, they don't like him. I overheard a few mention that his kids were better than him. Well, the son. The daughter is seen as a gold digger and a bit vapid."

"Even with the possibility that they attacked you?"

"I don't think anyone believes it was them. Sasha seems suspicious that Vlad had something to do with it, but that's about it. Most believe that it's a frame to distract from what's actually happening. I have no clue, as I don't know enough about any of them yet."

Duncan shook his head slowly but motioned for Trace to start walking again. "Come on. The fact you don't know the coven here better is a failing on your part. You ought to. You've known you were the mate of the royal prince for over five years, son."

"Duncan—"

"No, it's time. You have to stop letting what Ford did control your life."

"Don't say his name!"

"He only has power if you let him. How many battered partners, spouses, wives, husbands, et cetera, have you helped, donated to causes for, taken in, and more over the years? Do you still give to battered shelters and programs? Yet you won't let yourself move forward."

"It's not that simple," Trace mumbled. It's not like he hadn't tried! Trust was so hard to come by now, and even then, the past tended to sneak into his thoughts, and memories returned at the worst time to haunt him. He wanted a normal life; he'd just found that it wasn't possible. Not for him.

"You have the perfect mate waiting for you. He's gifted to you by Baast. Do you really believe that our Goddess would be so cruel as to gift you a destined mate who would hurt you?"

"I didn't think my last mate would, and look where that belief got me. Nearly dead." *Would have been if it hadn't been for you.*

"He wasn't the right partner for you, and you know it. You had doubts before you mated with Ford. I'm sorry for what happened, but I can't undo the past. You can have everything you always wanted, son. You have a mate who will care for you and cherish you always. That's what any parent wants for their child, and while you may not be mine by blood, you are mine by choice, so yes, I'm going to browbeat you until you accept that fact and do what's right for you both."

"You should have been a mother." Trace huffed but didn't dismiss what Duncan said outright. He knew what he said was true. Baast didn't make mistakes. Sasha wouldn't hurt him, not in any bad way. But could he be what Sasha needed? Sasha was a Dom, sorta. When threatened or angered, he was violent and lethal. What would he be like in the bedroom, though?

"Trace…."

"Thinking."

Duncan walked beside Trace quietly for a time, not speaking other than when they met up briefly with Vance as he headed out to investigate. Not long before they reached the edge of the "town" part of the tribe land, Duncan spoke again. "Son, I only push because I worry about you. When you lived at the council headquarters and worked directly for us, it was one thing. I could monitor you, make sure you were healthy and stable. I've done the best I could with you out here, but knowing that you've been struggling with a rejected mating all this time—that worries me like nothing else. Please try to work things out with your mate. Seek outside help if needed."

Trace froze, unable to do more than stare and blink at Duncan as he tried to process that last bit. *Outside help?* "Wha-what? What do you mean?"

"If it's too hard to talk to me about the specific concerns, then talk to a counselor. There are people trained in helping those that have been abused as adults. Others that help with depression and such."

"You think I'm crazy?"

"No, I believe you were hurt and are still suffering from the aftermath of what that vile filth did."

"That was—"

"Not something you just 'get over,' so don't even try it. Now I need you to see the doctor before you head back to the vampire den."

Yeah, sure, like I don't have enough crap thrown at me already. "Why?"

"He said he needed to see you before you returned. He wouldn't tell me why. The vamp doctor is a grumpy, weird male, and I have no interest in tangling with him. Nice vampire or no."

"It's probably about what I asked him to do before I left earlier. Thanks."

"And about what we talked about?"

"I said I'd have dinner and a moonlight walk with Sasha. I told Vlad Sasha is my mate. I'm trying."

"Good boy."

Trace stomped off, grumbling that he wasn't five. He didn't care that he probably looked like an oversized child right then. He was tired of everyone thinking they had the right to an opinion on his love life and future. That was between him and Sasha. Only!

Chapter Twenty-One

Trace was standing outside the main doors to the covenstead mansion when Sasha tracked him down. He'd been notified his fated heart had returned, but Trace had yet to enter the building, much less return to their suite. Sasha didn't have a clue why and didn't like not knowing. Summer stood off to the side, unobtrusive as always, but only gave a slight shrug when Sasha looked at him.

"Not helpful," Sasha whispered, knowing Summer would hear him. His personal guards weren't just strong and fast; they were two of the most skilled and gifted physically of all his people. Summer's hearing was so acute, technology couldn't match it, much to the annoyance of some of the techies in the coven.

"He's not said anything other than 'don't know why' since he left the doc's."

That got Sasha to move faster. He hurried down the steps to Trace, not bothering to wait to be invited into his space or warn him first. Not this time. "Mal'chik?" Sasha slid one arm around his waist. "What has you out here?"

Trace stiffened for a moment, but then he melted into the touch, leaning into Sasha a little. "Um… can we talk? Privately?" he added as he looked over at Summer.

What in Gaia's name is up? "In our rooms or in the garden?"

He reached up and touched his right shoulder with a trembling hand. "Rooms. Please."

Sasha slid his hand down to the small of Trace's back and gently led him inside the mansion and through the halls until he came to their suite. Once inside he closed and locked the main door. Returning to Trace, he smiled and held his hand out.

"No, I need to do this and say this with a clear head. Um, can… can you sit in your chair? This might be easier if we're how we are when you comfort."

"Comfort?"

Trace nodded and leaned into Sasha's hand slightly. "Comfort me," he said so softly Sasha almost missed it.

That made little sense, but Sasha agreed, willing to do most anything to help Trace be more comfortable. He just hoped he wasn't going to be disappointed or angry with the outcome of the, well, whatever this was. He sat in the overstuffed leather chair and waited as Trace knelt beside him. Instead of facing away so Sasha could play with his hair as usual, though, Trace faced him as he knelt at Sasha's feet.

That was new and arousing.

Later!

Sasha cleared his throat, pushing aside the thoughts of what he could do with Trace in such a position, and asked, "Okay, you have me here. What did you wish to discuss?"

"You sent Dr. Niko to check my scars."

"I did. Will you tell me what he found?"

"I—They—" Trace closed his eyes, took a deep breath, then let it out slowly before opening his eyes and meeting his gaze. "The main scars are still there, though not as deep, I guess you could say. But, um, the mating bite from… from F-Ford? It's g-gone."

"What?" Sasha croaked even as his heart raced and his head spun. "How? What does that mean?"

Trace shook his head. "I don't know," he whispered. "But Alpha Keith has declared my previous mating annulled, basically. We don't have a term for it, as it's not possible to do. To take a new mate, yes, but not to remove a past mating. Except you did. Somehow."

"Isn't that a good thing? To remove the mark of your abuser should be a positive thing, I would think. Wish I could take away the rest of them." He hated that Trace had suffered, but also that his back was a constant reminder of that monster.

The gulp was loud as Trace gave a shaky nod. "Yes, but it's not possible."

"Obviously it is."

"True. Um, the thing is, Dr. Niko said your bite should have left a mark, and that if I bite you with the mating bite, it will actually mar your skin as well. Something that doesn't usually happen."

That was one mark Sasha would be proud to bear. "We don't scar often, but shifter fangs and claws will do it. I know the bite will stay. It did on my sister." Hers had been bigger than what Trace would cause, but Trace wasn't a Chosen of Baast like Orin. Did that mean…. "Do you want us to mark each other?"

Trace looked away, his gaze not landing anywhere, it seemed, for a time as he twisted his long fingers together and fidgeted. "Um, I can't promise not to panic or worry. I don't know that I can be who and what you really need, much less want, but, er, yes?"

"For the bonds to seal properly and for us to both get the full—" Sasha considered his words carefully before he continued. "—benefits, you know us merely biting one another as we are sitting and kneeling now won't work. I could bond you without more of a link, but it's not as strong or complete as it ought to be, and you know how mating works on your end of things."

"I know. That was why I was outside for so long. I…."

HE WANTED this—he was terrified of what it meant—but he wanted what Sasha would do, what giving everything over to him could and would mean. He hoped. It had been so long since Trace allowed another male, lynx, or human—and never a vampire—to master him. The knowledge of what was to come, the fact he didn't really know what Sasha intended to do to him, had his cock hard already, even as his nerves amped up. He hadn't even managed to say he wanted sex yet, and already he was losing his mind!

But the moment he fully gave in to his desire and what he knew was the truth between them, his inner lynx had rejoiced and demanded they come back inside and give themselves to their mate. The thing was, Trace had never been anything but submissive with any partner, and with Sasha, all he truly wanted was to give, to please, even if his past did make him wonder if this was really the best idea.

Apprehension clogged his throat as he worked to get the words out, but he wouldn't refuse to answer any more than he would refuse Sasha's passion or need of him. "Yes, Sir."

Sasha stood and moved so he towered over Trace, but wasn't pushed against him as he would be with the chair behind him. He looked down at Trace and cocked his head, the edges of his plump lips curving as his gaze heated.

"Then strip and lie in the center of the bed, legs spread."

Was this how Sasha normally did things with his lovers? Trace had no clue, of course, but even as he debated refusing or asking why—and why they weren't discussing things before Sasha went straight to the sex part—he raised his trembling fingers up to the top button of his shirt and slowly began the process of slipping each free of the shirt until it fell open. Sasha didn't take his eyes off Trace, the hunger in his eyes growing as each came free and more skin was exposed. That hunger gave Trace the strength to continue, to slip the shirt off his shoulders and fold it neatly. He stood, then walked slowly into Sasha's bedroom before setting it carefully on the lounger beside him.

"You would look delicious with pierced nipples," Sasha murmured before licking his lips. The motion exposed his fangs, the sight of which made Trace whimper and his cock swell more. Gods, he was so hard it hurt!

"I-it wouldn't stay, Sir. Not with my shifting."

"I know, but it would still look good, and you could handle having me redo it each time, couldn't you, mal'chik?"

Ford had called him "kit," like the adults often called the kittens. His human Doms sometimes used "boy" or "pup," though he hated "pup," as it made him think of the wolf shifters, which he didn't have a problem with, but that wasn't what he was. But there was something different about how Sasha said "mal'chik" now than when he said it typically that made Trace's pulse race. It was so much better than "boy"! Trace wanted to kneel at Sasha's feet and worship them, but that wasn't what Sasha wanted.

He wasn't entirely sure he could manage this. The nightmare he'd lived through still wanted to invade, was trying to push into what Sasha and he were doing now.

"Trace? You with me or back in time with someone else? I don't share with ghosts," he growled, his tone no longer playful or sensual. The power and edge in it snapped Trace back to the present fully and made him tremble.

"Sorry, Sir. I didn't mean—"

"Don't apologize for your past, mal'chik. Now answer my question."

Question? Oh! "Yes, if that's what you want. I like the look, just never bothered because of healing every time I shift."

"Good boy. Now do as you were told. Don't make me tell you again."

Trace nodded as he trailed his hands down his abdomen, making sure he caught Sasha's gaze again before he slipped the button of his jeans. He took a deep breath and then slowly lowered the zipper, exposing his black boxer briefs. They hugged his body but did little to hide his straining erection.

"Jeans first, then briefs."

Doing as commanded, Trace stripped, folding each piece of clothing until he stood before Sasha in nothing but his bracelets, bangles, and rings—all of which he now knew had come from Sasha. As a shifter, he had no qualms about nudity like the humans he'd known, but somehow in front of Sasha, with him watching, it took on a whole new aspect. Plus Trace hated showing anyone his back. Even the short time it would take to turn and climb onto the bed was longer than he liked exposing it—the fact the scars weren't as bad as they had been didn't lessen that in the least.

There was nothing for it, though, so Trace turned and climbed onto the huge bed and lay down as Sasha had bid him do.

"This won't be like what you endured before, but I won't go easy on you either, Trace. I will take my pleasure, and you will serve me before I allow you completion tonight. You say you want more. That you want to serve me. That you want my full bite and to give me yours. Then you will start by sharing your body with me how I see fit, and doing so at my leisure and for my pleasure tonight."

Trace nodded, not meeting Sasha's gaze. It wasn't like he hadn't wanted Sasha's touch since the first time they met. Trace had wanted the infuriating vampire like he had never wanted anyone or anything before. He was simply afraid of what would happen if he let the male close. Now it was too late. Sasha had bound him to him while Trace's lynx was in control. The craving for Sasha was worse than ever, as was the want—no, the need to please Sasha. So here he was in Sasha's bed, a place he'd sworn he would never be, and he'd gone there by choice! Best or worst, when he left the bed, they would be mated. He just hoped his lynx was right, because he was certain this was forever.

Sasha moved to the head of the bed and pulled up two padded cuffs attached to chains. "These chains are strong enough to hold a vampire, so they will hold you, but the padding will protect you from chafing or injury." He slipped the cuffs around each wrist carefully, making sure it was tight enough to hold but not so tight as to hurt. "I know you could simply shift and get free, and I don't have a way, yet, to stop you from that, but it will displease me greatly if you do so. Do you understand me?"

"Yes, Sir. No shifting. I'm to stay as you put me because I'm here for your pleasure."

"Such a good, beautiful boy. Thank you, love."

Love? Fated, yes, but the vampire can't mean he's falling for me? Can he?

When Sasha moved away, Trace tugged his hands enough to test the restraints, and sure enough, he wasn't getting out of them unless he shifted. Still, if things went horribly wrong, he knew he could—cold comfort, but it was better than nothing.

Trace then watched as Sasha repeated the same with cuffs to his ankles. It was when Sasha pulled out a third set of cuffs, these larger, that Trace squirmed, unsure what was going on.

"Be still, mal'chik. I'm not going to hurt you."

Stilling immediately, Trace watched as Sasha buckled the larger cuff around his upper thigh. It had a chain binding it to the bed as well, but it also had a small clip like he'd seen on many cuffs meant to hook to other cuffs. Was this intended to hook to the other thigh cuff? Why would you bind a male's thighs like that? It made no sense, but he chose not to ask, worried he would anger Sasha. The little he'd seen of Sasha's temper showed him he never wanted to be on the wrong side of the vampire. Sasha took the time to adjust the chains so Trace's hands were high and close together, but his legs were stretched out and spread wide apart.

"I love looking at you, you know. Such a sexy male." Sasha prowled around the bed, still fully dressed other than his feet, as he'd removed his boots and socks at some point Trace had missed.

Trailing his hand down Trace's foot, over his toes, Sasha even outlined the planes between them. He then stepped back before he slipped off his shirt but left on his sinfully tight jeans, ones that cupped his groin in such a way as to make Trace's mouth water. Sasha then climbed up onto the bed and began the torture he'd promised, though not in any way Trace would have expected.

The contact of Sasha's lips to the arch of one foot caused him to gasp and jerk slightly. Sasha's lips curved against the top of Trace's foot, allowing him to feel Sasha's fangs, though they didn't scrape or prick him—yet. Sasha proceeded to kiss and nibble his way up Trace's leg, pausing at his ankle, taking his time to lick and nibble around Trace's knee, up to Trace's hip bone, completely ignoring his needy cock and heavy sac desperate for Sasha's attention. He knew Sasha had said he was here for Sasha's pleasure, but it was hard to remember when he was that close to his rock-hard and leaking dick.

Trace trembled and squirmed as Sasha licked and nipped the tender flesh at the juncture of hip and groin. Sasha moved back down to his thigh, licking a long swath of skin, causing goose bumps in his wake. He moaned but gasped a moment later when the sudden strike of Sasha's fangs sinking into his thigh replaced the tongue.

It should have hurt, he was sure of it. Having something plunge into your flesh should cause pain. This didn't, though. Instead it felt…. He didn't have the words or concept for it. Trace arched up on the bed, pushing his thigh against Sasha's mouth as he pulled the life-giving blood into himself. Trace knew there was a main artery there, but vampires could seal bite wounds, so he wasn't scared. The feeling, though, oh Baast!

Sasha didn't feed more than a moment or two, but Trace was trembling and wanted Sasha to bite him again.

"Mmm… delicious, mal'chik."

Trace whimpered, unable to form a coherent sentence to make his wishes known.

"Don't worry, I'm not done yet." He started all the way back down at the other foot, giving it the same treatment, licking, kissing, and nibbling his way up, ignoring the part of Trace that really needed Sasha's attention.

Eventually Sasha moved so he was kneeling beside Trace as he continued his torture up Trace's body. Nipping his fingers, biting down on Trace's wrist hard, but not enough to break the skin, teasing the soft skin at the crook of his elbow and licking and tugging on the fine hairs of his underarm.

Licking around each nipple but not giving either any real attention or pressure had Trace writhing and shoving his chest up into Sasha's face. "Please, Sir. Please…."

"You're here for my pleasure, mal'chik, not the other way around. You can make all the noise you want, but be still."

Trace fought his body's need to thrust and shift, and whimpers and moans fell nonstop from his lips as Sasha pinched one nipple hard, keeping the pressure on it as he licked and nibbled the other. The pressure increased as Sasha tugged on one at the same time he pierced the other with his fang, then sucked on it hard.

"Gonna come," Trace groaned. His body was on fire and his need was blinding. He wanted to bite Sasha. He needed to bite him at the point of release to seal the mate bond, but in his current position, there was no way! His lynx teeth had dropped and his claws were out, but that was all the shift a regular lynx shifter could do outside of a full shift. Oh Gods! "Please.... Wanna bite!"

Sasha licked his nipple once—the other still had the immense pressure pinching and pulling it—then raised his head. "You're going to come the moment I release your nipple."

"Bite. Mate."

His smile was feral, fangs extended, one tinged with blood still. The sight—not something he thought would ever excite him—only pushed Trace closer. "Yes."

Sasha rose up so his neck was even with Trace's mouth, pressed a light kiss to his lips, and then pushed his neck against his teeth at the same time he tugged one last time on the pinched nipple, then let go.

The pain and pleasure that twisted and fought for dominance in Trace's body set off a chain reaction that started in his nipple, raced down to his balls, up and down his spine, and out his cock. A second white heat spread throughout him, encompassing his entire being until his world was heat and strength and Sasha and love. He bit, the flavor of Sasha's blood as it rolled across his tongue for the first time, the taste and power coming from Sasha, merging into something he couldn't describe or name....

When he came to sometime later, Sasha had a cool, damp cloth and was cleaning Trace's chest.

"Welcome back, love."

"Um...."

Sasha chuckled. "Wow."

"Um-huh. I kinda hope it's not like that every time."

That only seemed to make Sasha laugh harder. When he calmed, he said, "No, I think that was because we both sent out our bonding at the same time, and I had you a little ramped up at the time."

"Yeah, just a bit." Trace tried to think, but his mind was still a bit floaty. "Wait, but you didn't... I mean, I came, but what about you? That's not right."

"Mal'chik, I am more than pleased with you, and if you must know, you satisfied me quite well." Sasha looked down, and Trace realized Sasha no longer had on his jeans, and Trace could scent Sasha's seed in the air. He also realized he was no longer in the restraints. Damn! He'd wanted to know what those thigh cuffs were for.

"Oh, *oh*!"

"Oh, indeed."

Chapter Twenty-Two

"Dimka, tell him I'm right." Trace flopped back in his chair, eyes squinted as he stared at his mate. "This is the best course of action at this point."

"Don't drag Dimka into this. I will not have you used as bait, Trace." Sasha all but vibrated in his seat as the four of them sat discussing the current standstill in finding the ones behind the attack.

Trace hadn't been attacked again, but he hadn't been alone either, so how would they get to him, tempt anyone wanting to come after him? No one would go after Sasha directly. That would be suicide, pure and simple. "How else would you suggest we draw them out? I refuse to be under close guard for the rest of my life, Sasha. It's not going to happen. I have things to do, a life, work. As do Dimka, Summer, and the guards they command. I understand that, as your consort, I will have to deal with some of the guard nonsense, but to this level? No."

"Sir," Dimka said, leaning forward. "He's right. Plus now that the bond is sealed on both sides, he should be stronger, and you should know his safety even better. We would never let anything happen, but things need to change."

"Your people are becoming more and more antsy too," Summer added. "It's not healthy for everyone to be so nervous, even within the walls of the coven. And with your uncle here, that won't change. You're letting him walk free as long as he doesn't leave the grounds. He keeps trying to stir people up against you. Well, more against Trace and the no-killing law you have in place, really. But it's the same thing."

"And he keeps trying to go after Tatiana," Trace tacked on. "She's been through enough, losing her lover, fleeing here while pregnant, giving up everything to make sure her unborn child is safe. Just because we're the only ones who know—well, and Jalin, of course—doesn't mean the others aren't picking up on the stress. Nor is any of it good for her."

"Ugh!" Sasha bellowed and threw his hands up. "You three are impossible. Fine, but bait doesn't mean actually alone, Trace. I will not lose you. They almost killed you the last time. Being my bonded, fated heart ought to help you some with your life span—you have mine now—but it won't stop them from ripping out your throat."

"Such a cheery fellow, you are." Trace scrunched his nose at Sasha. "I was thinking that since they attacked last time at a club, they likely followed me and waited until I was alone. They didn't want even the humans with the tribe around. Generic humans were okay for the initial contact, but otherwise no. So we need to have me get belligerent, publicly, and defy you. For me to go out *alone* and see if we can't get them to come out and play."

"I don't like this."

"Nor do we," Summer said. "But they—whoever *they* are—want to use him as a catalyst against you, both for the tribe and the coven, from what we pieced together before. I still say it's not Vlad, but to be sure, we won't let him or any of his people know anything other than what we feed them. He can think you can't control your fated heart. It won't hurt if he's not in on it for him to think that, as he already has that opinion."

"But how do we make sure Trace is safe if he's not properly guarded?" Sasha hopped up and began pacing. "I mean, bait means you have to stay back, so how do you make sure we can get there in time? That nothing goes wrong? That we don't lose him if they snatch him?"

"Did you know that the tribe's second, Vance, had tracking apps installed on all the tribe's cells? Not everyone has it activated—Alpha Keith won't force you to—but mine always is on. At any given time, Alpha Keith or Vance, his beta, could find me by my phone. And when all this started, Dimka put a tracker on my BMW, though he didn't tell me right away," he added, giving Dimka a playful glare.

Dimka grinned. "My prince said not to let anything bad happen to you. I'm going to do as he says, sorry."

"Yeah, you look so sorry. Not." Trace shook his head. "The point is, they would have to take me from the car and take my cell and leave it behind to make it where these two couldn't find me. Maybe. You still could, though," Trace added, looking back at Sasha. "As you proved the first time."

"And if they don't want to kidnap you, but kill you as they tried 'the first time'?"

"That's why I will be out in public, but not that cut off from one of you three or Keith and Van."

"Wait what? When did they get in the middle of this?" Sasha ground out. "No way am I endangering Keith. Jason would kill me if anything happened to his husband."

"I said both of them together, and Alpha Keith is a Chosen of Baast. He's not so easy to take on, Sasha. He, Vance, Chance, and Kelley have been training with some of Summer and Dimka's guards, so none of them should be all that susceptible to whoever is after me."

"You've been training the shifters to be vampire hunters?" Sasha asked, glaring between his guards.

Summer gave a tight nod and smile. "We have, sir. If you want Trace and Jason, as well as your nephews, safe, this is the best way. The lynx guards need to be able to handle more than humans and shifters. And while each of them is powerful in their own right, shifter versus vampire, vampire wins in a one-on-one fight."

Dimka smirked. "We've merely evened the odds a bit."

"I don't like it, but I will agree to your insane plan. However, nothing will go wrong."

"It's cute that you think a pronouncement will make it happen in a case like this. It won't, but things will still go right, simply because we plan ahead to make sure they do. Now relax. They're good at what they do, and I won't do anything I shouldn't when dealing with the nutcases. Now to tempt them."

"And how do you plan to do that, Trace?"

"He's going to storm out and go out clubbing to show you that you don't own him." Dimka shifted in his chair, not quite looking at Sasha. "I will have gone out for the night to check on Dr. Niko before this. Summer will ask you, publicly, if you want him to call me to go meet up with Trace. You will snap no and go do something else, declaring that if he won't listen to reason, he can have things his way for once and to hell with him the rest of the evening. Or something to that effect. If there's anyone here that is in on what's happening, they will relay the information, which will help us speed up things. I hope there's no point to the in-house acting, but there's too much at stake right now to chance it."

"Vlad had better not be in on this," Sasha ground out. The barely leashed violence sent a chill skittering up Trace's spine. He was certain he wanted nothing to do with whatever happened after the culprits were caught. Knowing Sasha was violent and lethal when needed was one thing, but seeing it…. Yeah, no. That was one thing he wanted no part of, thanks.

"For your sake, I hope not too."

SASHA HAD tried to force Trace to eat, but he couldn't. They were supposed to have a real date, but the need to mate the night before had hijacked that, and before they could replan it for the following evening, Summer and Dimka had approached him with the plan to draw out the ones behind the attack. Now he stood in his closet at the covenstead, dressed for a night out, hands shaking and breath coming too fast. Going out wasn't the problem. The idea of facing the ones who had bit and nearly killed him again was.

He wasn't sure how, but Sasha seemed to know Trace wasn't comfortable with biting thanks to those creatures. The bond hadn't worked that way with Ford—or the asshat had ignored the signs and his pain, which was just as likely. Still, the idea of Sasha biting his throat for feeding, even after the mating, the giving of himself, the bloodletting.... That, however... he couldn't stop the flashes from overtaking him if Sasha even teased his pulse points too hard there. He hated not being able to give that to Sasha—what kind of mate to a vampire couldn't let them feed the most common way? Ugh!

Thankfully Sasha didn't push or act bothered.

Now he needed to get it together and go have a temper fit before he went dancing. This wasn't his style, to lash out like they wanted, but it made perfect sense. Most of the vampires wouldn't know better, as they didn't deal with him on a normal basis before all this insanity began. Though he hated that it would look bad for Sasha in front of his people, Trace would simply have to find a way to fix things later.

For now....

Trace took a deep breath and squared his shoulders before he turned and strode out of the walk-in. He stopped long enough to gather up his bangles, bracelets, and rings, then his wallet and keys before he headed for the door. The smile he flashed Sasha was anemic at best, he was positive, but Sasha's wasn't any better, as they were both sick with nerves.

"You don't have to do this," Sasha whispered as he came up behind Trace and wrapped his strong arms around him. He pulled Trace to a stop and then tight against his hard body.

"Yes, I do. We do. I can't live like this for the rest of my life, nor can you. It might take a few nights, but I doubt they will wait all that long. The longer they take, the more likely whatever they're hoping for will fail, that you will figure it out. They can't afford to give you time. They shouldn't have tipped their hand how they did in the first place. That was either the sign of stupidity or overconfidence."

"Or both," Sasha agreed from behind, his head resting against Trace's shoulder. "I wish we had time for me to mark and taste you a bit before you went out. I hate the idea of them putting hand or fang on you."

"Just think of all the fun you can have reclaiming every inch of me after this is over," he murmured hoarsely. Damn, his dick perked up at the thought. He wanted Sasha all the time, and suggesting things like that wasn't helping him get out the door. What he wanted was to be at Sasha's feet, or on his hands and knees. Oh yeah, that would work nicely.

Sasha slid one hand around to cup Trace's cock and balls, squeezing firmly but not too tightly. "Be good, and maybe I'll remember where I put the key to the toy chest I have."

That wasn't a whimper. That totally was not a whimper that escaped him!

"Love the noises you make for me," Sasha purred, giving Trace another firm squeeze before he let go and stepped back. "For now you have to go yell at me and then storm out. Just remember I'll make you take back every word later."

Oh damn. He swallowed hard as he tried to remember how to speak. "Promise?"

"Mmm-hmm. Now go be a brat so I can teach you not to be one."

"Evil fang boy."

"That's *Sir* Evil Fang Boy to you."

Trace huffed out a laugh as he took hold of the doorknob. Once he had calmed, he focused on the drama of the night, ripped it open, and stormed out. "I don't fucking care what you want! I'm sick of being stuck here under lock and key like some damned damsel. I'm not a girl and I'm not one of your vampires!"

He continued out, throwing snide comments out as he went, grumbling if vampires got in his way. He tried not to be too rude to anyone, but he didn't allow any of them to bar his path out of the mansion either. When he hopped into his BMW and sped out of the drive, making sure to squeal the tires, he fought the urge to wince—he had never treated his car that way and hoped never to do so again. Still, if he was going to act the drama queen having a hissy fit, he figured he needed to do it right.

Trace didn't allow himself to drop the attitude even on the drive over, knowing there was a chance he might already have picked up the attention of whoever they were after. Honestly he hoped he had. He kept an eye on his speed, as he didn't want to attract the attention of the human police. That was one complication he did not need.

He had suggested he return to the same club the vampires attacked him in before, though he never wanted to set foot there again, but Dimka and Summer both said no. If it were them, they would suspect a trap. So he chose one of the other clubs he'd taken the humans in the tribe to over the preceding months. If they had been watching him as they claimed, they would know he'd been there before. The fact he went there now, when upset, would seem logical—he hoped.

It didn't take long to get inside; the bouncer knew him, and in no time he had a drink and was close to the dance floor, sipping his Coke with a cherry in it. It was the way he usually acted in the clubs when he went out with the others, only he didn't have the human mates to guard this time.

It took until the third night, Trace returning to his lynx tribal home— once even finding that weird bird scent again and sending word back to the council about it—not back to Sasha, before something changed.

"Looks like the prince isn't so good at keeping ahold of his pets," rumbled a voice that haunted Trace's dreams when Sasha wasn't there.

"Thought you were kept under lock and key, kitty boy." *Yep, and there's the psycho bitch now.*

"I thought you two left the area," Trace snapped. "Don't you know better than to stick around?"

The male moved behind him and wrapped his hands around Trace's wrists, squeezing so tight he imagined he could hear the bones grind. "Move it."

The female danced along against Trace, blocking what was happening from the others. It would look more like they had picked out a third for some fun, the way she kept rubbing against him.

"Not into little girls or psychos, so could you stop trying to maul me with your boobs?" *Please let Dimka and Summer be close!*

She whipped out one of her hands to wrap around his throat so fast he felt it there but never saw the movement. "Watch your mouth, you fuzzy sack of shit. You're just a means to an end. You only live as long as we need you. How comfortable you are is up to you, though, so be a good boy, and we won't have need to hurt you." She squeezed enough that he could still breathe but not speak. "Understood?"

He couldn't reply, but using her hold on him, she forced him to nod as they slipped out the back of the club.

"Don't play with the *puta, princesa*. We need to get him out of here. The last time your idiot cousin showed up and ruined everything. That's not going to happen again."

"Don't worry. I have the car right around the corner from the alleyway."

"Good."

Trace fought them as they shoved him down the alley farther away from the club. Dammit, when would his cavalry show up? *Any time would be good now, guys!*

Getting into the car was not on his to-do list. As the male tried to shove him into the backseat, Trace twisted and bucked, lashing out with his legs as best he could. He still couldn't scream, thanks to the bitch, but he could make it hard to hold him. He only worried they would tire of trying to control him and decide to kill him. The male wanted him alive, though—he didn't know why, but was thankful for the change in plans!—so he fought and hoped.

His vision went spotty as the female tightened her hold and yelled at him to stop kicking. There was ringing mixed in with both their voices. Then, before he completely blacked out, he heard Dimka and Sasha. Then the pressure let up on his throat, and while the world still swam and was covered in dark and light spots, it stopped trying to gray out completely.

CHAPTER TWENTY-THREE

SASHA PINNED Ivan, Tatiana's youngest brother, against the wall, blood pouring down his throat and chest where Sasha's fingers dug in enough to break the skin. "How dare you touch my fated heart! Are you *okhu`el?*"

"Let go of me," Ivan hissed in Russian.

"You are out of your fuckin' mind, boy. You dared to touch my fated heart again!"

"Sasha."

Summer's voice broke in to Sasha's rant. He snapped his head to the right and glared at his friend and guard. "What?"

"He's unconscious, sir. We have your cousin restrained and in the vehicle. Trace is in your car waiting. Let us take care of Ivan for now. You can interrogate him later. For now you need to clean up and take care of Trace."

Trace. Right. He released Ivan, who slumped to the filthy alley ground with a thump. Sasha looked at his hands, only then realizing how gruesome he had to look. "Dammit. Don't suppose you have any water or something? I need to clean up before I get to Trace, and my kit is in the car… which is where Trace is."

The rumbling chuckle from Summer was not appreciated, though the appearance of the pack from his trunk with water, wipes, and such was. It didn't take long for him to clean up, change his shirt, and put his things away. "Thanks, brat."

Summer smirked. "My pleasure, sir. Now go take care of your boy. I'll finish up things here. I'm glad they picked loudassed clubs and dirty alleyways. Makes things easier for us."

"Yes, much easier than it used to be, that's for sure. Just make sure there's nothing left of any camera feeds from back here."

"No worries. Go on, sir."

Sasha only paused long enough to make sure Dimka and Summer had both idiots removed and restrained before he climbed into his Hellcat, where Trace waited.

"Hon? Mal'chik?"

"I'm okay, Sasha. But can we get out of here, please? I'd really love to go back to our suite, take a scalding shower, change, and maybe never see either of them again. Yeah, that sounds about perfect right now. By the way, who the hell are they?"

"One is my cousin, Veronika. The other is Tatiana's youngest brother, Ivan. She's going to be livid when she finds out he was in on this. So is Vlad, for that matter."

Trace turned in his seat as much as he could and faced Sasha. "Does this mean your uncle is behind this?"

"Possibly, but I won't know until I find out from them what is going on. Considering how easily the two were caught, I'd say no. I can't believe my uncle would plan something this poorly. Ivan and Veronika, though…." Sasha shook his head. "Stupid, the both of them. Both are spoiled, entitled morons that wouldn't have half a brain if you put the two of them together. Well, maybe half. They did manage this long to pull this off, so I have to give them some credit. But still."

Trace slid one hand over, placed it on Sasha's thigh, and gave it a slight squeeze. "I just hope that this will be the end of it."

"Oh, it will be, if I have to hunt down every one of their associates personally. Seeing you at Ivan's mercy again…." No, that was not something Sasha could handle even contemplating, much less deal with the reality of again. "I'm not that strong, Trace."

They were both quiet, much to Sasha's relief, as they drove back to the covenstead. He wasn't looking forward to the coming "talk" with the two behind all this. Nor was he eager to confront his uncle, who would wish to plead for his daughter's life, Sasha was sure.

Treason only had one punishment.

They should be glad Sasha was willing to be merciful for Trace's sake, if for none other.

SASHA SAT in the large ornate chair in the main chamber of his mansion, Trace to his right in a comparable, though slightly less ostentatious version. If it were anywhere but the US, it would be his throne, though that's basically what it was. He hated it, though more for why he was there than for the chair itself. It was actually rather comfortable, as his mother had had it made for him for his coming of age, long before they knew how young he would be when he'd first have to sit on it to rule instead of to sit beside his parents.

Before him was his uncle, unbound, as they had found no evidence he had anything to do with the attacks or the reason behind them. Indeed, what he'd so far learned painted his uncle—and Vlad's older son, Karl—as victims as well. Much to his annoyance. His current rant, however, was wearing out what sympathy he'd earned himself.

"Vlad, do shut up," Sasha snapped.

Vlad inhaled sharply as if to begin another long string of noise, but Sasha held up his hand to stop him. "Did you know what your daughter, along with her fiancé, Ivan, was planning? The family you yourself tried to browbeat me into marrying into when you arrived."

"No! I do not agree with you bonding with your animal," Vlad spat, gesturing at Trace, "but I would never agree with attacking him. Especially not with what tribe he's a part of. That's… that's suicide," he sputtered.

"Agreed. It's also stupid." Sasha reached over to run a hand down Trace's arm, though he didn't touch skin. Trace hadn't done so well with direct contact since Sasha's interrogation of his prisoners. Trace hadn't witnessed any of it, but he seemed to know, on an instinctive level, perhaps, that Sasha's methods were painful for the ones being questioned. Had they been more forthcoming with their answers, it wouldn't have required so much pain… or blood. That was their mistake. Both had acquired the delusion that Sasha working with and bonding a shifter somehow made him weak. Veronika even went so far as to claim his love for Jason, his best friend and a human whom he considered part of his family, made him soft. They both were disabused of those ideas.

"Beyond that, touching of another's fated heart is a serious crime. Treason when it's the royal prince's heart, as Trace is my royal consort. You know the punishment for that." He made sure there was no question in his tone when he glared down at his uncle.

"But she's your cousin! It's that boy. That Ivan!"

"It doesn't matter, and no, it wasn't. I spoke to each of them separately. She knew exactly what she was doing. She planned for you to be dealt with as well so she and lover boy could rule my coven. As if those loyal to me would ever allow themselves to be subjugated under the likes of them." Sasha snorted before he continued, "His father has been contacted and informed of both the charges and the sentence."

Trace spoke for the first time since they had entered the room. "My liege? Will you allow his father and mother the chance to say good-bye? Or at least his sister, Princess Tatiana?"

"Royal Prince Yuri, no. Princess Tatiana and, once Princess Zamira arrives shortly, they may say their good-byes."

"Why not Yuri?" Vlad demanded.

"You know full well he is not welcome here, *Uncle.* I will not allow him near Princess Tatiana or near my royal consort. Besides, he did not request to visit, only to know when I planned to marry his daughter." *Disgusting male!* "Now if you have nothing further, I have things to do. I only provided you this formality as a courtesy, as you are family. Once things are over, you will not return to any lands or territories that are mine until—or unless—invited. Am I understood? That goes for your only child as well."

"I have two children."

"You have an only child… that you have publicly claimed, at the least."

Vlad ground his teeth but said nothing else.

It took only a short time for Sasha to be in the main corridor with Trace again, though Trace still wouldn't touch Sasha's skin, but at least he was beside him and still talking.

"Thank you for allowing them to say good-bye, Sasha."

"I'm not heartless like some would like to claim. I would like to focus on something else for now, however."

"Hmm? What's that?"

"You. You are my royal consort, and as such, you will have a certain amount of power and sway at times. You are a trained diplomat, mal'chik, so all this shouldn't be too difficult for you to deal with, other than the fangs part," Sasha added with a wink.

Trace gave an anemic smile, but at least he offered the attempt. It gave Sasha hope they would be okay once Trace came to terms with everything. "I know I am, and I suppose I do need to begin learning what you will require of me here. Will I still be able to serve my role for Alpha Keith and the Glacier Rim Tribe?"

"I don't need an assistant, hon. I want a partner. Don't worry. You will be able to still have your job. You'll have an assistant, remember? He'll help you keep track of any appointments or plans that will require you be here. He will simply need you to let him know your schedule there so he can keep it all straight." Sasha paused and turned to smile at Trace. "Even

I make sure that I don't allow this to be all I am. I run a very successful hospital where I make sure the humans are well cared for, remember?"

"True. Thank you. So where are we going?"

"I thought I ought to show you around the parts of the mansion that you haven't gotten to see yet."

"Oh?" Trace perked up. "What parts would that be?"

He took Trace's elbow and tugged him through a door one down from his own office, then flipped on the lights. "What do you think?"

TRACE BLINKED as he stepped into the large office and stared. "Um, what is it?"

"It's your office for when you're here. I know you have your office there on the tribe land and all, but that doesn't do you a bit of good when you're at the covenstead. So I had this set up for you. You are, of course, free to redecorate as you wish, just as you are in your rooms." Sasha's voice cracked on the last word.

Looking around, Trace took in the large wood desk, the delicate inkwells, the assorted pens, both fancy ballpoint and nibbed quill, and he noticed there were even the items needed for making wax seals on letters and parchments. Along with plush carpeting over hardwood floors, gorgeous draperies, plush chairs, and plump throw pillows and cushions, there were also many little Egyptian flairs scattered about the room. Near the desk there was a small shrine to Baast set up along the wall. One wall was nothing but bookshelves, part of which were already full of books. He wandered over, trailing his fingers over the spines, noting the names of such things as histories of the coven or the Tolstoi family specifically, or particular other families of note, or areas around the Americas and the world, and a few he couldn't read even with his extensive language knowledge.

"I have more I'd like to add, and I see there's certainly plenty of space."

"Add whatever you wish, just remember that this, while it is your office and does have locks, is a part of the more public part of the estate. Others will be in here, so don't place anything here you wouldn't wish others to see."

"I know you're older and *wiser*, but I'm really not an idiot, Sasha."

"That's not what I meant, mal'chik."

"I know." He looked around again, knowing it was killing Sasha, the not knowing what Trace thought of the room. "Other than adding a few personal touches and maybe a little feline flair," he finally said as he turned toward Sasha, "it's perfect. Thank you."

Sasha held his hand out and waited. Trace sighed but slipped his bare hand into Sasha's, shivering as their skin met.

"Does my touch truly revolt you so?"

"No, it's not that. It's…. I don't know how to explain it." Trace paused as he tried to order his rampaging thoughts into some kind of useful order. "Can we…?" He gestured toward one of the chairs and tugged Sasha over, waiting for him to sit before he moved back over to the door. He locked it, then walked slowly to first stand before Sasha, then kneel in front of him. He worked to control his breathing as he stared at his hands.

"I was afraid of you for a long time, but I'm not now. Not really. I'm having a hard time reconciling the fears, the brutality I've witnessed, the executions you plan, with the passionate, protective, loving male I know you are. You have shown me nothing but care, loyalty, and l-l-love since I was attacked. Before that in a lot of ways, really. I don't understand it, but then, I don't understand how you managed to remove a mating bite or to win over Duncan either." Trace paused as he caught his breath and fought for control of his body—neither trembling nor shifting right then seemed like a good idea. Well, not if he wanted to get this all out.

"When I heard about Tatiana, I was so angry, but I was scared too. I still couldn't admit to even myself that I wanted you. That my lynx was right about you, but the idea that someone else would get to bond with you made me ill and near violent all at the same time. I know it doesn't make any sense—it doesn't always to me, and it's my head—but that doesn't change anything. Still, to know you are capable of being this… violent, brutal killer is hard to handle. The part of me that lived through F-Ford—" He gulped as he forced himself to continue. "—whispers that you could turn that on me if I were to displease you enough. That you could succeed where he didn't in killing me."

Sasha leaned forward. "Mal'chick, I swear to you, I would never abuse you. I would never use my powers or abilities against you like that. I would never use your love against you."

"The rest of me knows that, truly. It's not that I don't. It's that I'm still dealing with a past that may never fully leave me. Can you handle that? Can you accept that, even years, decades, who knows how long down the road, something could cause a trigger, and I might pull away or panic for things that *he* did? It's one of the sad side effects that those who choose to love people who have been battered and abused have to deal with. Even as your fated heart, even though you managed to remove his mating mark, I still went through all that. I still almost died in a relationship. It's why I give so much to domestic abuse shelters and such. Why I wish more places would understand that men can be victims, not just the abusers."

"Hon, Trace, I don't care about that as long as I know why you are having trouble. I'll always be willing to help you. As for the shelters, maybe we can work to help more? For now let's focus on getting through the current issues. You look tired, and we have more visitors coming."

"True. Tatiana's mother is coming. That should be… interesting. She said there's a ritual she wants to do before her mother and entourage leave that has to do with you taking her in?"

"Yes, it's very old and rarely done now. It will make her my little sister, sort of. Adoptive and sheltered, basically. It's not long or elaborate, but it is something taken quite seriously and will likely shake her mother horribly. I'm not sure how she will take it."

"After things settle we should discuss the ritual you need to do with me, the public one, and then you need to think about choosing your surrogate so you can begin filling your home with laughter and love."

Sasha sat back and stared at Trace with his eyes wide and his mouth slightly open. "You mean…. Um." He cleared his throat. "You mean the royal consort wedding and for us to have a child?"

Trace nodded. It was time Sasha had the family he had obviously always wanted. "Just, um, let's get through all this first, yes?"

"Yes, my sweet boy. Yes."

CHAPTER TWENTY-FOUR

TRACE LOOKED around the small clearing and smiled. The blanket was spread, the basket set out with small finger foods he knew Sasha liked and could eat. He'd also thrown in a few items he hoped he could actually manage to have Sasha use. Now he just had to hope he could convince his nerves and the fear set on loop to shut the hell up long enough to allow him this—to allow them this.

"Sir?" Vasily said as he stepped into view.

"You don't have to call me that. Trace is fine."

"It's not proper, sir. I'm your servant. Prince Sasha gave me to you to serve. Now I have the last of the items you wanted set. Carlton, one of Kelley's men, has made sure this part of the forest is cleared of all shifters, and I'm the only vampire other than the doctor on your tribe's land. Until Prince Sasha arrives, that is. Do you need anything else?"

He couldn't help the sigh that slipped out. Sasha had told him he'd have to have a valet of sorts, though he hadn't really expected to get one—he'd thought the male was only to be his assistant. Try telling that to Vasily. Trace still wasn't sure what to do with the boy. He was a trainer and a diplomat for the lynx council, but now he was a royal consort to a vampire prince and had a vampire boy who followed him around to help him all the time. And of all valets to get, he found it almost funny Sasha had to give him Vasily—the boy he had rescued from Vlad that first night, whose excellent training had been wasted under Vlad's abuse.

"No, things look perfect. Thank you. I've told you that I don't want anyone within hearing range. That includes you."

"Yes, sir. I know. I will return to the main compound and await you."

"Thanks."

Vasily smiled softly. "You will be with the prince, so I won't worry. Thank you for trusting me with your preparations. If you need nothing further?"

"Have a good night, Vasily."

"You as well, sir."

Moments later Trace sat on a fallen tree trunk, alone. He took a few deep breaths as he worked to keep his nerves at bay and his mind focused on what he intended for the evening.

When he heard the slight fluttering of leaves that didn't quite match the wind, he smiled. "Hello, Sasha."

Sasha moved up behind Trace, slipping one arm around his chest and nuzzling his ear. His cool breath tickled Trace's neck when he spoke. "Mmm, hello, mal'chik. Will you tell me what all this is about yet?"

"Us. More." Trace pushed back into Sasha's touches and hummed. "I wanted to bring you here to try to…." *Dammit, why is it so hard to get the words out?* He'd practiced a whole little explanation a few different ways, but when Sasha was there, nope, the words wouldn't come. Words were what his life entailed, but when he needed them most, nothing!

"Do you need me to step back, love?"

"No! No, I want more. More with you." Trace closed his eyes tight and fought to push the words out. "T-take me… here… please."

Sasha twitched against him but didn't otherwise move right away. "Stand up."

Trace stood but didn't turn. Sasha plastered himself to Trace's back, somehow lining himself up so his now-rigid cock pressed against Trace's ass, even though he was much shorter than Trace. Trace wanted to know if he stood on the log or if he was using his abilities, but couldn't make himself look.

As Trace debated what Sasha was doing, Sasha continued to nibble and kiss up and down Trace's neck, sucking Trace's ear before following the edge and whorl with the tip of his tongue, making Trace tremble and whimper. "Take you how, mal'chik? How far do you want me to go?" he rasped.

I want you to fuck me and feed on me! Why can't I say that? I want to say it. Goddess dammit!

Instead of speaking, Trace rubbed his butt against Sasha's hard dick and pushed his neck into Sasha's nips, hoping he would get the idea.

"Mmm… you want me to fill you, mal'chik? Because if you don't stop rubbing against me like that, that's exactly what's going to happen."

Trace let out a deliberate moan and rubbed himself against Sasha more.

"I know it's hard for you to give up control, Trace. To give up your body even to me, but there are times when letting someone else have control—" Sasha maneuvered Trace over to the blanket.

"—is what we both need. Please, Sir," Trace finished for him.

"You give yourself freely? This isn't like before, Trace. I cannot do this with you if there is even a touch of another's influence in this."

"After...." Trace paused and took a couple of breaths as he worked to find the right words. "After what happened with F-Ford, I didn't think anyone could want me. Love me. Not really. But even more, the idea of trusting someone with me, with my body again... still terrifies me. However, I know you will never betray my faith in you. You can be violent and a killer, but are also loyal, loving, gentle, and—" Trace finally turned to face Sasha. He slowly lowered first to one knee, then the other, before he bent and kissed the top of each foot. He then sat back up and bowed his head. "—I believe in our bond and in you."

"I love you too, Trace." Sasha ran his fingers through Trace's hair a few times, the touch as soothing as it was inflaming. "Will you give yourself to me now?"

"Yes. I already gave you the mating bite. Now I want... I want to give you me."

Sasha stepped back. "Then strip and lie on the blanket facedown."

Trace stood and quickly divested himself of his clothing, pausing when he went to slip off his boxer briefs to watch Sasha remove his clothes. All that pale olive skin coming into view took his breath away, as did seeing the defined muscles of Sasha's pecs and abs. He wanted to spend hours licking every inch of his mate. When Sasha removed his slacks, taking his underclothes with them, his long, thick cock bounced up and smacked his belly, leaving a wet spot. Trace wanted to taste so badly he mewed.

Sasha gazed up at him and smirked. "I meant all of it, Trace. Hurry up. Naked and on the blanket."

Losing the last bit of clothing and lying down on his already painfully hard dick wasn't the most comfortable thing in the world, but he did as commanded, hoping Sasha would hurry.

"Lube?"

"Basket."

He watched Sasha reach into the basket and retrieve the lube, his cock bobbing with each motion. Then he was back. He slipped his arms around Trace, pressing his chest to Trace's back, rubbing his body against Trace, amping Trace's need higher. Trace turned his head and parted his lips in invitation. Sasha pressed his lips to Trace's, delving as deep as the odd angle would allow. It wasn't graceful, but it was hot, and with Sasha grinding against him at the same time, he had Trace ready to come already.

Sasha pulled back and trailed kisses down Trace's neck, then his shoulder and along his spine. Sasha slid his way down Trace's back, trailing licks and kisses as he went. When he reached the small of Trace's back, he pulled away slightly but then began to run his hands up and down Trace's sides and ass, pulling Trace's cheeks apart on every other pass.

Eventually Sasha stopped as he held Trace's cheeks apart and blew cool air across Trace's hole before licking from balls to the top of his crack. He did that a few times before he focused in on licking and nibbling along Trace's taint, lightly scoring it with his fang. When the wet heat returned to focus on his hole, Trace mewled and scrabbled his hands in the blanket, no longer able to control his body or his sounds. He'd tried to be good, but it felt too… he couldn't think of a good word with Sasha touching him… to be still and quiet.

"Love your sounds, mal'chik. Want to hear you." Sasha returned to his sensual torture, licking and stabbing with his tongue around and into Trace's hole, using his fingers—or so he assumed—to pull him apart more and delve deeper.

"Oh, um, Goddess! Sasha, Sir… can't… gonna… stop, please…. Cherry!"

Sasha froze, then moved away, leaving Trace panting and trembling on the blanket, overheated yet suddenly cold. He immediately appeared at Trace's side, petting his head, and asked softly, "Mal'chik, what's wrong, love? Are you hurt?"

"N-no. I was going to come if you didn't stop. I want you to penetrate me, not to just get me off like you always did before. Please."

"Oh, Trace." Sasha continued his petting, his voice still soft, though it now carried a wry edge. "I wasn't going to quit because you came. You will be more relaxed and looser if you're not so ramped up, though."

"Oh. Um, sorry?"

"Do you really want me to stop, or should that have been more of a lemon kind of thing?"

Trace knew he was bright red but nodded anyway. "Sorry? Please don't leave or stop." *Please don't be disappointed in me!*

Sasha bent down and took Trace's lips in a kiss that began gentle, teasing his lips open, light touches to his tongue as if saying hello, before taking over and turning Trace's insides to mush. By the time Sasha pulled back, all he could think was *more* and *want*.

Sasha moved back behind Trace again, this time trailing his nails up and down Trace's back. The pressure was not enough to hurt, but the light sting quickly brought him back to the needy edge he'd been skating on. He couldn't believe Sasha wanted to touch his back, the scars there—and they were still there, though slightly lessened. Still, the fact Sasha was kissing and touching them diminished the ghosts attached to them.

The sharp sting to his asscheek brought his focus back to Sasha and what was happening now. "What?"

"I told you I don't share. I'm the only one here with you."

"Yes, Sir. It's the scars on my back. The touching and scratching… feels like you're making them yours somehow."

"They are mine, mal'chik." Sasha scratched across Trace's back, digging in harder, the sting bordering on pain before he drew back and Trace heard the pop of the lube bottle. A moment later the cool liquid hit his oversensitized hole. Sasha used one finger to push inside, the breach startling in its abruptness. "So hot, Gods, but you feel so good. So tight. Damn, but you're going to feel so perfect wrapped around me, love…." As Sasha continued his litany of dirty words and praise, he added more fingers to his thrusts and twists. He returned his other hand to Trace's back, again digging into the flesh there, claiming the scars. "These are my marks on you. My markings, mal'chik. Every part of you is mine."

"Please, Sir. You, not your fingers. I need you."

"You'll have me. I promise."

He shook with anticipation. When Sasha nudged his opening, Trace tensed, the ghosts of his past pressing in on him, but Sasha wasn't Ford!

"It's me, mal'chik. Let me in, love."

Sasha. It was Sasha, and he would never abuse Trace. Trace knew that!

As Sasha slipped inside Trace, Trace stretched damn near to the limit. Sasha was big. He knew that already, but it felt as though he'd gotten even bigger somehow. Sasha pressed in farther, and Trace couldn't hold in the words any longer. "Fuckin' hell! You're going to split me in two."

Sasha stopped moving.

"Don't you stop. Please don't stop," Trace begged.

"Never want to hurt you the wrong way, Trace." Sasha moved again until he pressed his hips against Sasha's butt. He then stretched out over Trace, his lesser weight wonderful as he sandwiched Trace between himself and the ground.

"Oh Goddess," Trace groaned. His trapped cock throbbed, but even that only added to the moment. He was glad Sasha had chosen not to make him come first after all.

He clenched around Sasha, loving how Sasha gasped and trembled slightly. Sasha pulled almost all the way out before slowly sliding back in. The shudder that went through Trace made Sasha chuckle.

"Like that, huh?"

"Yes, Sir."

"Good. Me too."

Sasha set a slow pace, driving Trace insane. He touched and kissed and licked Trace as he leisurely fucked him, never speeding up or letting Trace move. A nonstop plethora of mewls, whines, and pleading came from Trace, but Sasha ignored him, seeming to not be in any hurry to finish. Trace, on the other hand, was a trembling mess.

"Oh my Gods, please, Sir. Please… I need…."

"You do beg so pretty." Sasha pulled Trace up to his hands and knees, never pulling out. He then wrapped his hand around Trace's cock and stroked base to tip with sure, steady strokes, just how he liked it. It only took a moment or two before Trace shook so hard he collapsed to his forearms. "Come for me, mal'chik. Give me your pleasure."

White-hot light shot up and down his spine, then from his spine to his balls, the pressure building until the demand from Sasha and his own body combined to tip him over the edge. Bliss shot out his cock even as sound blasted from his very core. Sasha sped up his thrusts but never stopped, drawing every tremor, every shot, every overwhelming moment of perfection out until Trace could only feel—nothing but Sasha existed.

"That's it," Sasha whispered, and Trace felt him kiss his shoulder as he slowly pulled out of his body.

"No, you…."

"Shh… I'm not done with you, love."

Sasha rolled Trace over onto his back, then carefully slipped back inside his now-hyperaware yet sated body. They both shuddered when Sasha was fully seated this time, and Sasha smiled down at Trace, his fangs descended.

Trace licked his lips as he focused on Sasha's fangs, then tipped his head to the side to bare his neck fully.

"By all the Gods, you are beyond perfect, mal'chik."

Sasha bent Trace in half as he set a pounding rhythm, driving into Trace. He dipped his head and took Trace's mouth, delving deep, letting his fang nick Trace's lip as they kissed. Trace wanted to show Sasha just how much he accepted the vampire, the fact Sasha was a vampire, so when he pulled back at one point, Trace curled up enough to press his lips to Sasha's, then flicked his tongue out to first touch and then trail up one fang. Sasha moaned and thrust harder, digging his fingers into Trace's hips hard enough that he knew, even with his healing being as good as it was, he'd have lingering bruising—and he relished the thought.

When Sasha shifted position again, he hit Trace's special spot, making him yell. With a decidedly wicked grin, Sasha continued to pound that spot until the pressure overwhelmed Trace. The jolt of pleasure shot through him only a moment before Sasha plunged his fangs into his throat, making him come completely apart. He cried, whimpered, and mewled so loudly he could probably be heard all the way back to the main compound, but he couldn't be made to care right then. The sweetness of joining with Sasha drowned out his past, his fears, everything. In that moment they were all there was.

Eventually they managed to pull apart and clean up. They even ate the picnic Trace had packed in the basket—there was more than lube in the basket, after all. They didn't return to the main compound of the tribe land and then to the covenstead until almost morning.

What awaited them couldn't even take the bliss from Trace.

"Prince Sasha," Jalin said once they were inside the mansion. "Princess Tatiana's mother has arrived."

CHAPTER TWENTY-FIVE

"Preparations are ready, but are you, Tatiana?" Sasha asked as he, Trace, and Tatiana sat in her receiving room. "You don't have to do it this way. You can stay here indefinitely under our protection. You know that."

"I do know that, my prince, my friend, but this is how I want things. I do not wish to be connected to that coven or to that lineage any longer. You of all people know of the cruelty and crimes common among my so-called family and of what my father has done to me." She whispered the last as she laid her hands over her abdomen. "The only one I will miss of my blood is my mother, but that cannot be helped."

"Then I welcome you with open arms."

"As do I," Trace added. "I have also spoken with Alpha Keith and his mate, Jason. They welcome you as well as long as you will abide by Sasha's laws. You will get to meet them both soon."

Sasha turned to look at his beloved and smiled, proud of how far he'd come in such a short time.

"Ever the diplomat, kind shifter." Tatiana smiled. "I have no problem following his rules." She paused and looked around. They were alone—she had sent even her loyal servants away. "My child's father was human, so I do not behave as the rest of them do. There are others who are like me, my servants, and those I keep as part of my regular entourage. I have always been *high maintenance* for a reason. I demand to pick who I wish to have close and drive out those who do not align with my views. Still, they do not know what I'm to do shortly, not exactly, so how they react to the news should tell me quickly if I have any routing I need to do."

"I will notify Jalin so he can have them watched for that reason as well. Just to make sure, as we do not want any close to you to be loyal to those you are leaving."

"No. And thank you. Thank you both for this. My child needs to grow up in a place where safety and peace are not only allowed, but encouraged."

Trace cocked his head as he blinked, then stared at her a moment. "Tatiana? When Vlad first brought you, I hated you on principle. Now

I am so thankful because that same arrival means we can offer you the sanctuary and time to heal you need that was once given to me. If you require anything, please let me know. But for now—" He looked at his watch and frowned. "If you are really going to do this, we need to go. It's time."

SASHA SAT on his royal chair he still refused to call a throne—even though that's what Trace insisted upon calling it—with Trace in his similar one beside him. The higher-ranking members of the coven were gathered, but unlike usual, the rest of the coven had been invited, and they had opened up the gallery for them. Part of the walls could slide out and down to overlap to allow more to witness the goings-on when deemed appropriate. Such as now.

"Princess Tatiana, please come forth," Sasha called, his voice ringing throughout the gathered court. He deliberately did not glance at her mother, who was in attendance. Sasha wasn't certain having her there was necessary, but Tatiana said it would have more impact on his people to see the visual separation and joining, so he allowed it. He still worried about how it would affect the female. She had just lost a son and now was losing a daughter. This had to be.... He didn't have the word, even in his thoughts.

Princess Tatiana entered the room from the other end clad in nothing but the underdress she would normally never allow any to see her in, other than her servants—the ones helping her dress—or a bed partner helping her out of it in the midst of passion. Over it she wore a rich bloodred cloak that lightly brushed the ground, with a hood that covered her lustrous hair. It was held closed at the throat with the crest of her birth house. She wore no shoes or jewelry other than her family signet ring.

Slowly she approached Sasha and Trace until she reached the agreed-upon stopping point, then waited.

"You have come to us and requested not only sanctuary, but have chosen to forsake your birth coven and status. You have asked to become my little sister, my ward. And that your offspring be considered part of my house, though not in line to rule. Is this true and of your own free will?"

She looked up and met his gaze, a fierceness there he'd never seen before. "I have and do, my liege. I pledge my life and what will become my line to you, your house, and your line. You have always been my friend. Let me now be like a little sister to you. I know I can never replace the one you lost, but a family can have more than one of each."

"Nadia always loved you, you know. She would be pleased to know you are one of us now, my sweet. Remove the last of that which was born to you but that is not of your heart, and come to me."

Tatiana pulled off the ring and dropped it where she stood, then unclasped the cloak. It slithered to the floor, revealing the shift she wore.

She stepped forward, but before she could reach Sasha, her mother jumped up and cried, "Tatiana, don't do this! Please, child. I beg you. Your father won't forgive this. I can't lose you too."

Tatiana turned and looked at her mother, tears clinging to her lashes. "You sat back as he beat me. As he murdered my lover. As he belittled and tortured me for no other reason than the fact I was born female. But you wish me to return to him because you don't want to lose me? You lost me long ago, Mother. I'm sorry, but Sasha and Trace are my family now. They love and accept me *and* my child for who and what we are. Go home to your monster, if that is your wish, or fall on Prince Tolstoi's mercy and ask for asylum and see if he will help you find a place away from the monster you married. Royal Consort Trace might even speak on your behalf, as he has a weakness for battered spouses. For now I have an oath to make and a family to complete."

With that Tatiana turned away from her mother and stepped toward Sasha, only stopping when she was directly in front of him. She then took a knee. He held out his right hand and placed it on her head. Trace stood and moved close enough that he could do the same. "This is your wish?" they asked in unison.

"Aleksandr Tolstoi, Royal Prince of the Konstantin Coven. Royal Consort Trace Wilson Tolstoi. Please accept this most humble servant into your home and into your lives."

"Arise, Princess Tatiana Tolstoi, and greet your people. They are eager to meet their new princess."

As soon as she stood, Sasha draped a new cloak—this one a light jade trimmed in silver, the clasp Sasha's coven crest—around her. Trace knelt and helped her into a pair of matching slippers. Before she could move away from them and out to the crowd as planned, a commotion started by one of the doors. A moment later Jason stepped through with

Keith stopping at the doorway, which he took up most of, him being in his Chosen of Baast form.

"Prince Tolstoi, P-Princess Tolstoi, my apologies for being late. I have a g-gift for the new princess, if that is allowed," Jason said. Sasha was impressed he managed to get all that out in such a public venue with so little stuttering.

Tatiana looked at Sasha, a question clear in her eyes. She hadn't been formally introduced to Jason, though she knew a great deal about him. "Of course. You're family, hon."

He approached, a medium-sized pale blue silk-wrapped box in his hands. "The Glacier R-Rim Tribe would like to welcome the n-newest member of the Tolstoi f-family," Jason said as he held out the box to Tatiana.

"Thank you, Master Jason. And thank you, Alpha Keith," she added, nodding in his direction.

Keith took a step forward, his voice a deep, resonating growl in this form. "As you are truly a Tolstoi now, we welcome you. This gift is one of welcome and hope between us. It was Jason's idea and design, though he had to have help with the execution—he's an IT geek, not a woodsmith. We hope it pleases you."

She took the box and carefully removed the silk, handing it to one of her servants. Sasha knew she would use it for something later, just as he would have. A gift was a gift, but the silk was part of the gift. Finding a good use for it was just as important as whatever was inside. The box was simple, but within was a nesting doll! One unlike any he'd ever seen—a cute trick, since they were a Russian tradition and he had many in his coven who crafted and sold them all over the world.

Her gasp could be heard throughout the area, if the looks and craning necks were anything to go by. She immediately took it over to one of the tables along the side and set the large doll down. Tatiana took her time looking it over. Sasha, with Trace following behind him, joined her. Jason, to the side, smiled as Keith stepped up behind him—still in his Chosen form.

"It's beautiful. This is... this is Sasha's father."

"It is. I already had a couple of these contracted when I found out about today, so you get the first one," Jason whispered as he looked at Sasha but didn't meet his gaze. "I hope you don't mind."

"Of course not, hon. Thank you." Turning back to Tatiana, he added, "Well, you going to open it?"

"I was admiring the detail and artistry, but of course." She opened the first level, and the next one was Sasha's mother. Sasha had to fight the urge to take the doll and demand to get to keep the set himself. Beneath that was Sasha; then Nadia, Sasha's sister; then Chosen of Baast, Alpha Orin, Nadia's fated heart. After that was Trace in his lynx form. Sasha would recognize a generic lynx from Trace, though Tatiana might not.

"That's Trace," Sasha murmured.

"I figured it was him. I was positive. I've only seen him a couple of times in his lynx skin, but thought it had to be him. It's so well done! Particularly as it's not done by Russians."

Beneath that one was a doll that wasn't as detailed but was obviously meant to be Tatiana. And inside that one was the traditional baby.

"How did you manage to add me to the doll so quickly? It takes a lot of time and work to make these. You can't just up and change them at the last minute."

Jason smirked. "You can if you had designed the inside to hold more than the single baby. Changing it so it held a new doll and one baby was doable. Unfortunately the Tatiana doll isn't as fancy as the others. My artist said he can keep working on it to finish fancying it up after this, if you will allow, but I didn't want to miss welcoming you to the family."

"You're not in the doll," Tatiana said, a slight frown on her face. She turned to Sasha and asked, "Why isn't he?"

"I didn't order the doll. You'd have to ask him why."

She turned back to Jason. "Why aren't you part of the doll? Everyone knows you're family to Sasha."

"Not official like you and Trace are. He's my best friend, and my grandfather asked him to watch over me when he passed, but he didn't adopt me or marry me or anything."

Her brows pulled together as she seemed to think about what Jason said, but Sasha was too busy not liking what Jason implied to worry about her take on it. Jason didn't think Sasha considered him "really" part of his family? How could the man miss something so simple?

Trace touched Sasha's lower back, pulling him out of his musings. "Sasha, right now Tatiana needs to go mingle. We need to make sure everything goes as planned, and did you notice that Jalin had Dimka walk Tatiana's now ex-mother, I guess, out already? Jason's comment and your displeasure with it can wait."

"Thank you, and you're right. Tatiana," Sasha said a little louder. "It's time for you to go meet your coven as their new princess. I know you've met many of them already, but it's different now."

"I know, and thanks. You have no idea what this means to me." She kissed both his cheeks before she did the same to Trace. Tatiana then turned and walked out on Jalin's arm into the crowd that awaited her. Before the party that would follow, she would be able to go dress properly, but meeting a few of the higher-ranked members first would help her, as this was her home now. Thankfully she was already popular and well-known. She had visited off and on since they were small children.

"SASHA, THANK you for tonight." Tatiana hugged him tight, tears still occasionally streaking down her cheeks. They were in his and Trace's sitting room this time, having seen Jason and Keith out and escaped the rest of the coven already. "But there is something I am not happy with."

Sasha sat back in his chair as she retook hers. Trace settled on the plush rug beside Sasha's chair by his own choice, as had become his norm. "And what is that? I thought things went quite well. I know it had to be hard to hear and respond to your mother, but—"

"No, not her. What bothers me is what your human, Jason, said, and the fact he's not in the doll. He doesn't truly believe you see him as family? Or that his station is lacking? I don't understand, and by the scowl on your face at the time, you seemed disturbed by what he said as well."

Taking a deep breath and holding it a moment, he tried to sort his thoughts and failed. "I'm not entirely sure why he's relegated himself to not as important, but I don't like it."

"You're a prince, Sasha," Trace said, looking up at Sasha, one hand curled around his calf. "He's merely a human, a common, stuttering geek that you became friends with as a side effect of a promise to his grandfather."

"He is my friend and family. He was my only family before I met you, Trace. How can you relegate him to of no import like that?" Sasha snapped.

"I'm not. I'm telling you what he said earlier, just rearranged a little. He doesn't doubt that you're his friend or that he can count on you. He knows you would do anything for him and for Sean and Zeke. But see himself as worthy of being true family of a royal prince? He still turns red and stutters over being sought out for judgments or advice as the alpha mate. Put him behind a computer and he could rule the world. Otherwise he still feels that he's a little lacking outside his circle of friends, family, and loved ones."

"And I don't notice him act like that anymore because… I fall into that category of people he's comfortable with, so he doesn't act the same as he does with outsiders, right?" Sasha didn't like what Trace said, nor did he know how to fix it.

"So adopt him like you did me," Tatiana said.

Sasha snapped his gaze up to meet hers. "What?"

"Make him your little brother in truth, not just *like* family, but *be* family." She smiled softly at him. "I know it's a bit unconventional to adopt a human, but he wouldn't be in line or anything, so that wouldn't be a problem, and it could be seen by the coven as a stronger tie to the coven with the tribe. You have bonded to their trainer, and your brother would be married to their alpha. Instant covenant."

"But he's human, not a vampire," Trace argued. "Won't that be an issue? I don't know the laws yet, but the fact he's not shifter or vampire, I would imagine, would be a problem."

"That might be true," Sasha mumbled, considering the idea. Making Jason an official member of his family was something he wanted with a deep craving now that it had been presented to him. But what were the laws? And what would Jason say? "I will have to research that immediately, but no matter what they say, there is the issue of if he would agree." Would Alpha Keith try to dissuade him or encourage him? "If there's one thing I can say with certainty with Jason, it's that I never know what he'll decide."

"Then I will help you research," Trace said, his voice cautious but determined. "This is something important to you, but also something that could impact my tribe. Just promise you won't do anything he doesn't agree to do. Please."

Sasha cupped Trace's chin and lifted it so their gazes met. "I would never do anything against him, mal'chik. Just as I never would against you."

CHAPTER TWENTY-SIX

THREE DAYS later Trace was settled in his new office, staring at his new guard, trying hard to figure out what in Baast's name to do with him. "Let me get this straight. Dimka has permanently assigned you to me, but you chose to come early and introduce yourself instead of waiting for either him or Sasha to make the proper intros and explanations?"

The male was maybe six feet before you added in the thickness of his badass boots—then he was probably about six four? Then there were the leather pants, the leather corset-like jacket, and the streaks in his jet-black hair that were all in a deep crimson. He had at least a dozen piercings going up his right ear, with only three in his left... plus an industrial and one in the little nub part, two in his right eyebrow, one in his left nostril, and one in the center of his plump bottom lip. There were also numerous leather strips at his neck and wrists, various rings on his fingers, and his nails were done in black and tipped in crimson. All in all the effect was stunning but would stand out most anywhere but a club—and even in many clubs.

"Dimka was summoned by Prince Sasha on our way here. I chose to continue. It's not proper for you to have to borrow guards all the time, and as I've been assigned to you, I thought to introduce myself."

Trace sighed as he sat back in his chair. The male did have a point. Now that he'd accepted being Royal Consort Trace—and he was certain he heard capital letters when the words were spoken by any but Vlad—he had to accept the rest of the stuff that came with the station too. Ugh. "Fine. Can we start with a name? Oh, and while I don't personally object to how you're dressed, you do realize that you will not blend in most places I would go in the human parts of the world, right?"

"I am Sloane, and yes, I know. You are a bit conservative, but I can tone down my attire when needed." His lips curled down slightly as he touched the series of earrings on his right ear. "But, um, how plain will you require me to appear to be? Sir."

He couldn't help but smile at the butch little bad boy worried about losing his metal. "Just tone down the clothing when needed enough to do your job, and I'll be happy. I know full well that vampires have the ability to blend no matter what they're wearing, to a point. When they want to. How else would they hunt—those that kill humans, that is?"

"True. Thank you. Dressing as you are is just not me."

"Understood. Oh, and you don't need to call me 'sir.' Trace is fine."

Sloane smirked. "Take it up with Dimka, sir."

"Damn vampires and your annoying formality."

"Right, and you shifters don't have your own? You're a trainer and work for their council, right? I'm pretty sure you have a long list of things you have to follow as well."

"Just because you're right on this point doesn't mean I like you right now." They both chuckled. "But fine. I will speak to Dimka. Not like I've won that battle with Vasily either."

"And you won't with him. The serving class, especially those who are chosen to be valets and all, would never dream of not giving you the respect your station deserves. Especially now that he serves you after being rescued from his... previous owner."

Trace didn't like the idea but understood the principle. Still, though....

Sloane continued, unaware of Trace's thought, "If you befriend him, maybe after a few centuries he might, once in a while, use your name in private... maybe. You may be a shifter and commoner-born, but you are now our royal consort. The fated heart to our beloved Prince Sasha." Sloane ran his hands up the back of his close-cropped hair—the top and front much longer and styled to frame his striking face—before dropping them to his sides again. "As much as he likes to run off and play with his hospital and hang out with his human brother-friend, he is effectively our king, and you his eternal consort. Not all outside our coven will see you that way because you are a lynx, but for us, that's the beginning and end of it. I will protect you with everything I have, not because I know you—yet—but because I am loyal to my prince and will not allow anything to harm that which finally brings him happiness and peace."

"The whole medieval thing is still strange to me. Feels like I ought to be at a Ren faire or something."

Sloane shrugged. "It's just how our society functions. I know humans moved away from this for the most part, but it works, and honestly, I can't imagine trying to make vampires function where we had to vote and have a new leader every four years. We would tear ourselves apart within a decade. As bad as some princes and princesses are, this is still the best system for us."

"Just as tribes are for lynx. I get it. It's just the bowing and the sirs and the wishing to help me get dressed and all… it's…."

"Weird? Yeah, I wouldn't like that either. But that's what you get for bonding with our prince," Sloane said with a laugh. He sobered as he stared down at Trace's desk. "Mind if I ask what you're working on? I know it's none of my business, but you had an odd expression on your face when I came in."

"You'll hear soon enough anyway, so I don't see why not. These are the plans for two houses that will serve as shelters for battered partners, no matter the gender of the victim or the abuser. Domestic violence shelters. One for shifters and one for vampires."

"I remember during the ritual Princess Tatiana mentioning you having a soft spot for those in need. I didn't know she meant to this level. This will likely make you a target of those not wishing to lose their spouse, mate, whatever."

"I don't really care. The fact an abuser doesn't want to lose the one they hurt isn't my problem. Besides—" Trace flashed a grin at Sloane. "—isn't that why I have you? To keep all the big and bad from getting to me?"

Sloane stood a little taller. "True, and a worthy cause. Humans, sadly, do not own the market on such crimes. But why do you care so much?"

Trace took a deep breath as he looked Sloane over and made a decision. Talking about his past wasn't something he did, to the point he'd never let himself heal and had nearly cost himself Sasha. Setting up and opening the two programs was good, but maybe he should start answering that question? "Until Duncan saved me years ago, I refused to ask for help, so I can understand where each one of those I hope to help is coming from. Hell, even after he rescued me, I didn't want it, and without him, I would have died—quite literally, unfortunately."

Sloane twitched as he stared at Trace. "He what? What do you mean?" he asked, his voice dropping to a low rumble. "And who is Duncan?"

"This is not show-and-tell time, Sloane. I have no interest in getting into my full history, thank you. But I will say that my projects are personal, as I've been there, nearly didn't make it out the other side. The hard part for me, once they are running, will be not tracking down the pieces of filth that tore away at the body, heart, and soul of each of those we hope to help, and returning the pain they gave as sharply and as viciously as I can."

Sloane took a step back, his pale amber eyes going wide. "Dayum! Remind me not to piss you off."

"Never abuse your partner and we're fine," Trace snapped, then took a deep breath, working hard to calm himself. "Sorry. It's nothing against you or any vampire. It wouldn't matter what race you are. I hate abusers. Period."

"Got it, sir. I do as well." He smirked. "My mistress would be pissed if I even thought of hitting her."

Trace chuckled. "Ahh…. Maybe I'll get to meet her sometime. For now I need to finish up here and then get ready. Since you're here I guess that means you get to go out with us tonight."

"Dimka said you were going out but didn't tell me where or with who."

"The why is the more fun part. Tatiana and I are taking Jason out, but he thinks he and I are taking her out as a welcome-to-the-area kind of thing. So she can get a taste of Seattle from a human and lynx shifter point of view, not just where vampires tend to hang out."

"And why are you two tricking the human? Prince Sasha won't like anything that upsets Jason. We've guarded him since he was a babe, though he never let us teach the human's exes a lesson when they hurt him."

"I've heard the same grumble from Summer and Dimka and kind of agree with you, though I understand staying out of it. But it has to do with him saying he's not really family. Tatiana wants to work on showing him that he's wrong. On… including him in things that only family would be."

"But he is family, even though he doesn't have fangs. We all know that. Just as none here would ever harm him or would have approached him before he knew of us. He belongs to Sasha as much as you do, only in a different way."

"Now to make him understand that…."

"I LOVE this place, Jason," Tatiana said as she looked out the large window of the restaurant on the wharf as they enjoyed a very late dinner. "I've never been to any place like this before."

It was a little hole-in-the-wall eatery that had the best fish and chips Trace had ever had—and that included when he'd gone to England many years ago.

"That's because you're used to b-being treated as a p-princess, not a person, hon," Jason said, then smiled.

It had taken a little to get him to relax, but he had, for the most part. Now if they could get him comfortable with Tatiana enough to lose the stuttering….

Trace popped a fry into his mouth and chewed, enjoying watching the two as they adjusted to one another. He scanned the area and noted Sloane at one table in the corner and Summer at another. Eventually Tatiana would end up with her own guard, but for now it seemed Summer was acting as hers. He didn't see anyone for Jason, though he had a feeling there was at least one of the tribe's guards outside as well.

"She'll learn, Jason. Give her time. Sasha's not had her long. Though"—he winked at Tatiana—"you could help with that. You know, show her how to get along and be 'normal.' You and Sasha hung out for years doing all kinds of human stuff and all, so I'm sure you'd be a great big-brother type for her to learn from."

Jason frowned as he looked up from his Coke. "Um, she has a big b-brother already. Sasha. R-Remember?"

Cocking his head to side, Trace blinked at Jason. "She can't have more than one? Once upon a time, I had three brothers and two sisters, so I know families can have more than two children."

"Well, of course they can. Not everyone is an only child like I am, but—" He leaned in and lowered his voice. "—a vampire princess does not need a human acting like a big brother for her. She has a proper adoptive brother already. Someone that would be up to her—" He rolled one hand as he frowned. "—standards."

A fry thumped Jason dead center in his forehead, startling him and drawing Trace's attention. "What the hell?"

Tatiana sat smirking at Jason, brushing salt off her fingers, somehow still appearing completely prim and proper even in her surroundings. "Thank you for your attention, boys."

"Wha— Why did you do th-that?" Jason snapped.

Trace sat back, trying not to laugh at how indignant his friend looked.

"Shouldn't I get a say in if I think you're up to my—how did you put it? Oh yes, *standards*."

"Well, yes, but I don't get what his point is."

"No, you don't want to get it. Are you really that hung up on Sasha being a prince? I thought, from what he's told me about you, that you got over that and you two were as close as brothers, and that he was uncle and godfather to your son. Surely that means what Trace said made sense."

"Jason?" When Jason turned and met Trace's gaze, he continued. "If Sean calls Sasha uncle, then wouldn't Tatiana be Sean's aunt? Think about it carefully."

"Well… um…." He took a deep breath and pulled out his cell. After typing on it a few moments and getting a reply, he frowned. "It would seem the answer is yes, she is."

Trace couldn't help but laugh at the disgruntled look on Jason's face and the bright smile on Tatiana's. "So says your husband? Yes?"

"Yes. He said, and I quote, 'Of course she is. Your brother adopted her. Duh.'" He flopped back in his seat. "What the hell? How did I get a brother and a sister, and when? Why didn't anyone tell me this?"

"You're a wonderful friend and human, but you're also a bit of a ditz, Jason. You've called Sasha that for years. You told me he was family when we first met. How is it you didn't know he was family, then?"

"Well, yeah, family, but *like* family and *really* family isn't the same thing."

Tatiana looked over to Trace and asked, "Is it a human thing to not accept being part of a built family?"

He didn't know, as he had never fully accepted Duncan basically adopting him after his family had turned on him with the whole Ford issue. "No, I think it has to do with not seeing yourself as worthy of being included. Dammit, I need to talk to Duncan now."

They both stared at him. "Huh?"

"What?"

"Nothing. Look, the point, Jason, is that yes, you're family. You are my brother-in-law, whatever terminology vampires have that matches up. She's my sister-in-law. Same deal. As much as I fought being Sasha's mate, I have not only a mate but a family now, and that includes you, Sean, Alpha Keith… which is weird to think about—"

Just then Jason and Trace's cells rang.

Trace pulled his out and slid the little green phone icon to the right. "Hello."

"This is Taylor." *Why on earth is Keith's sister calling me?* "The doctors just called a meeting, so we're calling everyone in now. Get here as soon as you can. They have news about Sean."

Trace's heart raced, and the reinforced case to his phone groaned as he clutched it tight. "Is he okay?"

"As far as I know, yes. Just get here soon, 'kay? I don't know what they want to say, but even Sasha, Dimka, and Summer are specifically being called. Hurry."

She clicked off, leaving Trace to stare down at the now-dark cell. What the hell?

"Um…? Jason?" Trace looked over, and Jason looked twice as worried as Trace thought he probably did, though that only seemed right, as Sean was his son. "Come on. I'll drive."

They all grabbed their personal items, stood, and headed for the door, their guards quickly joining them, Summer in the lead, Sloane bringing up the rear. As they headed across the crosswalk, a car ran the red light and sideswiped a huge truck, throwing it into their path. Trace didn't have time to do more than shove Tatiana forward before the truck collided. Pain radiated out from his right side as he went airborne until he impacted something and the world went dark.

CHAPTER TWENTY-SEVEN

SASHA PACED the currently cramped living room of Jason and Keith's usually spacious home, unsure what to do or where to turn. They had stabilized Trace on the drive to Jason's—thank the Goddess—and he was already healing, though slowly. He was curled up in lynx form on a small bed they'd brought in, with tubes pumping him full of things to help.

However, Jason wasn't waking up. Even when they gave him transfusions of Keith's blood, they couldn't get Jason's injuries under control. Taylor, a nurse in the human world, was helping the two doctors as they tried to heal Jason, but when Sasha looked over at Keith again, he feared he would lose his friend and brother. Keith was unraveling, not that Sasha felt much better.

"Someone do something!" he bellowed when Jason cried out again.

"We're trying, sir," Dr. Niko replied as he and Dr. Lili kept working. "His internal organs are trying to shut down due to the extreme amount of damage."

"You should have taken him to the human hospital. He's human."

"Respectfully, shut up. The only reason he's made it this long is the alpha's blood. The human hospital couldn't have given him that. Now leave us be unless you plan to bring him over." Niko didn't pause, just kept working, checking and doing who knew what.

Keith continued to make little wounded-animal sounds anytime Jason came to enough to make any kind of noise. Otherwise he paced and looked ill—pretty much matching what Sasha was doing. His only deviation was to check on Trace, who thankfully rested peacefully.

Hours later, though he had no clue how many—time had lost meaning by that point—Dr. Niko came over and asked to speak to Keith and Sasha.

"What's going on? How's he doing?" Keith asked, his skin pale, his face wet, and his eyes bloodshot.

"We've done everything we can, even with the extra healing Keith's blood can provide. It's simply not enough. Jason has slipped into a coma, and his body is slowly continuing to lose ground. I'm sorry. If I had access to organs to transplant and we could be certain they would even be compatible…. But it would require multiple, plus there's damage to the heart and the spinal cord."

Sasha barely managed to catch Keith as he crumbled at the doctor's words. Of course a part of him wanted to join Keith on the floor, but someone had to take care of Jason's husband.

"There has to be something," Sasha pleaded, not caring how he sounded. "He can't die. He's too young!"

"My liege, at this point, there is only one way to save your human, but as he's bound to a shifter…."

Keith snapped his head up at the same time a chorus of "what?" rang through the room.

"That's not my choice to make." *Oh Goddess, I think I'm going to be sick!* He'd never made a vampire, though he knew how and had the right, as the prince. But the only human he'd ever offered to bring over turned him down—Jason's grandfather.

"It's also against the treaty pact you made with the tribe," Taylor snapped even as Sasha's head spun. Like he cared about the damn pact! Jason and Trace were all he cared about, and Trace was healing just fine, no thanks to the truck that had hit both males. But Jason… no, no, no!

Somehow, though he couldn't have said how, Sasha wound up sitting on the floor beside Keith, his head in his hands, his wet hands. At some point a fuzzy face pushed into his lap, letting out a soft mew. He pulled his hands away and looked down to see Trace. Trace had hobbled over and was wiggling into his lap.

"Sweetheart, you shouldn't be moving around so much. You need to heal."

"Mew, huff."

"Yeah, I still don't speak kitty, hon."

A moment later a very naked and battered Trace was sprawled across Sasha's lap. Trace curled against Sasha, nuzzling his face against the crook of Sasha's neck.

Tatiana had stayed out of the way the entire time but now came over with a blanket and tucked it around Trace. "Um, I don't mean to be rude, but as I'm new here, I don't know what pact you spoke of earlier. Why can't Sasha save his brother and your alpha mate? The last Chosen had a vampire for a mate, so it's not against your laws, surely. Nadia was bonded to Orin, after all."

"He promised not to," Taylor said. "Though...." She swallowed hard as she stared down at her brother, who looked more like a broken toy than the powerful Chosen of Baast alpha he was. "That was meant in the seduce-unwitting-humans-into-becoming-vampires way, not the save-one-of-our-own kind of way."

Sasha shook his head slowly. "He can't make that choice in his condition, and I don't have that right. He doesn't even truly see me as family."

"But Keith could," she countered.

Blinking slowly, Sasha turned to face Keith. Could he ask Keith to make that choice for Jason, and did they still have enough time? Jason was still alive—barely. He could still bring him over.... But would Jason forgive him? Would Keith be able to accept Jason changed like that? "Keith?"

"Daddy?" a sleepy voice said from the other side of the room.

Oh Gods! Sean had slipped out of his room and gotten past the guards.

Keith beat them all to Sean, scooping up his son and crushing him to his chest. His bloodshot eyes met Sasha's as he pressed Sean's head against his chest. "Save my mate. Please." He then buried his face in Sean's hair.

"Keith?" Taylor asked.

"Where's Papa?" Sean mumbled.

Taylor slumped her shoulders, but she turned to Sasha and nodded. He didn't immediately go to Jason, though, turning to Trace instead. He was the other concern. Sasha had promised not to do anything without Jason's permission, and this would be with Keith's, not Jason's. "Trace?"

"It's not my call to make."

"I made you a promise, love, so yes, it is."

"No, it's not. It's my alpha's. Jason is his mate. If he is willing to accept you turning his mate, then that is the only voice that matters. Go save our alpha mate."

Sasha swallowed hard, terrified of the possible outcome. He would get to keep Jason—something that thrilled him more than anyone but possibly Keith would understand—but he wasn't sure how Trace would see him after. His fated heart still had issues with some of Sasha's more vampiric nature at times, though things were much better.

He held the words of faith and love Trace had said not so long ago to his heart, then crossed his emotional fingers and called for everyone to leave except Keith. Trace refused to leave as well... of course. At least he stayed on the other side of the room.

Sasha lifted the battered and broken man he had come to love as one of his own into his arms. He took in his features and how his heart struggled to keep beating. "I'm so sorry, my friend, my brother. I hope you will forgive me my weakness, but I can't let you go. *We* can't let you go."

He then bent and sank his fangs into Jason's throat, draining him until he was at the very cusp before laying him back down.

"Keith, come here and assist. I want you to use your claw to make the cuts used to allow my blood to return Jason's life and health to him."

Sasha guided Keith in making the cuts over Jason's heart, deep enough to let Sasha's blood enter his heart. Once they were made, Sasha cut his wrist and let the blood soak the wound and enter Jason's chest cavity. The blood moved sluggishly at first, but as it continued to pour into him, the flow strengthened, and eventually the cuts closed on their own. When that happened, Sasha brought his wrist to his mouth to close the slit he'd had to reopen more than once.

Suddenly Jason seized and then stopped moving, even his heart. Keith, being a shifter with advanced hearing, noticed and panicked. It took Sasha time to calm him, but eventually he got physical control of him, and after repeating, "This is just part of the process, he'll be fine," Keith calmed enough to release him.

"He's dead," Keith whispered.

"No, not really. Think of it more as, um… a reset."

"How long?" Trace asked as he finally approached. "How long will Jason be 'not dead' like this?"

"I need to take him to the covenstead. He will awaken at sunset, starving. But he will still be Jason, just like I'm Sasha. He'll need a little extra care to adjust, but he will be okay and be able to return to his life here. We will both have to claim him, Keith. I can't have a rogue vampire, especially one I brought over, running around in my territory and not have him officially be a part of my coven."

"Mine," Keith growled as he glared at Sasha.

"Ours, actually. But he's always been that, just in different ways. The only thing that changes is he will need blood once in a while, and he has official membership in both our clubs now."

"And his life span."

"True," Sasha said and shrugged. "But then, as you're bonded to him, it does the same to yours. As Tatiana said: it's like when my sister bonded to Orin. But this time no one will hunt my family and take them from me." He wouldn't let that happen again. This time the lynx would have their immortal Chosen and vampire alpha mate, and he would have his family intact!

"You can't take him," Keith countered as if the last part hadn't been said.

"I have to, Keith. Your tribe isn't set up to handle a fledgling awakening. It's like when a teen vampire first comes into their fangs and abilities… other vampires are needed, or someone could be killed. You can come to the mansion, but we need to leave." He wasn't going to get into how young he'd been when his powers first appeared or that Jason was likely to be a little "more" because of being sired by him. Not right then at least.

"But Sean…."

"Can come. He'll just have to stay away from Jason until we make sure he's stable. It usually doesn't take long for the hunger to settle. The fact he's a brought over instead of one that's matured might change things a little. We'll see."

"I…. Trace?" Keith looked from Jason's body to Trace with wide, pleading eyes.

"I'll go with you and make sure Sean is cared for, Alpha. But you made this choice for Jason. You have to see it through now."

Keith nodded and gently wrapped Jason up as if he were sleeping and lifted him into his arms. He then walked out to his car, ignoring everyone.

Sasha turned to Trace. "Please get Sean and whatever you think they will need from here. It might be a couple of days. And… thank you." With that he followed Keith outside. He waited at his car, unable to process what had just happened. Jason, Trace, the turning, the pain, and dammit, he still didn't know what the doctors had wanted in the first place.

JASON SAT in one chair, and Keith stood beside him holding Sean as Trace watched the room fill with the others Sasha had invited to the meeting. It took a week, but Jason was stable, and Keith and Sasha had decided it was time to bring everyone together with the doctors again. This time they were meeting in Sasha and Trace's sitting room at the covenstead. Sasha sat in his overstuffed leather chair with Trace at his feet—by his choice. Sasha was a little surprised at the choice, considering some of the additional visitors that day, but he would never deny Trace anything. Both doctors, the guards, Taylor, Tatiana, Duncan, and of course Vance, Chance, and Kelley were there. The room had never had so many people in it, not that Trace had seen, and it wasn't really the right size, as it was a bit cramped. But it was private and secure.

"Thank you for all coming, and I do apologize for the unusual setting," Sasha said, nodding to the lynx. Trace smiled and curled a hand around Sasha's ankle. "Since Jason has been staying here, I thought it easier to meet here, and I know everyone is eager to hear what the doctors have to say. Niko. Petronia."

Dr. Niko gave a short bow and stepped forward. "Thank you. We have more we'd like to work on, but we believe we've found the key to why your son can shift, Alpha Keith. You fed Jason your blood and were...." He flicked his gaze to Sean for a moment. "Intimate with him just before he sired Sean, yes?"

Keith nodded. "Yes, you know that already."

"And that wasn't the only time you gave him blood. We believe that the theory Trace put forward is correct. The trials we've run back that what's in your blood should have just enough effect on your mate to temporarily count. It's difficult to explain without a blend of magical and medical terminology."

Dr. Lili added, "What it means is that for a short time, Jason had enough of what makes us shifters running in his system to let Sean be a shifter. Well, to be enough shifter to shift. He's not pure shifter, but he can shift, and being the bit he got through Jason carried the tag of a Chosen, he will still be powerful when he matures, we believe. Possibly be an alpha, in truth."

"That part we won't know until he's older, though," Niko said, his brows drawn together. "We also can't guarantee if it will help non-Chosen who mate with humans have shifter children instead of human ones."

"Though it might." Lili seemed just as frustrated as Niko. Huh, guess neither liked not knowing things.

"But that means Sean is healthy and safe shifting?" Jason asked.

"Yes. There is no reason we can find not to let him act as a normal, healthy lynx kit."

Sean let out a little whoop. "Yay! No more doctors? I get to play with Zeke and the others and be me?"

"Yes, sweetheart," Keith said, hugging Sean. "You can go back to just being a normal little kid. No more doctors all the time."

Sean wiggled so much Keith ended up putting him down. They all watched as he ran around the room acting like the hyper little kid he was.

"Is there a way to know for certain if these findings will help other mixed couples?" Duncan asked from the far side of the group. Until he spoke Trace had forgotten he was there.

"Without test subjects, not really," Lili replied. "With what you are being a mix of genetic and magic, it's more than just pure science that has to be taken into account for any research. I'm sorry, sir."

"No need for sorrys. We can take the results back to the council as a whole and decide how to go from here. If it proves to help, we might need to find a way to let the wolves know. I know they suffer the same limitation." Duncan frowned. "We don't have the best relations with them in most areas. As you and your tribe do here, Alpha Keith, perhaps in time you may again be called upon."

Keith looked up from Sean, all smiles. "If that proves to be true for all lynx, I'd be happy to speak to the wolf alpha and let him know so he can try to find out if it is for them as well. The Hunters are good people."

BY THE time the meeting broke up, Trace was nearly bouncing out of his fur, and his fur wasn't even out. He'd asked Duncan to stay behind. Now he awaited Sasha's return, as Sasha'd chosen to walk the others out of the mansion—Sasha carried a sleeping Sean curled up in his arms.

"What's up, Trace?" Duncan asked while they waited. They were sitting in the same area they had been in for the meeting.

"I'll explain once Sasha is back. But until then, how are you? I know you need to get back to Toronto and the council lands soon."

Duncan nodded, his lips curling up slightly. "I do. It will be good to get back to things, though I will miss you. I've not been able to see you as much as I'd hoped while I was here, but keeping Lili on task was too important, and you working things out with your mate was even more so for you."

"I am sorry for that. You could have visited. Even though you're part of the council, Sasha has given you leave to visit anytime I am here. The guards know this. I've also spoken to Sloane, my personal guard, so he knows who you are and will never bar you from anywhere I am." Trace truly missed seeing Duncan all the time, though they did e-mail and visit on the phone often. Ever since he'd moved to Seattle, away from the council lands, he'd seen less and less of his mentor and adoptive father.

"I know, son. But you needed time with your mate. I can't tell you how happy I am that you've finally claimed him and that things are working out for you. He'll be a good mate for you, even if he is lacking proper fur."

"There's nothing wrong with my fur. My fated heart just wears it for me, that's all," Sasha said from the doorway.

Trace hopped up and hurried over. "You're back."

Sasha slipped an arm around Trace's back and pulled him into a hug. "You knew I wouldn't be gone long. What's wrong, mal'chik? Why are you so worried?"

Taking a deep breath, pulling the scent of Sasha into his lungs and holding it there a minute, Trace forced himself to settle and release Sasha. He stepped back and slid his right hand down Sasha's left arm until he reached his hand, then entwined their fingers. "Come here. With me. Please."

Brows scrunched, Sasha nodded slowly and squeezed Trace's hand once. "Of course, mal'chik."

Trace led Sasha over to where Duncan sat, the male watching Trace with wide, concerned eyes. "Trace? Son? What's going on?"

Trace stopped in front of Duncan and took a couple of deep breaths. "Um…." He turned to Sasha. "Sir, I'd like you to officially meet my… my real father. The one of my heart." Trace heard Duncan's gasp but ignored it, knowing if he didn't get it all out at once, he wouldn't get the rest out at all. "Duncan. D-Dad." Goddess, he'd never called Duncan that outside his own head before. He hoped Duncan was happy with it, but he didn't look up to meet either male's gaze. He couldn't. "I'd like you to meet my mate. Not just my fated mate, but my real mate."

Sasha wrapped his arm around Trace's waist again, holding him tight. "Love you too, mal'chik."

Duncan cleared his throat. "Dad?"

"You've been more a father to me, more family to me than any by blood ever were. You call me son, and I know you've referred to me as your pseudoadoptive son. So, um, yes. If you please."

"Of course I please. Nothing would please me more. Just one question before I can welcome Sasha."

"Yes?"

"Do you love him? Not just did you give him the bite, but did you open your heart to him too?"

Trace finally looked up, meeting Sasha's gaze. "Yes, sir. I love him. And I know he loves me. It took nearly losing everything and then some to see what was in front of me, but I do now. And I'm never letting him go again."

"Nor am I, mal'chik. Nor am I."

EPILOGUE

"So," Liam Hunter, the alpha of the local wolf shifter pack, said as he stepped up with two young male wolf shifters in their human skins at his heels. He had others with him, but the others hung back or were part of the security detail. "What is all this about and to what do we owe the... pleasure of the vampire prince's attention tonight?"

"For two reasons. First, to formally reintroduce Jason as Jason Tolstoi Skyler and Trace as Trace Tolstoi. Secondly, and more importantly, we are here because we have possibly important information about mating and children for mixed couples," Keith replied, Jason at his side. Liam's reaction to Jason no longer being human had been a bit comical—at least in Sasha's opinion. The double take had been cute; the turning to Sasha and asking if it had been a trade since he'd mated a lynx, not so much. No other comments had been made, though, so Keith pressed on as planned. "Depending on if your wolf-human couples produce shifter or human children, of course."

That got Liam's attention.

"Excuse me?"

What got Sasha's attention was the sudden scent rolling from one of the two males with the alpha. The problem was, Sasha wasn't certain which one it came from—they were too close together, and both were standing too rigidly to tell which might be reacting to someone. He thought it was the new male, not Caleb Hunter—Liam's younger son. The problem was, Sasha didn't know who the other boy was. The pack sometimes took in other pack's sons to train, which could explain his placement at the alpha son's side. He hoped it was that and not that the male was supposed to be something important to Caleb. Of course, he'd heard Caleb was straight, so that ought to mean there was no possibility of anything between the two. He hoped he remembered right.

The two alphas continued to discuss the news about how to possibly help mixed couples, which Sasha was honestly happy for them over, though it had nothing to do with him. Early on Sasha noted Liam's nostrils flare and concern flit across his face for a moment but he quickly schooled his face and continued with the discussion, not missing a beat. Sasha however, scanned the group gathered, hoping to find who the match to the wolf might be, but couldn't place the mate. Lynx didn't give off the same mating scent to call their mate that wolves did. And whoever it was did a bang-up job of not letting anything show. Dammit!

So one of the young male wolf shifters and he presumed one of the lynx shifters, as he didn't think it could be one of his vampires. Fated hearts were so rare, and with him having found his, he wouldn't have believed another close to him would be so blessed so quickly. He could but hope, though.

"What about the vampires? What are they doing here?" Liam asked, drawing Sasha's attention back to the conversation.

"Which ones?" Keith asked, his tone hard.

"Prince Sasha of the Konstantin Coven, not your mate. We have no issue with Jason being here. He may have fangs and strange eating habits now, but he's still viewed as a lynx, just as he was when human."

"And he is, thank you. As for Prince Sasha, he is here because it was partly through his help we discovered the information about how to help our mixed couples as we just relayed to you. Also, he's Jason's brother."

Sasha stepped forward. "Besides, with all the extra vampires in the area, thanks to Trace's and my bonding ritual tomorrow, it's also for your protection and safety that we are here. Our visitors are all bound by my rules and laws, but just to keep them honest, I felt it best to accompany my family here. Besides, Trace is going to explode if I don't let him share our news with the tribe soon, so we had to come to where they would be."

Liam frowned. "You think we can't protect ourselves from your kind?"

"I believe that you ought not to have to, Alpha. They are here in my territory because of the bonding ceremony tomorrow. But that means we all have to deal with the influx of outsiders. I have excellent guards and warriors, but most covens are not like mine, as we all know. It is no slight to you that I wish to make sure that my visitors behave, good wolf."

"And with both alphas in one spot, some might be tempted to take advantage," Keith added.

"Exactly."

"That's all f-fine and dandy," Jason interrupted. "What I want to know is what's Trace's news. Sasha said there was something and Trace is nearly b-bouncing."

Trace laughed lightly. "Let's make sure Alpha Keith is ready for us to move to the announcement portion of the evening and then I will tell you our news."

"As I'm going to have our pack healer get with the doctors that have been working on the children issues for the tribe, I'm interested now in your news. Since we have a pact with your coven—and we recognize you, Trace, as being a part of both the tribe and the coven, so don't even go there, boy—any big news of yours might be important for us to know as well."

"That was actually why we wanted to wait until tonight to share, so both tribe and pack could be told together."

"So, out with it, Trace," Keith rumbled, his brows rising as he smirked down at Trace, his arms folded across his chest. Liam mimicked his stance—Sasha wondered if they realized they matched as they stared down at Trace.

Trace beamed as he pressed against Sasha's side. Sasha slipped an arm around Trace's waist, but couldn't give him more physical shelter, as Trace was taller—dammit. "Jason, Keith, you know how some within the coven have been pushing for Sasha to have an heir, and how some outside the area have been grumbling about Sasha taking a male for a consort for that very reason? Or that's been one of the excuses, at least."

"Y-yes, of course." Jason stepped closer, his face darkening. "That's why you chose a s-surrogate finally, though I still don't like that others believe it's their place to butt into your lives like that."

"Jason, hon, it's okay. You know I want children. I just wanted to have them once I'd found a partner so any child I had could be raised like I was, as a child of love, not merely as an heir with duty and obligation as my only function."

"Exactly. That's the way to do things."

"I know. Relax."

"But what has that to do with things? You chose the surrogate. Surely that appeased them."

Trace sighed loudly and mock glared at Jason. "The news is that—" Trace's expression flipped from scowl to brightest grin, his voice rising slightly as he continued. "—Dr. Niko confirmed that she is with child, Jason. Sasha will finally have the heir the coven is so worried about him having, and we will have our first child to spoil and teach and love."

Before he registered the movement, Sasha found himself scooped up in Jason's arms. "That's wonderful! I'm so happy for you, hon. I can't believe you're going to be a daddy!" Jason hugged him tight.

Sasha laughed, returning the embrace. "*We* will be fathers. The child is Trace's child as much as he or she is mine. The fact I own a hospital and keep in touch with human science and insist my personal physician is so well trained is no coincidence." He winked. "The child will be ours, in both heart and genetics, *and* you and Keith will be uncles. Again."

Jason let out a whoop, and everyone laughed as Sasha wrapped his arms around Trace, happier than he thought he could or would ever be.

"I love you, mal'chik," he whispered.

"And I you," Trace replied.

TEMPESTE O'RILEY is an out-and-proud pansexual genderfluid person whose best friend growing up had the courage to do what they couldn't—defy the hate and come out. He has been their hero ever since.

Tempe is a hopeless romantic who loves strong relationships and happily-ever-afters. Though they love writing M/M—they have done many things in their life—writing has always drawn them back (no matter what else life has thrown their way). They count their friends, family, and Muse as their greatest blessings in life. They currently live in Wisconsin with their children, reading, writing, and enjoying life.

Tempe is also a proud PAN member of Romance Writers of America®, WisRWA, Fantasy, Futuristic, and Paranormal Romance Writers RWA, the Paranormal Romance Guild, and Rainbow Romance Writers. Tempe's preferred pronouns are they/them/their/theirs/themselves. To learn more about Tempeste and their writing, visit tempesteoriley.com. You can also visit them on Facebook, Twitter, or join Tempeste's Temptations Facebook group for all kinds previews, news, fun, and more.

WHISKERS
of a
Chance

TEMPESTE O'RILEY

Chain of Fate: Book One

Jason Grant runs his own IT business from home, owns his own home, and has the best friend he could imagine. What he doesn't have, or believe he will ever have, is love. When Jason catches a glimpse of his new neighbor on moving day, his libido ignites and his fascination in piqued. He even manages to concoct an excuse to go over and meet the man who makes him hope and want for more than he has in years.

Keith Skyler is a shifter in a world where his kind is known only to a few, but they don't often mix and they never mate. Keith has been hoping for a mate since before he can remember, but gay lynx don't have true mates. As far as he knows, they don't have mates at all. However, while moving his little family across Seattle—and away from their tribe—his reality tips and spins more than he thought possible.

When these two men meet over a dish of five-cheese broccoli-noodle casserole, sparks fly. Who knew a welcome-to-the-neighborhood gift could give both of them their chance at love?

www.dreamspinnerpress.com

CAGED
SANCTUARY

Tempeste O'Riley

Kaden Thorn, a dental surgeon who lives a quiet life, has no hope of finding the love he craves. A vicious gay bashing cost him the use of his legs and confined him to a wheelchair. He has given up hope of finding a Dom or even a nonkink partner to love him. When his best friend practically forces him to attend a dinner party, the last thing he expects is a strong Dom who can see beyond his wheels.

Deacon James is an architect and a demanding Dom, but he has spent the past couple of years without a sub or partner. When an employee invites him to a dinner party to meet his girlfriend, Deacon smells a setup but agrees anyway. He prides himself on being an excellent judge of character, and when he meets the younger dentist, he sees past the chair and finds a sweet submissive man who more than piques his interest.

Kade's fears and demons continue to haunt him, challenging Deacon to use everything he's learned as a Dom to earn Kade's trust and submission. Deacon's determined, though, willing to battle all of it to have Kade by his side and at his feet.

www.dreamspinnerpress.com

Dreamers'
DESTINY

Tempeste O'Riley

Liam Grady is the owner of the Feathered Quill, a quirky little bookstore in Asheville, and—though he doesn't realize it yet—a dream walker. His last relationship failed almost a year ago, and he's not had the interest or nerve to pursue anyone he's met since.

Cameron Danu is a tattoo artist from rural Georgia. Cameron is left without a job after his boss, José, is forced to close the shop after a heart attack. When Cameron learns José has set up an interview for him at a small tattoo parlor in Asheville, he hopes for a fresh start in a new town.

Fate brings Cameron and Liam together, and they realize they've met before—in their dreams. A chance encounter and a winged tattoo might lead them to their destiny—if fear doesn't turn their dreams into a nightmare.

www.dreamspinnerpress.com

TEMPESTE O'RILEY

DESIGNS
of
DESIRE

Desires Entwined: Book One

Artist James Bryant has forearm crutches in every color from rainbow for fun to sleek black for business. He even has a pair with more paint splatters than metal. After his family's rejection and abuse from a man he thought loved him, James only just gets through the day by painting. He lives in constant fear that he's not worthy of anything, let alone love.

As CEO of his company, Carrington Enterprises, Seth Burns is a take-charge kind of guy, and he is instantly smitten by the artist helping with his newest project. When he witnesses James suffer a panic attack, a protective instinct he never knew he had kicks in. He truly believes nothing is unobtainable—including James—if he's willing to put in the time and effort.

James is shy and confused by Seth's interest in him as a person. With Seth's support, can he work through his fears to finally find the true love he deserves, or will someone finally land the crushing blow he won't survive?

www.dreamspinnerpress.com

TEMPESTE O'RILEY

BOUND by DESIRE

DESIRES ENTWINED SERIES

A Spin-off of *Designs of Desire*
Desires Entwined: Book 1.75

Despite his past abuse, James has come to terms with his relationship with his Dom and lover Seth. Seth treats James with all the trust and love his sub desires. There is only one thing left to do to make it all complete: Seth needs to put a collar on James.

www.dreamspinnerpress.com

TEMPESTE O'RILEY

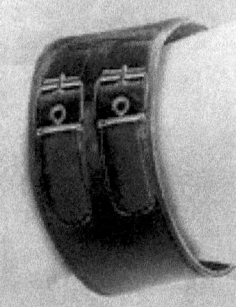

DESIRES' GUARDIAN

DESIRES ENTWINED SERIES

Desires Entwined: Book Two

Most people see Chase Manning as the party-boy twink he seems on the surface. Only James, Chase's BFF, knows the depth of his loyalty and the extent of the wounds Chase carries inside. When Chase meets Rhys Sayer, things don't go well, but he can't shake his attraction to the huge, sexy man.

Rhys is a man of contradictions and fear—a strange combination for a PI and bodyguard. He's in a bad place emotionally when he sets eyes on Chase for the first time. When Chase puts the moves on him, Rhys insults him, thwarting any possibility of a relationship. Rhys doesn't see himself as a complicated man, but he dreads the very kind of connection he desires.

Just as they're trying to overcome their uncertainties, Chase is put in harm's way. Luckily Rhys and their friends have all the right talents to help Rhys save the man of his dreams.

www.dreamspinnerpress.com